by

WINIFRED AIRE

CHIMERA

Annabelle published by
Chimera Publishing Ltd
22b Picton House
Hussar Court
Waterlooville
Hants
PO7 7SQ

Printed and bound in Great Britain by
Cox & Wyman, Reading.

This book is sold subject to the condition that it shall not, by way of trade or otherwise, be lent, resold, hired out or otherwise circulated without the publisher's prior written consent in any form of binding or cover other than that in which it is published, and without a similar condition being imposed on the subsequent purchaser.

The characters and situations in this book are entirely imaginary and bear no relation to any real person or actual happening.

Copyright © Winifred Aire
first printed in 1998
reprinted in 2004

The right of Winifred Aire to be identified as author of this book has been asserted in accordance with section 77 and 78 of the Copyrights Designs and Patents Act 1988

ANNABELLE

Winifred Aire

This novel is fiction – in real life practice safe sex

On a rack against the wall were organised some leather lashes, a dog whip, a whalebone lash, and several sheaves of birch rods. He approached the woman cautiously. It would not do for her to recognise him, perhaps point him out in public... he shrank at the prospect. He tried to raise the black silk bag, but a complicated series of tapes had been tied to keep his features, and incidentally hers, anonymous. For a moment he regretted it. He loved having his cock sucked, and Chastity so infrequently agreed to do so. On the other hand, this one was completely exposed. He gazed long and thoroughly at her uncovered body. He had never seen a woman naked before. Chastity, of course, always wore a heavy nightgown to bed, and his few experiences with whores had been hurried affairs in the dimness of their cribs. There was something else, too, he had wanted to do, but never tried...

Chapter One

'I cannot, sah, ah just cannot.' The tearful voice was that of a beautiful young woman. The Southern accent was strengthened by the power of her emotions. Her blonde hair, worn long over her shoulder in soft bottle ringlets, glittered in the sun. That part of her skin that was observable was a creamy white tinged lightly with pink. But her large blue eyes were brimming with tears, and she hid her exquisitely tiny nose in a barely larger lace kerchief.

'My dear Annabelle, you must surely reconsider.' The speaker was a tall young man. His brown hair was slicked smoothly down, the meticulous brushing not marred by the glossy broad hat he held in his hand. His grey frock coat was impeccably tailored. Though young, lines of character and experience surrounded his eyes, giving him a thoughtful look. His tight trousers showed the hint of a shapely calf, and, for those caring to notice it, a pleasing bulge at the crotch. 'You will surely become my wife.'

'After all... after all you know?' she wailed, and dropped weakly to the white-painted seat in the tiny arbour. 'Ah am shamed for life!' Her accents were that of a young Southern aristocrat, now trembling with suppressed tears.

'Precisely because of that,' he said in his careless British accent, 'I will have you. And you will be a loving and obedient wife, as I shall be a loving and pleasant husband. In public.'

Annabelle looked up at him. 'Sir Peter, whatever do you mean?' There was an agony of fear in her voice.'

'Are you still a virgin?' he asked deliberately. He was looking down at her figure. The low cut of her peach-coloured dress exposed the pale full mounds of her breasts.

'Why sir...' the outrage in her voice was genuine, as genuine as the surprise.

'You have confessed to a reprehensible and unnatural lust for women, my dear. I merely asked you the next logical question. Are you a virgin?'

'Yes I am,' she sobbed again, her face staring at the floor. 'Since I had... had... Sara, I have not had any other. Not a... man. The very idea repels me.'

'Nonetheless, you *shall* have one,' he continued implacably. 'Me. Do you understand? I will not have it that my future wife will become known throughout society as an unnatural woman-lover.' Sir Peter Stone stared down at the young Southern belle. 'We will make our nuptial agreement now. We will live, in public, as the most respectable and proper couple we can be. In private, you will follow my every wish and command...'

'What?!' There was genuine surprise and outrage at this statement from the cool young Englishman. The fire of her Southern blood rose to her eyebrows, and flushed the tops of her breasts.

'You will have one major duty, besides pleasing me. You will select our household help. All the maids. I do not believe we shall require a butler. And you will make it clear to them that their bodies are at my disposal. That, after all, is not so unusual here in the South, I believe, though of course, most people of your class are much less open about it. My disposal, my dear, shall also be yours.'

She turned her surprised face up at him and gasped again. 'You are not repelled by my person? You are not repelled by my... perverted desires?'

'I believe, my dear, that because of my love for you, I will be able to tolerate it. Just as you, my dear Annabelle, shall be required to tolerate my lust on your body. Merely because you dream of being thrashed by a woman while engaging in concupiscent activity should not be a barrier to such a loving and appropriate match as the one I am proposing.'

'Oh, dear dear Peter.' Her magnificent bosom heaved and he dropped to one knee beside her, grasping her white-gloved hand in his. 'Why... when I meant repels me, I was not trying to be personal...' She looked askance at the bulge high up in his tight fitting breeches.

He fell dramatically to his knees beside her, and a faint shadow of maidenly hidden regret covered her pretty features.

'My darling Annabelle, will you consent to be my wife?'

'Of course, dear Peter.'

'Then I shall ensure that your secret shall not only remain one, shameful to you though it may be, but that you will be able to indulge in it to your heart's content. After all, if there is no cure, the next best thing is to control one's appetites judiciously, don't you agree my dear?' There was a strange glitter in Peter's eyes as he peered into her own.

'Yes,' she whispered. 'Yes, oh yes. I shall be yours from this day on forevermore.'

He rose and dusted off his knees. His crotch was at the height of her eyes, and she could see that the bulge there, which she had carefully avoided examining even at a distance before, was now larger.

'I shall address your father at once, and ask him for your hand,' Peter said. He lowered his voice. 'But in the meantime, we must bind this agreement between us. I will not let you go, but I wish a token of your affection.'

'Anything, my dear,' she breathed. 'Anything at all.'

'Very well my love. Abhorrent as it will be for you, I am afraid you must help me satisfy my lust.'

'Now?' she squeaked in trepidation. Her white-gloved hands clenched on the handle of her parasol.

'Yes indeed,' he said. 'Remember my dear that this is your wifely duty, and I shall expect you to assume your duties from this moment.'

She lowered her lashes over her large blue eyes. 'Yes, of course my darling. I shall do whatever my position requires.'

His hand dipped to the waistband of his pants, and he undid his fly. Within the folds of cloth of his trousers and linen she could see a mass of dark hairs, and a long snake of flesh that peered at her blindly, gaping from a tiny mouth. She examined it fearfully, then her gloved hands involuntarily stole up the material of his pants until she could barely touch the monster with the tips of her fingers. It stirred at her touch.

'That is a cock my dear, the organ of generation. John Thomas. It fits certain parts of your own sweet flesh…'

'I know that, dear,' she said somewhat abstractly. 'I've seen the animals in the plantation, you know. I was just wandering where you proposed to put—?'

'My dearest Annabelle,' he interrupted patiently. 'Obviously you are expected to be a virgin on our wedding night. But for now, your dear mouth will be sufficient...'

He held up the limp but swelling monster before her face. First she smelled at it deeply. It smelled somehow bitter, repulsive yet powerfully masculine. So different from her previous smells of the juncture of human legs. She opened her pink lips wide, and he gently placed the head of the cock on her waiting tongue.

She held the huge tip on her tongue for a brief moment, and Peter indulgently looked on. Then she covered her front teeth with her gloriously red lips and closed her mouth softly. Her lips fitted behind the broad flanges of his penis and she stroked the two lobes of the bottom half with her tongue. His hands descended softly but firmly to the top of her golden head as she explored the large morsel. Her eyes closed and she was lost in the sensation. The taste of the tiny drop that came to her tongue was strange: slightly salty and musky. She tickled the tip with her tongue, then stroked the pulsing flesh beneath the lobes of the head.

Peter shifted slightly, then pressed his hips forward. Annabelle tried to move backwards but was held by the insistent pressure of his hands on her head as the silky shaft slid between her lips.

'Hollow your cheeks, my dear, and suck me,' he ordered. His voice was soft in the noon light. Far away they could hear the sounds of a boat on the river. Annabelle did as she was bid, her cheeks moving in and out as she exerted pressure on the shaft and its mighty head. Shyly her gloved hand rose to support her bent torso by grasping his leg. A thrill ran through her at the touch of the muscular column and she sucked away lustily at the other shaft, slightly less thick, that was filling her soft mouth where barely anything but the most delicate of viands had gone before. Screwing her eyes upwards she could see his face turned down to look at what she was doing with her mouth. His eyes were glazed and he seemed to be in a trance. Peter spread his legs to firm his standing, and a lascivious, almost incredible idea took hold of Annabelle. Slyly, so as not to startle Peter and cause him to stop her, her other hand stole up between his legs until she could touch the shaft. She knew he would not notice. The tips of her fingers encountered the hard yet silky shaft that was joining her mouth to his mysterious crotch. She moved her head rapidly back and forth to distract him from her explorations. He grunted softly, like a baby settling for the rag teat. Then her exploring fingers encountered another object. It was a pendulous bag hanging below the base of the shaft. In its viscid depths her fingers could feel something floating: a large jewel. She touched the surface fearfully for a moment. She had seen male animals, but had had no idea men were constructed on such similar lines.

'Darling Annabelle,' Peter's voice, strained and jerky, broke into her reverie and she hastily snatched her hand away. 'Darling Annabelle, I am sorry but I must... I must move in your mouth.'

Peter's hands clutched at her head more roughly than she cared for. It would disarray the careful coiffure she had spent hours on. Then incredibly the shaft was shuttling in and out of her compliant mouth. She gagged reflexively, but held her ground as she knew every Southern belle should. The shaft seemed to swell and incredulous gasping sounds were coming from above her head. She sucked harder, trying to capture the head as it dashed from her lips-protected teeth almost to the back of her throat. Then the shaft suddenly jerked once, then again and again. She clutched Peter's muscular thighs to keep her balance, her nose full of the intoxicating smell that emerged from under his linen. A sudden wash of liquid gushed into her mouth. Caught by surprise she almost pulled away, almost threw back the essence he was pouring into her. Then her training, the habits of maintaining her position instilled in her by her background, came to the fore. She swallowed rapidly as the flood seemed endless and there was real fear of it running out her lips and down her chin. Such a ludicrous sight she would be, were that to happen. Peter pulled back slightly, and her breathing eased. She swallowed quickly again, then licked the insides of her mouth delicately. Only now did she become aware of the flavour of what she had swallowed. The first tiny drop she had tasted had been but a bare shadow, a harbinger of the real thing, and she blushed to think that she had paid no attention to the taste until it was almost gone.

Annabelle sighed deeply, then withdrew her hands from their supports. She hoped he did not think her forward for holding on to the only support that offered. Peter pulled back, watching as his softening prick withdrew from the soft lips, stained slightly by her lip rouge.

'May I?' she asked shyly, her tiny white-gloved hand raised hesitantly to his crotch.

Peter smiled thoughtfully. 'In some circles it might be deemed unseemly, but seeing as we are to be married, and seeing what our nuptial agreements are to be like, you may of course my dear. Consider it your second affianced duty.'

Fumbling a bit, she managed to reinsert his still hard member into his pants and rearrange the linen. She got the hang of it quickly: not unlike dressing a doll, Annabelle thought as she buttoned up the entrance. Then she rose to her feet with a brilliant smile.

Helping her to rise, Peter kissed Annabelle fondly. 'I shall now go to solicit your father's permission for our wedding, dearest heart.'

Arm in arm they walked back from their stroll, their figures outlined against the green of the lawn and the Spanish moss that hung, decorating the ancient trees.

Annabelle's mother watched the young couple approach with some puzzlement. The girl had been a trial to her for a number of years. She had had eligible suitors by the score, but rejected them all coldly. True, some of the young bloods from New Orleans's less wealthy households were probably after Annabelle's inheritance. Some of the best families had lost all their young men, and those that had remained... And Annabelle, after all, she was the only child of General Maxwell Hughes, who had been chief of the Confederate army's commissariat! Still, some of them would have made good matches, very good matches indeed for her daughter. Now here was this young Englishman, whose manners were indeed exquisite, but who knew what his antecedents were?

'General, a word in your ear if I may?' The young Englishman was as polite and as cool as ever. Annabelle, beside him, her face impassive, dropped into a convenient chair held by one of the liveried servants. They may have lost the war, Annabelle's mother thought, but someone had to keep up standards nonetheless.

'What? Of course my boy, of course.' The General sipped the last of his rum on ice – his one peculiarity, that drink, and the cause of many a rumour – and led Peter off to the sitting room.

'As you know sir, I have been visiting your beautiful house not merely for the pleasure of hearing you discuss your campaigns, and the pleasure of madame and your company, but for another, more selfish reason as well...'

The General harumphed. He had not become fully accustomed to having this young fellow call Miz Maxwell 'madam'.

Peter cocked an eyebrow at the older man. 'As I was saying, I have been extremely enamoured of your young daughter, and I feel my life will not be whole without her. I would like to request the honour of her hand.' He raised a hand in admonition as the General stirred. 'No, please sir, hear me out. I realise she is your only daughter, and you must therefore feel some trepidation at losing her, but as I intend to settle in New Orleans, that does not present an insurmountable problem. As for my prospects, I am sure you are aware that they are at least moderately acceptable.' He slipped a hand into his waistcoat and withdrew a sheaf of papers. 'Here you have a copy of my letter of patent. Here a letter of credit from my London bank for twenty thousand pounds. And here, finally, a copy of a letter from my business agent discussing the rents, which come presently to the sum of three thousand two hundred pounds, sixteen shillings per annum.'

He raised his hand again, as the General was sputtering in his seat. 'More importantly, if I may say so sir, is the fact that Annabelle and I have come to an agreement and find ourselves extremely well suited.'

The General's snowy eyebrows arched in surprise. Annabelle had so far, and without good reason, turned down a number of qualified suitors. 'This is all so unnecessary...' he started to say.

'Please sir, I beg of you, have I your permission...?'

'Of course, my boy, of course!' the General said, suddenly realising the implication of Peter's words. Why, he would be the father of a Lady, a true aristocrat. And no matter how much they prided themselves on their American heritage, no matter how much he and his fellows saw themselves as true gentlemen, General Maxwell like most of his class, place, and time, had a sneaking suspicion that they were not yet *true* nobility. And here, in one step, he would enjoy a social promotion. He rose and rang the bell for the servant. 'Bourbon or rum?'

'Rum of course,' said Peter, and in one stroke banished forever all doubts from the General's mind.

Chapter Two

'How are you this morning, my dear?' Peter's raised hat and smooth bearing were as cool as ever. Annabelle blushed slightly, remembering how passionate he had been in the garden not three days back.

'Why Peter, I did not expect to meet you here. This is my friend, Mrs Jakes. We are on our way to the milliners to choose...' she blushed slightly and appropriately '...some things.'

'Mrs Jakes,' Peter bowed and raised his hat again.

'Won't you come with us, Mr Stone?'

'I say, Sir Stone actually.'

'Oh, indeed. Then I shall have to be calling you Lady Annabelle,' Mrs Jakes said sweetly.

'No, darling Heather. We shall always be friends,' Annabelle said, linking her arms with her friend and with her fiancé.

'Annabelle has been telling me all about you,' Mrs Jakes said.

'Not all I hope,' Peter said. 'That would be awful, don't you think?'

Mrs Jakes chuckled. She was darker than Annabelle, and her figure fuller. She swayed slightly as she walked, and Peter could see the tiny beads of sweat gathering at her temples as they moved down the street. Around them, the bustle of New Orleans in the late morning muttered through the haze.

'I shall have to leave you ladies here,' Peter said. 'I have some arrangements of my own to make. Shall we meet here in an hour, then, for lunch?'

The two ladies bowed their heads in gracious assent, then continued their way to the shop of Mr Jurgens. He was an acquaintance of long standing, having supplied several generations of the town's womanhood with lace and fripperies, petticoats and fabrics: all the necessities of daily living. Even during the darkest years of the war he somehow contrived to keep his stock intact, forbearing even for long periods of time from pressing his customers for their bills.

He assisted the two young ladies through his emporium, exclaiming loudly and with heartfelt congratulations for Annabelle's coming good fortune. The two friends selected appropriate stuffs, then turned their hands to the choice of the best lace. Annabelle turned over the rolls of delicate material doubtfully.

'None of these is truly satisfactory Mr Jurgens. I shall have to dig into the storeroom myself,' Annabelle said gaily. He bowed his assent and turned to aid Heather in choosing a pale chiffon that had caught her eye. Annabelle wandered off into the rear of the establishment, away from the clerks, examining the shelves with interest. There was a slight movement in one of the bays, where older material was stored. Annabelle looked up complacently and was somewhat taken aback at the sight of her fiancé lounging in the bay, his appearance as dapper in this inappropriate place as it was outside in the hot sun.

'Peter dear, how did you come here?' Annabelle smiled graciously.

'Darling Annabelle, I could not do without you any longer.'

She smiled at the implied compliment, and he moved to enfold her in his strong arms.

'It isn't terribly romantic though,' she said doubtfully,

eyeing the piles of stuffs around them, and the curtains strung from the walls of the storeroom.

'But it is,' Peter said. 'I had this unaccountable urge for you my dear. My passion is uncontrollable. Come, I am afraid you will have to do your duty and indulge me my dear.' He smiled sadly at her and his lips descended towards hers, planting a kiss first on lips, lightly, then more strongly on the swell of her breasts barely visible under the crinoline.

'Here? You mean now?' she asked.

'My darling, I should not have to remind you of our previous conclusions. Yes of course here and now.'

'I was only fearful that we might be interrupted...'

'Of course not,' he said. 'I have bribed Mr Jurgens to give us some moments of un-chaperoned time. He will keep your friend Mrs Jakes occupied too. She is a delightful creature, is she not?'

'Oh, in that case,' she said, looking around for a convenient seat and finding it in a pile of stuffs, 'I would love to be of service my darling.'

'No my dear.' His hand stopped her. 'I think not that way this time. Here, lean over and support yourself on your hands.' He turned her to face a pile of fabrics and she obligingly leaned forward, supporting herself with her hands.

Peter raised her dress, then followed that with the hoop of her crinoline. He regarded the cotton covered white frilled drawers for a moment. 'Darling, I beg of you, do not wear these anymore. I long to think of you as available at any time for my wishes.'

He reached around and untied the ribbons that held her knee-length drawers to her hips. 'Free trade has always been one of my principles,' he murmured into her ears as his hands divested her thighs of the thin cotton. They slid to the floor and she stepped daintily out of them. His hands stroked the length of her smooth thighs, not neglecting the slight swell of the bottom of her belly and the mossy protuberance at the very lowest point. She shivered in anticipation. Notwithstanding the inappropriate surroundings, she was ready to surrender to his demands, to yield her maidenhood to his importuning hands. Peter nuzzled her ear, biting gently yet sharply at the delicate rim, then she felt the length of his body slide down hers. As he raised the back of her many-layered skirts she braced herself against the shelves. A shiver of anticipation raced through her body. He lifted the petticoats and neatly tucked them under her sash. She knew the entire length of her rear was exposed to his gaze, then could feel the warmth of his breath on the smooth round plumpness of her behind. Both of his strong palms now rested on the plump mounds. She blushed, but did not move as she felt him part the buns and peer at what had been until now a hidden treasure, even to herself. His mouth moved over the silky skin and she could feel his lips puckering and sucking at the smooth flesh. Then his tongue licked out and she barely managed to stifle a cry of rapture.

'Shall I beat you my dear?' his mouth nuzzled at her ear and sent a frissón of delight through her frame.

'Oh, ma dear, have I been so *terribly* bad?' she breathed mischievously. So confident was she in Peter's intentions, that she had no thought but that he would do all to please, and nothing to harm her.

'Yes indeed.' He too adopted a playful tone. 'You have kept yourself from me for an entire day. This inattention cannot remain unpunished.' Suiting his actions to the words, his hard palms seized each of her buns and pulled them powerfully apart. The rough fabric of his trousers scratched against the soft tissues exposed in the crack of her ass, where nothing but the softest of fabrics had been before. Annabelle shuddered at the delicious feeling. She closed her eyes and imagined what else he could do, ready if called upon, to yield her innermost self to her beloved ravisher. She felt his hands fumbling between them, while his other hand dug cruel yet delicious fingers into the soft mounds of her butt. Then she knew, by the cold touch of the horn buttons on his flies that his monstrous machine was free.

'I have a truncheon here, my dear. Stronger than any policeman's, and I shall give you a proper thrashing.'

Peter withdrew slightly, and grasped John Thomas firmly with one fist, then struck with his engorged cock at the softness before him.

'La, sir,' Annabelle cried out in feigned alarm. 'Surely you can strike harder than that?'

In a frenzy of lust Peter struck at her bare bottom again and again. The repeated fleshy lashing had a wondrous effect on both protagonists. Both the instrument of torture and its recipient glowed rosily with the repeated blows, and Peter's truncheon soon began to weep tears of anguish at its treatment. Nor was his other hand at rest. He smacked at her rosy bum with a fury, the sounds swallowed by the millinery-loaded shelves of the warehouse.

'Oh my dear… Yes, strike me more. I am such a terrible person,' Annabelle sobbed, though whether from true pain or from some other emotion that heaved her bosom and softened the expression on her face it was hard to tell. As for Peter, his normally pallid face assumed a hue of redness that in a less wholesome youth might have been deemed apoplexy. Sounds emerged from between clenched teeth until at last he gave a cry muffled by his teeth in the muslin-covered shoulder of his affianced. His truncheon burst, pulsed, in a frenzy of milky liquid that spurted onto the pink flesh before him. Guided by Peter's knowledgeable hand, the juices flowed down the open crack, liberally bedewing the tiny brown orifice, then dripping via Annabelle's pearly lower lips to bedeck her thighs and the tops of her stockings. Lovingly he gathered up some of the spilled spunk and offered it to her ruby lips. With a loving smile she sucked in the entire morsel, laving all with her tongue.

'I'm afraid I shall be away for a couple of days, my dear,' he said as he examined his clothes as the two lovers put themselves in order for respectable company.

'Away?' she said in sudden alarm.

He smiled at the panic in her voice. 'I must see to your wedding presents. From the groom to the bride.'

'Oh,' she almost squealed, 'what are they, my heart? And you did say "presents" did you not?'

'I did indeed,' he said warmly. 'Though they shall be a secret until the day.'

Chapter Three

The heavy trees shaded the dusty road, turning it into a cavern of mystery where the horses' hooves barely sounded in the soft covering. Peter would have preferred to ride, but he had to find out whether the road he had been told about was really suitable for a carriage. After all, he was intending to bring Lady Stone-to-be, as well as guests, in this direction, and it would not do to have to travel through impassable bogs or other uncivilised pathways.

Before him the path widened out somewhat, creating a mossy dell. A single shaft of sunlight penetrated the thick canopy. Someone was sitting on a stump making stifled sounds. Peter casually checked the pocket of his coat. The short-barrelled revolver was still there, and the nipples were all covered with their caps. Good. He urged the horses forward.

The young woman sitting on the stump paid no attention to the carriage. The once-bright gingham of her dress was stained and spattered, and a torn kerchief hung down from her coal-black curls. She wore her hair rather long, and it glittered in shades of blue and black under the single ray of sunlight.

Peter stopped his carriage and looked at the figure on the stump.

'What's the matter girl?'

Nelly barely raised her tearful head. 'Go away,' she muttered under her breath. The shame and the feel of the parson's hands between her legs still burned. And she knew that drops of his cum had stained her dress. The thought of that old man, his face flushed and his toothless gums uttering endearments almost made her want to vomit again, but she had spewed the contents of her stomach long before, as she had made the long way from the tiny collection of cabins that went by the name of Cabotsville.

'What are you doing here?' he asked again, in a strange accent, as if his mouth was full of alligator pear.

Nelly looked at him, really seeing the man for the first time. He was rather good looking, and he had about him an air of both inquiry and command, as if he was puzzled by the world, and yet satisfied that it was ready to do his bidding. He was dressed in fine clothes, that even at the distance she could tell were expensive.

'What are you doing here?' he demanded again. 'Where do you live?'

'I'm lost,' she said. 'Live somewhere back thea…' she pointed vaguely into the forest, then suddenly was conscious of her error, as he stood on the boards and examined their surroundings.

'Don't speak like a country bumpkin,' he was saying thoughtfully. 'Been in service, have you girl?'

She nodded miserably. Those had been alternately the most miserable and most delightful times of her life. Being a slave had forced her to become, paradoxically, fiercely independent, proud even, and just as fiercely determined to be her own mistress. On the other hand, the attractions of the soft life as the member of a rich household, where even the slaves and servants were pampered and enjoyed some of the comforts of the rich, had made her dissatisfied of her family's life in Cabotsville. To which, as she suddenly realised, she would never return. Not ever. *That* part of her life was over.

'I shall take you on as maid to my wife. Get into the

carriage,' he said matter-of-factly.

She stood in her place, frozen as much by surprise at his calmness as by fear. He cracked his long whip impatiently.

'Get into the carriage,' he ordered again. The whip cracked once more.

Without knowing exactly how it happened she found herself in the seat of the carriage. The young man ignored her, concentrating on his driving. The horses were lively and he handled them with great skill. A shyness, and a sense of her own pride, made her clench her teeth over her questions. They turned into an abandoned driveway after he checked on some written instructions. Nelly relaxed on the fabric covered seat and tried to imagine herself as the mistress of the mansion that opened up before them, being driven home after an evening's party.

Peter watched her out of the corner of his eyes and noted how relaxed and languid she had become. Her lips turned moist, and her lids half covered her dark eyes. Peter felt a tightening in his groin, and he knew he must resolve it in some measure.

The mansion he had been told about was in poor shape, neglected and abandoned now that the wealth of the pre-war era had given way to the poverty of the Reconstruction. The front door opened to his key, then reluctantly yielded to pressure and opened with a squeal. The once-white columns of the entranceway were stained with mould. Inside the house smelled musty, and Peter wandered through the rooms, ignoring the furnishings but concentrating on the structure. Nelly followed him in wonder, wanting to ask what he wanted with the ruin, afraid to voice the question aloud. Yet the young man with the strange accent seemed so sure of himself, so concise, that she felt compelled to follow.

They stopped at the entrance to the master bedroom. A huge four poster bed of imported African mahogany dominated the large chamber. The owners had lavished care on the room. The walls were stained with neglect, but the ceiling still bore traces of the figures and gardens that had been painted there. She peered around his shoulder, and then slipped into the room, surveying everything, wondering whether she would ever live in such a place, rule it as it should be ruled.

Peter watched the young woman roving about the room, observing everything, touching nothing. She had grace and carriage, and her full bosom held up the scanty fabric of her dress. Darker circles marked the presence of her nipples, and as she bent over an item he saw the fabric tighten over her bare ass. She approached the huge bed, large enough for three or four sleepers, and he moved rapidly forward. One hand went to her ass, the other to her shoulders and suddenly she found herself on the bed.

She squeaked in surprise and tried to struggle. His weight and clever hands kept her pinned to the dusty cover of the mattress. His face – she could imagine the cruel sneer on his thin lips – only an inch from the back of her neck. His breath was fiery hot on her nape.

'You may struggle. I shall like that, though you will enjoy it much less. And when we have had our fill of one another, we shall be in a better position to discuss our future.'

The words seemed to make no sense to her and she tried to hump herself up, against his punishing weight. Peter kept her pinned to the bed with one hand while with the other he swiftly and knowledgeably stripped off her dress. It tore in tatters, notwithstanding his efforts. At first she screamed: loud and high pitched, then she recalled the way to the old mansion, and fought on grimly, silently. Soon they were both covered with sweat. She could feel the slickness of his skin against her naked back and realised that he had managed to strip himself as well. He straddled her, pushing down on her shoulders with two hands while she lay exhausted beneath him.

Peter looked down at the smooth dark brown back. Her shoulders were broad, tapering to a narrow waist. Under his ass he could feel the smooth swell of her full buttocks. He stroked the length of her damp back, feeling the bump of each vertebra. She panted frantically and her back flexed and relaxed under his hand.

'I am Sir Peter,' he whispered huskily into her ear, then with a sudden burst of strength, he rose off her and flipped her over on her back. She stared back at him from eyes in which hate and fear were the major emotions. Her breasts, flattened somewhat, attracted his attention first, and before she had a chance to react, he had covered both bubbies with his hands. The dark nipples burned pleasingly against his palms. Nelly tried to resist, only to find that his hands were squeezing brutally against her full breasts. The pain of the grip was mitigated somewhat by the feeling of... she had no word for the feeling, except that it felt good. Peter's hand sought between her thighs. She clenched her legs together and instead he stroked the crisp black curls that pointed to the avenue between her thighs. She was too exhausted to struggle, and his words, so calmly spoken in that mushy voice of his, came as a surprise.

'I would not insult you by offering you money. I *will* have you however. I promise you will enjoy your fuck.' He smiled, as if reminiscing on something in his past. 'Let me assure you my dear, that you are entering a completely different life. One that will benefit you very much.'

Nelly heard his words, but their import did not penetrate. She wanted to laugh, would have laughed, but for the situation: here was this pecker about to screw her and babbling about something great in her future. Hell. She wanted to struggle again, but exhaustion and despair overtook her and she sagged back against the bed. Peter took advantage of the situation and his hand slid down between her legs, along the length of her plump cunny lips.

'What is your name, girl? Can't call you "girl" all the time. Awkward, eh what?'

'Nelly, sir,' she answered reluctantly, then immediately regretted not giving a false name. He lowered his mouth and kissed her. Not the brutal invasion of her mouth she had been expecting and dreading, but a true lover's kiss. His tongue hesitated on her lips, as if asking for permission, and reluctant, fearful of the consequences of refusal, she allowed him entry. With firm gentleness he explored her mouth with his own, and to her surprise Nelly found herself responding. His hand found its way between her slick legs again and this time the touch was not uncomfortable.

She parted her legs, still reluctantly, expecting an invasion by his stiff digit. Instead, he caressed the outer pouting lips of her cunny, his finger-pads bringing a thrilling feeling to her frame. Then the invading fingers crept higher, and he toyed with the stiff little curls that adorned the base of her belly. Nelly shivered in anticipation and closed her eyes, while his mouth explored the smooth surfaces of her face, nibbled at her ears.

'Ahhhh,' an involuntary cry expressed itself from her lips as his mouth nibbled delicately at her ear, while the tips of his fingers found the hood at the tip of her mound and the tiny glistening button she knew was hidden there.

Without being conscious of it, her body arched in response.

His body spanned over her and, peering down between the full flattened mounds of her breasts, she could see the pink threatening head of its cock. She parted her legs wider, raising her knees, and he thrust forward. There was pressure against the hole she so loved to touch, and then the large object was pushing deeply into her body. She expected to feel pain, but instead, the invasion filled her tissues with pleasure. She clutched at him with arms and knees. Her heels and fingernails dug into his back and she clamped her lips onto his. He called out deeply into her mouth, his tongue invading her, and kissed her savagely back. Grinding his pubis against her, he forced himself deeper and she rose to welcome the intrusion. Then he tried to pull back, but Nelly was having nothing of that. She yowled deep in her throat and her hands raked at his flanks, not willing to relinquish her hold. He drove into her again, then tried to retreat for a second thrust. She let go his lips to take on air, then with a sudden twist, rolled around on the bed until she was astride him. Her eyes closed, she rammed herself down on Peter, taking her pleasure. Her rough farm-hardened hands pinning his shoulder to the bed while she rode his loins to a climax.

Her body was aching and she tiredly slipped off his cock, which stood erect over his belly. The pale epicene face was looking at her in puzzled surprise, and he rolled the top of his torso onto her, taking one of her nipples in his mouth. Nelly moaned deeply at the touch, and his fingers searched again at her moist interior. The crisp curls at the base of her belly were slick with her juices. Her pleasure was beginning to rise again, and she clutched at his head to bring his lips closer around the aroused nubbin of flesh. Peter raised his head forcefully against the pressure of her hands. He saw the fierce determination and lust on her face, and grinned faintly. Then he abandoned her chest, though she clutched at him with all her force. Surprisingly, he did not try to get wholly away. And his lips seemed to be making their way deliberately down her quivering belly. For a brief moment Nelly entertained the fantasy that he was actually going to kiss her down in her pussy, but the thought was too impossible to contemplate seriously, banished from her mind when she saw his pale skin against her darker flesh. Still, his skilful fingers were in her hole, and she shoved her pubis against the pleasant touch. Her body was less demanding than it had been before her sudden climax, and she was ready for more, even if it came slower this time.

But his head did not stop when it came into contact with the bottom of her belly. Indeed, his lips continued their downward passage until they touched the prominent hood that hid the tiny button she loved to finger.

'Oh lawd, oh lawdy lawd,' she found herself reverting to the language of childhood as warm flexible lips engulfed the cowl of her pussy and sucked the thin inner lips. She found herself ablaze with passion, her hands involuntarily grabbing at his smooth soft hair, pushing him down onto her cunny. It might happen only once in her life, but she was determined, for this time at least, to benefit from a man's mouth. Then his tongue touched her engorged clitoris and she screamed once again. Her body was trembling, almost unable to control itself when he licked her once again, his tongue going the length of the inner lips, while his fingers scoured the insides of her vaginal tube.

'Ahhhh God! That is so good. Do it again you peckerface. Suck my slit. Lick it! I'm gonna cream on yo' face. Fuck, fuck…' She screamed and babbled worlds she did not know she had ever heard. And all the time that delicious tongue was threading her lower lips, licking delicately and soothingly at the tender tissues, re-inflaming them in ways she had not anticipated. And the man seemed to be willingly participating in what must be such a humiliation for him! Nelly wanted to cry with joy and triumph. Her fingers, strengthened by work, tore into his scalp, urging the oral digit deeper and deeper into her interior, as for the first time she took her own selfish pleasure from a man, a reversal of fortune she feared would never come again. She creamed once again, and before the last of her shivering peaks was over, he had pulled back and flipped her over on her belly. His shirt pulled up, his smooth belly glued itself to her sweaty soft behind and the stiff rammer that jutted from the base of his belly pushed into her again. One of his fingers urgently explored her tight sphincter, and she would willingly have yielded that orifice to his cock as well. Instead he moved in undeniable demanding rhythm to a climax that flooded her interior for a second time.

Lying on top of the young woman, his hands idly toying with her charms, Peter considered for a while. Her breasts were firm, the nipples softened now as her passion was spent. She smelled clean and acted respectably. Yes indeed, a very good choice for the pleasure-mate of his future wife. And Annabelle would need someone to shepherd her through the flames of her passion. Who better than this strong-framed, deliciously proportioned young woman?

Peter rose from the young woman and examined his cock. It was glistening with their mingled juices. He looked around at the covered furniture. 'How do you like this house?'

Nelly stirred languorously. She knew it would

eventually come down to this, and though it had been terrifying at first, she was pleased that this strange strongly gentle man, and not the terrible old parson, had been her first.

'It's a very nice house,' she said idly.

'How would you like to live in it?' he asked, buttoning his fly.

For one brief, brutal moment her heart leaped and she actually thought he meant... he meant... but then the other, more real possibility occurred to her, and she thought why not?. She was no longer a virgin anyway, and being a man's kept mistress would not be too bad. His actual words surprised her.

'My wife needs a personal maid. One who can perform various services. Discreetly. Would you like the job? Have you ever been in service before?'

'I've worked for Colonel Hawthorn's sir. Yessir, I would like the job.'

He smiled briefly. 'Good. It will be very convenient then. You'll be paid, oh... twelve dollars a month. No, double that.'

Nelly gasped at the thought. *Twenty-four dollars*? It was an inconceivable sum in a place and time in which the average man of her class and colour earned a few cents a day.

'Let me explain,' he said. 'I shall expect absolute obedience from you. Absolute. Is that clear?'

'Yessir,' she said. Her eyes were fixed fearfully on his own intense orbs.

'My wife will require your personal attentions, as shall I from time to time. Nothing that passes here shall be mentioned or hinted at outside. Is that clear as well?'

'Yessir,' she said again. The implications of what he was saying were starting to sink in.

'So long as you keep to our agreement, you shall be rewarded as I have said. And moreover, I guarantee you added emolument as time passes by. Are we in agreement?'

'Yessir,' she said for the third time, then added, 'What is emol... emolmate, sir?' She quailed slightly from the fishy eye he turned on her, though Peter was merely thinking that he had better invest in her education.

'Money,' he said succinctly. 'Your pay will increase as you show your devotion and obedience. And please, I know you are capable of speaking proper English, not that horrid patois. Do so in our company, at least.'

Nelly nodded, satisfied.

Chapter Four

They rode through the golden afternoon between massive tree boles hung with Spanish moss. Annabelle clung gratefully to her new husband's arm. She felt with relish the play of the hard muscles underneath his coat sleeve as he handled the matched greys with ease, now spurring them on with a touch of the whip, now easing them with the reins. A tiny shiver coursed through her body as she saw the play of the whip, wondering how he would handle her, knowing that she would require some gentling herself.

The wedding party had been superb. She was the envy of all her friends, though there was some muttering when the new couple departed towards the end of the festivities. Annabelle knew that some of the overheard mutterings were the product of envy. Surely no bride since before the war had been married in such a lavish fashion. And, she knew by the tingling between her legs, at last she would taste the true joys of marriage, and of whatever delightful surprise Peter had hinted at that awaited them in their future connubial life.

Peter smiled down at her, and her lips crept shyly to his. The horses ran on and he diverted his attention to steal a kiss from the proffered red lips. The wedding had been magnificent, the envy of all New Orleans. She had been the most glorious bride they had seen since before the war. Her heart swelled at the sight of her brand new husband. Annabelle's joy and satisfaction were tinged with some surprise and concern. She wondered why Peter had insisted on this lonely drive out of the city and into the countryside. And on their wedding day too.

The horses slowed and her musings stopped as she became conscious of her surroundings. They were facing a gate that looked slightly familiar. Two obviously new stone lions topped the elderly gateposts. The iron gate, newly painted, opened into an avenue of majestic trees that wound off into a plantation of tall sycamores and hickories.

'My dear,' he smiled down at her. 'Are you properly wet?'

'Peter?' Annabelle asked in confusion. Then she reddened, divining his meaning, and her thighs clenched involuntarily.

'No, you mustn't do that,' he said quietly, still smiling. 'To the contrary. Open your legs my dear. I want to see your hand giving you pleasure.'

She blushed, but only for a moment, then a brilliant smile lit her face. Yes, this was to be her new life. As they rode between the trees down the newly cleaned avenue that still seemed vaguely familiar, her own hand dove between her thighs. She pressed her fingers against her sensitive clitoris, mashing the soft virginal lips of her cunny. She was grateful she had remembered Peter's demands, and was wearing nothing underneath her petticoats. She felt so free, so randy this way.

Peter watched his bride frig herself. Her eyes were slightly closed and her breathing was quickening. As the first tiny shudder shook her frame, the carriage burst into the sunlight of a clearing. A majestic mansion, newly painted white, its gingerbread and tall columns glinting red in the setting sun appeared before his eyes.

'Look my dear, your wedding present,' he said softly.

Annabelle languidly opened her eyes, which suddenly widened into two blue orbs. 'Oh Peter! It's the Hennely place! Why I never! I always thought of it as the most magnificent mansion in the world. How on earth did you know...?'

'I asked your mother, my dear.'

'It's wonderful, dear Peter. The best present I could ever have.'

'Now, continue as we drive up.' The command was delivered gently, and for one moment she did not know what he meant, then the tautness of her breasts reminded her of what she had been doing. As they rolled up over the crunching gravel drive she wondered if the servants were watching, but the pleasure of frigging herself for her husband overlaid any other considerations. The carriage stopped before the house and the tall double doors flew open. A young bronze-skinned woman in a maid's apron and cap came out and walked hurriedly down the steps, then made an attempt at a curtsy. Annabelle, her hand still in her lap, examined the other, the blood rushing to her head. The hand started moving of its own accord. Besides the cap and apron, and high-buttoned boots on her feet, the young woman was completely naked. She had dark brown breasts topped with wide black nipples. Her sides and flanks were a smooth dark brown. Her lips were full, and her complexion was the kind Annabelle longed to run her hands and lips across.

Peter leapt lightly from the carriage and ran around to help her down. 'Your maid, Nelly. You will have to choose the rest of the staff, but this is your second present.' He helped her down. Annabelle's eyes were riveted to the maid's.

'Nelly, this is your mistress, my wife, Lady Stone. She will instruct you in most of your duties. Carry the luggage in please, then serve us a light supper.'

Annabelle was swept towards the double doors of the

house. As Peter picked her up to carry her over the threshold, she cast one look at the maid. Nelly was stretched out on one leg as she lifted one of the cases down from the portmanteau. The muscles in her legs were taut, and her breasts were held up by the tension in her shoulders. A flush of juices ran through Annabelle's veins and she wondered what the night would bring.

The workers, Peter noted, had done a fine job. They had concentrated on those rooms and chambers he and his new household would occupy first. The rest of the mansion would wait until Lady Annabelle chose what to do with it. Smoking his after-dinner cigar, the warm darkness lying like a blanket on the land, he contemplated his next steps, then rose languidly.

Nelly was clearing the last of the dishes from the fine supper he had sent on ahead.

'When you are finished, please attend Lady Stone and myself upstairs,' he said as he passed by the polished mahogany table. It shone like silk. She was shaping up to be a fine servant, damn if she wasn't.

Annabelle was standing before the large poster bed. She wore a sheer silk gown Peter had imported from London. Her tiny pink nipples and surprisingly large areolae made dark spots against the fabric. Even from the distance of the door he could see that the nipples were hard and erect. From the tips of her breasts, the gown fell to her tiny feet, enclosed in red morocco slippers. And hidden in the folds Peter could barely see the soft sweet dark triangle of her mons.

Without speaking he admired her from the doorway.

'My dearest bride,' he eventually said, and Annabelle's eyes grew wider at the sound of his voice, a faint blush suffusing her cheeks and descending down her perfect white neck. 'My darling, tonight is to be the night of your entry into that dearest and most precious of states: connubial bliss.'

Her perfect pink lips parted slightly, but she made not a sound, and Peter congratulated himself on the excellence of his choice. Only the movement of her bosom quickened as she regarded him.

'In the trunk over there you will find a gilt leather box. Please bring it to the night table and contemplate the contents, while I retire for a moment.'

In his dressing room, Peter divested himself rapidly of his clothes, then, after his ablutions, pulled on a bed gown of embroidered heavy silk. With nothing on underneath, and with his thickening rod parting the skirts at every step, he returned to his bride.

Annabelle was seated on the love seat, by the side of the bed, the box before her on the night-table. The box was open as instructed, and she was examining the contents with wide eyes. Peter sat himself down by her side. He took one of her delicate hands in his, and together they examined the instruments that were arrayed within.

'My dear,' he started by saying. 'All of these are for you, for our mutual delectation. However, I beg and order you, not to use any of them before I have first taught you its use, hm? Once I have showed you, you may feel free to use it as you please.'

Annabelle nodded, her eyes first on his manly face, then on the attractions of the box. Holding her soft palm in his, they explored the box.

'This, my dear, is a tawse. In its naval form it is known as the cat o' nine tails. Notice how smooth it is, sliding between your fingers. Unlike the crude one favoured by Jack Tar, these will leave no unsightly scratches on fair skin.' Annabelle's hand was quivering, and images of what one could do with the instrument filled her brain.

'This,' continued her new husband, moving her hand to a new instrument, 'is a whalebone lash. Notice the white smoothness and flexibility. It is made of the same substance as those awful corsets I have forbidden you to use, but here we shall employ the creature of the deep to create pleasure, not an instrument of torture. And here, my dear,' their hands moved to another instrument nestling in the blue velvet, 'is a most peculiar object.'

Annabelle stared at it, wide-eyed. It was in the shape of a male member, such as the one she knew was even now peeping out of her husband's gown. Made of ivory, it reproduced the male member in perfect shape. There were two more beside it, one of some dark black wood, the other, much smaller than the other two. The black one was double ended, as if two members had been joined at the base. The small one glistened as if oiled.

'These, my darling, are called *godemiches*. They are of French design, as are all the best instruments. You shall find their use much gratifying. This one, of course, is for when I am too fatigued by exercise to continue. The double one is for the enjoyment of such tribadic pleasures as we shall engender and attempt. I am sure your new maid will appreciate its use. As for this, the smaller one, it is of course for your fundament.'

Annabelle blushed at the very idea, a moment of outrage colouring her cheeks, and then she recalled not only her vow to her new husband, but the fact that this was all new and exciting, as well as the feel of his tongue on the article in question during their meeting at the milliners.

'But why, dearest,' she managed to utter, 'do you need this latter? Surely you can use…' She blushed as she motioned to the erect pillar of flesh that jutted from her husband's gown and was even now rubbing against her skin.

Peter laughed. 'Of course, my dear. And I shall indeed introduce you to the pleasures of Sodom. But ain't two better than one?' He bit gently at her ear and his warm tongue laved the pearly convolutions. 'One for the front, one for behind.'

Annabelle could say nothing to that, but a deeper blush ran through her frame.

Slowly, so as to savour every minute, her led her hand through the contents of the box. They were interrupted in that delightful pursuit with the arrival of Nelly. Peter looked at her with approval. Unbidden, she had yet used her time well to change her stockings and apron, so that they were both spotless. Wordlessly, she stood at the foot of the bed.

Annabelle looked up from the box, and Peter took it gently from her hands. He rose to his feet, then bent down and picked his bride up. He kissed her lips gently, and she responded with a passionate embrace. In two steps he had deposited her on the soft sheet, which Nelly had deftly uncovered.

'Please show yourself to me,' Peter said quietly, his hands by his side. The tip of his cock was parallel to the floor, and Annabelle's eyes looked at it for a brief moment, before she looked away, embarrassed at her temerity. Her eyes lit on Nelly, and another blush suffused her face. Between her legs she began to feel a heat that was like nothing she had experienced before. Without her volition, it seemed, her hands stole to her sides, and she pulled up the smooth lines of her nightdress. The man and the other woman looked on as the glowing flesh of the young Southerner became visible. Her legs, the thighs smooth and pale, showed first, then the moss covered cleft at the entrance to her femininity. Her belly, which had not been seen by man or woman for many years, was a rounded cupola of whiteness, topped by the dimple of her naval. Her proud breasts were flattened on her perfect ribcage, and the pale pink contrasted exquisitely with the white mounds. Finally she lay there, her legs spread apart so that Peter could see the red crack between her legs. Her inner lips were tiny, all but hidden by the outer rolls, and he longed to throw himself onto the waiting flesh of his bride. But that would have to wait. First, he bent over her and filled her mouth with a kiss, his tongue exploring every bit of her waiting lingual cavern.

The kiss seemed to last for an eternity to Annabelle, and she sighed in disappointment when Peter withdrew. But then he was positioning himself between her widely splayed legs and she fortified herself happily for the pain to come. Instead, he crept backwards until his mouth was between her legs, and applied himself to sucking her femininity.

Though she had experienced it herself, Nelly had never seen a man lap at a woman's pussy before, and she looked on with interest as Sir Peter began licking the length of his bride's split. Nelly compared the other woman's cunny to her own. The skin was deeper pink outside, fading into pale white, and the inner lips and clitoral hood were smaller, but the pink inside was the same shade of her own. She watched entranced as Miss Annabelle jerked, her hips reaching for the air, her hands clawing at the bed sheets. Then Sir Peter was motioning her down beside him, and she knew what was expected of her.

The two of them started licking at Annabelle's cunny in earnest. Annabelle sobbed above them, her hands clawing at the bed, then finding a place on the two heads. She played with their hair, the one head napped, the other covered with smooth light hair. And her hips lived a life of their own, quivering delicately, then shaking violently as a particularly skilful lingual action brought new, untouched sensations into play. Peter began biting her thighs in between sticking his tongue to her hymeneal barrier. The hoped-for pain brought an even more violent reaction to Annabelle's frame. She cried out aloud, aware that there was no one to hear her save her household, and they were both busy with the parting of her legs.

Peter muttered something to the dark haired head beside him. She withdrew, her lips and cheeks glistening with Annabelle's juices, and looked at him in surprise. He nodded, and she immediately complied.

Annabelle looked on, hypnotised, as she straddled her head. The two brown thighs, their muscles taut, lowered the offered cunny over her face. She had a bare moment to study the organ, the culmination of her desires. The lips, both outer and inner were visible, and Annabelle envied their owner the darker complexion, so different from her own. Then her face was surrounded with the earthy clean scent of a woman, and Annabelle set to work willingly, licking with all her might at the offered morsels.

She was an inexperienced tribade, and occasionally her teeth grated into Nelly's flesh as she slobbered and licked at the dark organ above her. The smell was intoxicating, better than she had remembered from her far off adolescence when she had forced her then slave to cater to her wishes. Now she was free to indulge without the slightest censure. She noted that Nelly's clitoris was larger than her own, and it stuck out of the clitoral hood. She wished she could suck on the nubbin, and suiting deeds to wishes, she sucked away at the proffered morsel. A violent quiver that ran through Nelly's frame rewarded her. At the same time the movement of Peter's tongue in the cleft of her legs had not slackened, and her own climax was rapidly approaching. She howled out in delight, sucking rapidly at every available inch of skin, as her first climax rose from her groin into the depths of her stomach and beyond. The quivers in her loins turned to violent shakings, and she almost dislodged her husband's pursuing mouth.

'Oh God, more. Please more. Oh darling. Oh darling, I've got to have you all again,' was all she could mutter as her climax subsided somewhat.

Peter raised his head from his wife's sopping quim. The beautiful willing maid, her thighs spread around the golden hair of the new bride, was staring as if hypnotised at the blonde-topped split between the white thighs. Her own were still quivering from the hidden tongue and lips of her mistress, and she too wished this could continue forever.

'Nelly!' She was jerked out of her daze at the sight of the pale golden fuzz. 'Please hand me the paddle.' Sir Peter's hand was held out in expectation.

Nelly knew it would not do to dawdle. She reached for the case that had been left on the night-table. She was not sure what he meant, but among the instruments, things she had not seen since the bad days before the war, if even then, lay a thin-bladed instrument that could conceivably be a paddle. Her choice must have been appropriate, since Sir Peter merely said, 'Thank you,' before turning back to his bride. He waved the paddle in the air and it wafted a scent of something exotic to their nostrils. It was slightly flexible, covered with leather.

'Sandalwood,' Peter said casually. 'I do love the smell. Mingled with your own exquisite scent, my dear, it will be heavenly.'

He let Annabelle have one last look, her face peering from between dark thighs, then motioned the maid off her mistress's face, and rolled Annabelle over on the bed.

The white mounds of her ass shone in the candlelight with a pearly sheen. Bending rapidly, he kissed his bride while at the same time, raising the paddle and bringing it down sharply on her shapely behind. Annabelle tried to howl at the sudden stroke. Her sensitive skin raised an immediate red patch that complemented her white complexion. Kissing her deeply, Peter began lashing the pale mounds with all his might.

Annabelle howled at the sudden sensation. 'Oooaaah. Oh dearest. Don't stop. I can hardly bear it. Ooooooo.' Then her mouth was stopped by something warm and incredibly soft that was shoved between her lips. Tipped by a harder nubbin, she could barely recognise the breast between the lashes of pain. She seized on the offered morsel, her lips and teeth sucking heavily at the breast with the greatest of pleasure, while her hands clawed alternatively at the sheets and at the willing body before her. The blows suddenly changed tempo, and Annabelle knew that her husband had turned the paddle over to her own maid. To her own maid! She was now being beaten so pleasurably that she did not even notice when the tit was jerked from her mouth.

Peter watched for a moment as the maid beat his new wife. Soon, very soon, he would have to commit the final act of the evening. In fact, as his massive straining erection told him, he needed some slight relief right now! He advanced and parted the brown thighs displayed so enticingly before him. His tumescence was a glowing bar of iron, and he did not hesitate to quench it in the proffered wet hole. She growled deep in her throat when she felt the knob push into her sopping orifice. She had never treated another woman in this way, and she found that the excitement burned in her loins at the sights and sound of the paddling. So the thrust of the male member in her hole came as a delicious relief. She pushed back with her rump, intending to impale herself fully, while still conscious of her duty. Her strong hand rose and fell, bringing the paddle down forcefully on the proffered mounds.

Soon all three of the actors in the drama were breathing heavily. Peter found it increasingly difficult to restrain himself from pouring his juices into the maid's hot cunny. He shafted her brutally, digging as deeply into her soft female flesh as he could with each stroke, his balls smacking against her thighs with his wild movements. He fondled the full muscular mound of her buttocks, parting them and admiring the sight of the little clenched hole above the grasping lips that held his shaft so firmly. As he withdrew he saw his shaft was covered with a sheen of slime, and he felt the quivers as the maid reached the start of a series of peaks. Hastily he withdrew, before he could spew himself fully into her, and watched as the pink hole gasped desperately after the withdrawing shaft.

'Oh... oh... oh...!' Annabelle was crying out with each blow.

Nelly echoed her, though she was muttering into Annabelle's ear with each blow, 'Take that, you bitch. Come on you pink bitch, take that... and that... and that...' each word emphasised by a blow.

Sir Peter stopped her abruptly. Roughly he rolled Annabelle over. Her face was bedecked with tears, and she moved gingerly from the pain in her behind, but her face was smiling, and her lips, upper and lower, blushed a full pink, moistened by the juices of her passion. Wide-eyed she watched as Peter dropped his dressing gown. He allowed her to inspect him, prick completely erect, for a long delicious moment. His body was hard and muscular, and the... thing... sprouted like a pillar from a nest of dark brown hairs, the same colour hairs that speckled his breast and shoulders, though more curly and thick.

Supporting Annabelle with one hand he placed some cushions behind her. Her full pale breasts rose proudly, and she was smiling through her tears. Peter gently parted her thighs, exposing the pink slit between full lips. He knelt between the columns of exquisite flesh.

'Nelly.' His command was as gentle as before, but there was no mistaking the air of command. She took the proffered paddle, and looked for the box to return it. 'No,' he said.

Nelly saw that the bride's eyes were fixed hypnotically upon her. There was a strange expression on the tear-bedewed face, a compound of lust and fear.

'Strike her breasts,' Sir Peter said. 'Keep a steady pace. You will stop when I tell you.'

He lowered his head and began licking at Annabelle's exquisite lower lips. For a moment Nelly shied away from what she was to do. Then she had a good look at Annabelle's face. Her mistress was pleading, her glance longing, but it was not for release from the exercise. To the contrary, her lips were moving silently, and she seemed to be saying, 'Yes, yes… oh please, yes.'

Slightly puzzled, but willing nonetheless, Nelly raised the paddle. The look of gratitude on her mistress's face was all the encouragement she needed, and the paddle came whistling down.

The pain was as exquisite as she had always known it would be. Annabelle shrieked wildly as the blow struck her nipples.

'Oh, more, more…' she moaned, her hands reaching for the exposed dark flesh that towered above her. Peter watched the sight for a brief moment. His wife was splayed before him, and above her knelt the maid in her lustful glory. The dark breasts were moving entrancingly, and Annabelle was drawing red weals as she dragged her nails across the maid's muscular stomach. But all that was as nothing compared to the smack of the flexible leather covered paddle as it whistled down and cut into the soft sensitive tips of Annabelle's pale breasts. Her flesh was already a fiery red, and the nipples stood out as prominently as fresh cherries, when Peter threw himself forward. With one swoop he found the juicy, barricaded entrance to his wife's split. He pounded forward. The tip of his broad cock parted the nether lips and slid between them to the thin maidenhood. Without stopping it rammed through the barrier, tearing its way deep into the virginal canal. Annabelle shrieked as she felt the thrusting, tearing pain. Then there was a foreign object lodged where nothing had ever been before. It burned its way like molten fire up her innards, exacting pain and pleasure as it went. Then the entire weight of her new husband's muscular manly weight was resting on her splayed loins.

He fell upon her like a lion seizing his prey. His hands gripped her breasts painfully, his thumbs exercising the nipples. His loins fell upon hers, though she shrank at the sudden weight. Then the marvellous hard pole was at her virginal opening, shouldering her quivering tissues aside brutally, piercing her to the very quick as he lunged forward with all his strength.

Annabelle shrieked gratifyingly, knowing she was expected to do so as his hard shaft tore into her. In reality, it had not been at all painful. First had been the pressure of the blunt nozzle against her, between her, then a short tearing sensation as her maidenhood had burst under his onslaught. The pain had come – bearable but painful – when the shaft had thrust up her channel, widening the cavity in her body. She groaned and bit his shoulder as Peter set to work to fuck her.

'Ahhhh,' she shrieked in a paroxysm of joy. Her questing hands abandoned the dark skin and muscular belly above her and sought for the junction of their bodies.

Raising himself slightly, still jogging his rump to force himself more deeply into her, Peter allowed her to explore his flesh and their joining with her delicate hands. She fondled the ball bag roughly, not understanding their delicate nature, and patiently Peter allowed her the pleasure. Then she pinched her own distended flesh, feeling again the pleasure of the torn membrane, and her face lit with joy. Peter stopped the beating hand with a gesture, and brought his own lips down to cover those of his bride. Then he set to work to bring her to a climax again, this time using only the instrument of his manhood.

His cock pumped in and out of her splayed body. His hands roved over her ass and thighs, and his mouth sucked at the flesh of her neck, at her ears, kissing the tears away from her face. He motioned peremptorily again, and Nelly too started using her mouth on the supine woman. The two alternated their kisses on Annabelle's cherry lips, their tongues taking turns to explore her mouth, to suck at her breasts, to tickle her ears. Sir Peter's muscular buttocks were straining against the wide V of his new wife's body. Annabelle was moaning endearments, and when her climax approached she moved as if demented. Suddenly she stiffened and clutched at Peter with all her might, her nails drawing blood from the skin of his back.

'Oh, dear Peter. I'm… I'm… oh this is so *good*!'

'Yes, spend, my dear. Spend with my cock in you. That's what it's called. Let yourself go, dearest.'

Obedient to her husband's commands, Annabelle allowed herself to be swept away by the rapture of her senses, as her sopping thighs squashed against her husband's loins and she felt as if she was completely melting. Then Peter joined her. He forced himself into her as deep as he could, the tip of his cock was clipped by her inner recesses, his hairy scrotum mashed against the split of her thighs. His cock pulsed, once, twice, a third time, and Annabelle found that the torn membranes of her insides were flooded with his exudations, which served as a balm to her bruised tissues.

The happy conjugal couple lay in silence for a brief moment, then Peter started moving inside his wife once again. She opened her eyes, their brightness echoing his, and blushed. 'Oh Peter,' she marvelled, 'so soon again?'

'Yes, my dear,' he said. 'But there are other pleasures awaiting,' and without a further word he withdrew from her insides.

Annabelle tried to clutch at him, wondering what she had done. Peter avoided her embrace, and turned to the maid.

'Lie down,' he said to Nelly. Nothing loath, the maid lay down on the bed, spreading her legs.

Peter raised Annabelle and spread the pink opening of her maid with one hand, exhibiting the soft, wet, pink interior, framed so charmingly by darker lips.

'Mount her, my dear,' he said, smiling at his new bride.

Annabelle threw herself onto the maid's dark body. She fumbled around until she could find a comfortable position, where her newly inflamed cunny could come into contact with the other woman's slick lower lips, then she set to work to rub herself furiously against the curl-covered mound. The sensation of the friction between their two parts sent Annabelle into a delicious frenzy. Her own vagina was seeping juices, her own and her husband's, which lubricated the wiry connection between the two mounds. She thought she could feel every hair on her maid's pussy, and the touch of the other woman's erect and larger clitoris sent her into a passionate storm of exultation and delight. She pushed her tongue daringly into the other's mouth, exploring and marvelling at the softness of the tissues, their sweet surrender to her demands. Her hands rove over the maid's body as she rubbed herself into the other's organ of pleasure. Suddenly there was another source of pleasure as a white hot streak drew itself over her buttocks. Annabelle shrieked into her maid's mouth, unable to contain the sensations she felt.

Peter raised his hand. In it was a simple string lash, which he brought down again and again in time with Annabelle's movements. She screamed again, as the pain goaded her to greater efforts, as if she wanted to penetrate the maid's supine body. Nelly aided Annabelle's efforts, her strong hands clutching at her mistress's buttocks, parting the soft mounds so that the sting of the lash could reach every inch of flesh. Overcome by her passion and excitement, Annabelle stiffened on her companion as wild waves of pleasure coursed through her. She fell forward in a swoon, and her husband rushed to her side.

She was restored by a sip of brandy and some smelling salts, to find Peter's handsome face peering into her own.

'Are you yourself, my darling?' he asked anxiously.

'Oh Peter.' She threw her arms around him, quite overcome by the concern and love in his voice. 'That was so marvellous. We are going to be the happiest couple on this earth. Oh darling...'

'You enjoyed the sensations, then?' There was a smile beneath the mocking tone, and she replied by throwing herself into his arms.

'Once I have rested for a moment,' she whispered shyly into his ear, 'we must commence again.'

Chapter Five

Annabelle stretched luxuriously. For a moment she could not remember what she was doing in the strange bed, and then a smile crossed her face as she realised where she was, and no less importantly, *who* she was. Finally, a wife. And not only a wife, she thought, but the wife of such a glorious husband, one who not only knew, but actively abetted in his wife's weakness.

She stretched again, and the twinges of last night's activities reminded her of her paramour. She opened her eyes expecting to see the manly body of her beloved beside her, but she was alone on the silken sheets. She examined the rumpled fabric carefully. It bore marks of the previous night's exertions, including some minute bloodstains, which attested to her previous status and its final disposition.

The sun was shining brightly outside. She rose and the fabric of her nightdress, heavily embroidered silk imported by Peter at great expense, scratched comfortably against her nipples. They grew erect, and she explored her secret places with her hands. She was pleased to note that though the bruises on her backside still stung mildly, that of the wound between her legs only sent shivers of anticipatory lust up her frame. At that thought, she started and hurried through her morning toilet, wrapped herself in a light morning gown, and set off determinedly to search for her husband, the tingle in her loins having long become a fierce demand.

Peter was already at the table, having consumed a cup

of coffee. At the sight of Annabelle in her long gown he paused, then watched her move about the room, as she came to his side intent on a good morning kiss. She leaned over to him, still blushing slightly at the memory of the previous night. As she bent down her décolletage opened. Peter grasped for her breasts suddenly. As she squeaked in surprise he rose abruptly. She found herself instantaneously spread on the breakfast table. Crockery and silverware crashed to the floor. Under her tender bum she could feel bumps and objects poking into her. Fearfully she watched as he rose. For a moment she winced, expecting the tearing pain of the previous night.

The broad head of his cock pierced her without any preparation. At first she felt pain, not the lacerating pain of the loss of her maidenhood, but the pain of the dryness of her channel. But very soon the pleasure of the long shaft filling her interior brought down her own juices.

'Oh, Peter,' she cried when his mouth had released her. 'Oh Peter dear, how could you have known?' Her legs tangled with his, and she slid her smooth skinned limbs up and down, rubbing fiercely against his more hirsute appendages. Daringly, yet sure of her own authority, she ran her hands across his muscular buttocks, enjoying the play of the male strength under the hairy skin. She sought his mouth with her lips, sucking in the invading lingual member with all her might. His own fingers digging into her soft and bruised posterior brought about a tide of pleasure that she felt she could not contain.

'Oh Peter dear... Fu – fu – fu...' She found it difficult to articulate the word, even though he had told her that among married couples its use in private was not only permitted but perfectly laudable.

'Say it,' Peter breathed into her shell-like ear. 'Say it, dear wife.'

Needing no more encouragement, she muttered shyly, while her insides were a storm of emotion, 'F-fuck me, Peter dear. Oh... ah yes. Do fuck me. So hard, it's so *good*,' she wailed as her hair was mixed with the scuppernong jelly in an exquisite silver dish they had been given by one of her father's friends.

Willingly, Peter shuttled his inflamed prick in and out of her delightful hole, his loins smearing the breakfast materials on her backside and the front of his thighs.

Peter jerked suddenly, once, then again, then he pinned her roughly to the table, his cock screwed in deeply with all the power of his horseman's muscles. She screamed in pretended anguish and felt the essence of his pleasure flood and lubricate her interior. His cock hosed his semen deeply into her, and the weight of his loins spread her on the ruined breakfast, pinning her like a lovely pink butterfly beneath a giant pin.

Nelly watched the couple on the table impassively. Internally she sighed at the breakage of crockery. They were a lovely couple, and she really admired the picture of the master's pale ass surrounded by Miss Annabelle's paler thighs. Then Sir Peter turned his face from his wife's heaving tits and saw her. In the absence of instructions to the contrary, she was still wearing the previous day's uniform.

'Come here,' he said, sliding out from his wife's embrace. Annabelle clutched at him, reluctant to have him withdraw. The pale thighs were still sprawled apart. Nelly examined them. The slit was still a glowing red, and a runnel of male juices ran from between the nether lips and pooled on the table. The hairs that covered Miss Annabelle's lower belly were a pale golden fuzz, and her tiny pink clitoris was barely visible, peeking through the plump outer lips. The master pulled her to him. He kissed her deeply, his tongue seeking hers, and she responded with alacrity, wondering what was to come.

'Clean her,' he directed, pulling away. With two fingers he opened the gluey lips, exposing the red channel to the maid's eyes. Her pink tongue peeped delicately from between her dark lips as she considered a response.

'Exactly,' Sir Peter whispered. 'With your tongue.'

Nelly obediently knelt over the table. Her lips sought for the salty-sour-bitter mingled flavours of the man and woman. At first she was reluctant. Then the thrills of the sensation overcame her and she set to work with a will, licking and sucking at the delicate flesh.

At the first touch of the tongue Annabelle quivered and sighed deeply. She raised her head slightly from the jelly dish and saw the black close-cropped curls of her maid between her thighs. Her husband, his cock drooping forlornly from his hand, was being stroked to a new erection, and in the meantime, Annabelle's pleasure knew no bounds as she felt the rough tongue of the maid explore her gluey interior. She wondered what it tasted like, the essence of her husband's lust and her own intermingled, so that when the member in question was presented to her own pink lips, she was not at all loath to suck it in and gulp at the length. She sucked until she could feel the tip nudging at the back of her throat, and with an effort she controlled her gag. In the meantime Nelly was applying her entire attention to her mistress's slit, and her tongue was twirling between the distended lips, visiting the tiny boatman beneath her hood, and laving the length of Annabelle's nether lips with long caresses of a soft yet insistent tongue.

Sir Peter motioned to her, and the maid stopped her ministrations to the mistress's pink shell. Without a word he indicated the position he wanted her to take.

Doubtfully, but with growing curiosity and lust, she climbed onto the table, glad she had no skirts to hike up. Her knees spread, she straddled Annabelle's flushed face, her own nose a few inches away from her mistress's humid forest.

Annabelle sighed happily and her tongue reached for the black hairs that clustered in tiny ringlets on the mound above her. She parted the full lips with her fingers and examined the enclosed groove. To her surprise, the interior of the nether mouth was as delicately pink and sweetly moist as her own. For a long minute she perused it. The long furrow, the tiny hole, the little pearl-like pink bead that was the set of pleasure, then, with the rise of pleasure in her own belly, her tongue and lips were drawn uncontrollably up to that before her and her tongue shot into the tight depths. She was in heaven. The slightly salty taste of the serving girl's interior brought involuntary spasms to her frame. She pushed her tongue in as far as it could go, titillating it rapidly with vibrations of her lingual finger. Then, in the throes of her delight, she pulled the dark skin closer, her nails digging into the full buttocks. Her nose nuzzled at the darker muscular entrance above the hole she was licking. Undaunted, she pushed forward, breathing deeply at the musky scent of her maid. Nelly was grunting above her and at the feel of the nasal invasion of her rear, she settled herself more comfortably on her mistress's face amidst the broken crockery. Her own fingers gripped the other girl's delicate pink lips. She lowered her own and as the pleasure of Annabelle's tongue in her cunny moved her frame, she sipped delicately at the juicy petals. Then she looked up triumphantly, inviting Sir Peter by her looks to take advantage of the pale splayed legs and channel she held open with her fingers.

Peter grinned at the picture of his servant perched on

his wife's face. His cock was still flaccid, moist with his joint spending with Annabelle. He moved forward until he was poised at the entrance to the golden-furred mound.

'You do it,' he said.

Nelly leaned further forward and her lower lips escaped Annabelle's mouth. The pretty young wife sought again for the delicate morsel, and Nelly settled herself more forcefully on the blonde curls.

'Punish her if she does it wrong,' Sir Peter smiled from above. 'Come, help me rise again.'

Nelly stared at her employer in doubtful surprise. He encouraged her with a brisk motion. She pinched the pink lips experimentally. Beneath her she could hear a muted 'Ahhh', whether of pleasure or anger she did not know, but she tried again, and was rewarded with a deep thrust of the tongue under her. She pinched harder and Annabelle's tongue set to work, lashing the dark cunny to a frenzy.

'Clean me and make me rise,' ordered the young man. Nelly sniffed first at the glowing cock. The smell was delicious, even perfumed, overlaid by the harsh male odour. Then her pink tongue peeped out and she licked the spongy knob. Harshly, Sir Peter seized the nape of her brown curl-covered neck and thrust his half-erect male appendage into her waiting and willing mouth. She hollowed her cheeks and sucked him in, providing friction with the pressure of her tongue against her palate and with the pressure of her lips. Sir Peter sighed with satisfaction, and still holding her neck, he began moving her head forward and back in a rhythm that soon brought him to full tumescence.

Nelly enjoyed the feel of the male member growing in her mouth. Paradoxically it gave her a feeling of great power, and she was sunk in a reverie where *she* rather than the pale body beneath her was the real bride, when she was brought rudely to her senses. Annabelle's teeth bit deeply into her fleshy cunt lips, and the girl shrieked with pain. Automatically, in a reflex kindled by a flash of uncontrollable anger, she twisted the pink lips beneath her hands viciously.

'Oh God! Ahh yes!' She could hear the muffled shriek from between her thighs, and, recalling her employer's tastes, she set to work to wreak her fury on the body beneath her. Her fingers curved like claws and she tore at the soft mound of flesh.

'Oh yes, please Nelly dear, oh please.'

Nelly obediently increased the pressure and cruelly twisted her fingers in the luxuriant blonde curls. Pulling hard, she exacted another yelp and delighted scrabbling at her feminine port.

'Oh my dear, oh my dear. Yes, I'll do anything. I'll be good,' Nelly could hear the mouth beneath her mumble, and then the marvellous tongue began stroking the lips of her slit, exciting a flash of sheer pleasure, so that she rammed herself deeply onto the proffered mouth.

In the meantime Peter's cock had grown to its original magnificent erection. He pulled back from the dark face and examined the twinned women on the table. Blonde curls were peeping out from under and between Nelly's dark chocolate covered thighs. Her own tight-curled dark head was framed by pale pink legs that clutched and quivered with every twist of her strong fingers in the golden fleece beneath them. Peter watched for a while, idly stroking his cock until he could bear the sight passively no longer. He leaped onto the table, scattering silverware as he did so. First he knelt by Annabelle's head and planted a kiss on her sweaty, musky-smelling forehead. Then he crouched behind Nelly's pouting bottom, his bag swinging perilously close to his bride's perspiring brow.

From below, Annabelle watched the male member come into sight, armed and ready like a lancer, and she cried out the harder.

Peter crouched over the upraised bum. He parted the full dark buttocks and ran his thumb along the crease, dipping into the pink valley. His wife's tongue rewarded the tips of his fingers with a brief lick, and as he peered between his legs he could see her blue eyes gleaming up at him. His thumb stroked again and dipped nail-deep into the puckered anal hole. Nelly gave a gasp. Peter aimed his cock at her flowing cunny and pushed forward. The velvety movement of his wife's tongue complemented the slick tightness of the maid's dark pussy.

Nelly shuddered and gasped as her mistress's tongue and her master's cock penetrated her together. Then the three of them started moving in unison as if they had practised the choreography of love all their lives. Nelly moved herself backwards and forwards, impaling herself onto the pink pillar that skewered her from the rear. Her fingers dug deeply into her mistress's slit while she played roughly, pinching and squeezing, with the tiny nubbin of pearly flesh that fronted the love channel. Annabelle, moaning and gasping with pleasure, licked furiously at her husband's pistoning manhood and at the prominent pink extrusion of her maid's vaginal parts. Her own hips were jerking furiously, and soon all three of them were trembling with the imminent arrival of their various climaxes.

'Oh my God. Oh honey. Oh yes. Let me have some more. Fu… fu… fuck me with your mouth.'

Nothing loath, Nelly obeyed her mistress's furious commands while surrendering herself to the pleasure of her master's demanding movements.

'Ah, yes sir. Do me... do me,' she uttered, in semi-trance herself. She shuddered almost wordlessly, crying out aloud, as the first of a series of crests hit her and she began climaxing. She knew her insides were running with liquids, and Miss Annabelle was licking them all up. 'Oah, Miss Annabelle. Oah, Sir Peter,' she gasped as the waves hit her and her hips jerked. 'Yes! Do me... do meeee!'

Stimulated by the women's cries and by his own passionate embrace, Peter shot off load after load of spermatic libation into the clutching interior. Then he collapsed on the woman's backside, while his obedient and loving wife licked up the residue of his seed as it oozed between Nelly's distended lips and his own tumescence.

When at last Peter pulled away, Nelly would have moved too. But Annabelle gripped her hips, and with a sharp smack kept the maid in place. Carefully and thoroughly she lapped at the residue of her maid's and her husband's lovemaking, while Nelly quivered again and again in the throes of later comings.

At last Annabelle relented and allowed her maid to recover. She rose and stood shyly before her husband. Her hair was covered with jelly, and her gown was covered with the remains of their breakfast, which she had not had a chance to eat. But she was smiling, shyly yet happily. Her husband tilted her face up to his and kissed her delicately.

'Nelly,' he said over his shoulder. 'Please run a bath for Lady Stone, and then you may clear away.'

Nelly, her knees stained with the remains of food, her insides happily satiated, bobbed a curtsy as she had learned by trial and error he expected, and darted ahead while the young couple wandered slowly upstairs.

Newly installed gas lamps dimly lighted the street below. The tall dark man sniffed delicately at the brandy that had been brought to his room by an obsequious waiter. He regarded the shimmering surface of the liquid critically.

'Faster!' he said without raising his voice.

'Unghh,' the woman crouching at his feet grunted and her head jerked rapidly up and down in his lap. Languidly he raised his gloved left hand and picked up the long riding crop from the table by his side. Without watching, he brought the quirt slashing down on the plump pink buttocks exposed beneath her black stays. 'Not so roughly,' he added without raising his voice.

She suppressed a scream and tried to maintain a smooth pace.

His hands drifted slowly to her mousy curls, then he pulled viciously at her hair. She cried out into his cock.

'Ahh,' he said. 'I do so love that feel.' He smiled and his mismatched eyes glowed. The green one was inflamed, the red colour of the sclera contrasting strongly with the bright green of the iris. 'Nothing quite like it, eh? Your throat trembling against... this,' and he jerked his cock forward so that the tip jerked against the back of her throat. She moaned again, but afraid of him, did not otherwise protest. His eyes caught the sight of the newspaper he had ordered earlier, and his hips stopped their thrusting motion. She relaxed slightly, even allowed herself to balance against his knees, since her hands, bound behind her, offered no support. The lash mark still stung, but at least he was allowing her to get on with it.

The newspaper covered her head, bobbing up and down as he read while she sucked at his thick tumescence. She wondered how long it would take before he flooded her mouth. Her jaws were tired. With any other customer she would have speeded the process along, but this one was too… too scary, she admitted to herself with a shiver.

'Aha!' He exclaimed suddenly, and she could feel his entire body stiffen. The paper fell in drifts over her head. Then he was conscious of her mouth on him. His fingers grabbed her ears and he jerked himself fully into her.

'Yes, that's it. I've got you now!' he cried exultantly as his cock shuttled between her lips. She was gagging, about to bite him and be done, when he stiffened convulsively. A stream of thick liquid jetted from his cock and flooded her mouth. She gulped hurriedly, trying to keep the remains from staining his trousers, but he was too impatient. He jerked his cock from her soft mouth, then wiped it casually against her cheek as he stood up. The 'Society at Large' page was clutched in his hands, and he stared at it fiercely, his face twisted in an unpleasant grin.

He tossed a gold sovereign at her. 'Get out,' he said, his mind not even on her, absently buttoning up his flies.

She rose and reached quickly for her clothes, the gold clutched in her fist, but not before casting a glance at the column that had so attracted his notice.

None of the squibs meant anything to her. Not even the one that said:

English nobleman marries Southern Belle.

Chapter Six

Sir Peter looked critically at the silver tray.

'A proper tea is *quite* the done thing, my dear. I'm afraid that…' he sighed, 'it will take a while to bring the habit to the Colonies. Nonetheless, we can but try. Sandwiches? Very good, though I do wish we could find some proper cress. Tea pot warm? Most gratifying. Some small pats of butter and well-sliced bread? I must say she does one proud, your maid.' He frowned for a moment. 'Though I do think we should consider more staff.' He raised his eyes and smiled at his new bride. 'Once we have properly settled in, that is.'

The afternoon had turned out to be dismal. A warm torrential rain was falling, and they had returned from a stroll before being drenched to the bone. Now they were seated in their new parlour while the rain drummed on the roof overhead.

Gratified by his words, yet put properly on her mettle, Annabelle bent to pour the tea. She knew she presented an enchanting sight in her new crinoline. Its mild peach hue had been chosen with an eye to enhancing her perfect complexion, and its cut was enough to entice the most jaded of men, which her new husband assuredly was not. So she knew, as she bent over the tea cups, that she showed a proper amount of her perfect pale breasts to her husband's appreciative eyes, and she wondered what he would do to encourage her. From the corner of her eye she could see her maid, dressed now most conventionally, albeit in lavish fabrics of black velvet and starched white lace, hovering modestly by the wall. The blood rushed to her cheeks at the thoughts and imaginings that that slim black figure was *hers*! Hers to do with what she most wished. For a brief second she paraded the images of her fantasies, long suppressed before her mind's eye, knowing them all to be possible. All to be acted out in time, and she trembled at the thought of those brown hands lashing her, with instruments of pleasure, with bare pink palms, forcing her onto the slim dark body that lay beneath the sober maid's clothing.

Her lips and eyes were moist as she looked up at her spouse. As if sensing nothing, Peter was delicately sipping at the fine bone china and sniffing appreciatively at a cucumber sandwich. Demurely, Annabelle helped herself as well, and they discussed how they would arrange the garden.

'Would you play for me, my dear?' Peter asked, indicating the piano that stood by the side of the drawing room. Smiling with pleasure, she rose and sat on the broad piano stool.

Peter stood behind her as she played, entranced by the sight of those slight fingers coaxing such beautiful sounds out of the black and white keys. The muscles in her exposed shoulders moved in synchronisation with the music, and he could feel his manhood hardening as he watched her play, absorbed in the music. In a trice he had opened his flies, and began rubbing the tip of his cock against her exposed shoulders in time to the music. At first Annabelle did not notice the priapic intrusion, but soon the silken feel of his flesh against hers brought about a flush that arose even as the chords became more entrancingly sensuous and the rubbing of the male member against her skin brought about an exquisite sensation. Romantic, full chords rolled lushly out from under her fingers. She sighed even as her shoulders quivered, and her nipples could clearly be seen in their erectile state under the thin muslin dress she wore in the humid heat.

Peter's hands moulded her shoulders, and not gently. He strained the full length of his member against the nape of her neck, rubbed it against her creamy shoulders. The pace of her playing slowed to a dreamy waltz. Seizing a fistful of his wife's golden hair, Peter rubbed his reddened cock furiously across her back. He leaned forward and with his other hand dug inside her bodice, popping out her full breasts and squeezing the nipples fondly. In time with the music, he started moulding her breasts until his fingers sunk into the soft mounds.

'Ohhh, yes my darling,' she mouthed, the chords becoming ragged.

Peter twisted the lovely pink nipples with his fingers until they flushed a deeper red.

Her eyelids dropped, and Annabelle moaned deeply 'Aaaaa... punish me, my love. Rub your cock into my hair. Punish my bubbies. Hit them... please hit them.'

Peter, ever ready to oblige his bride, obeyed on the instant. One hand held out an inviting milky-white teat, while the other rose and descended in a slap that was timed to perfection to the music. Again he raised his hand, waited an instant, and brought it down on the beat. Without losing the beat, or his grip on the lovely woman now writhing on the piano stool before him, he shifted hands and slapped deeply onto her other soft mound. It jounced merrily in his grip, and Annabelle's cherry lips opened once more in a cry of pleasure and pain.

'Diddle me. Ohhh... darling. Come and put your lovely member into me.'

Not waiting for another command, Peter pulled at her

shoulders and laid her on the padded bench. He lifted up her skirts to cover her face, and flipped the hoops over her head. Nelly hurriedly came forward and unloosened the tapes, and dragged the hoops off, just as Sir Peter exposed his wife's naked cunny. He glared at it lustfully for a moment, then parting her knees roughly, he threw himself on the supine and trembling body. With a single lunge he was lodged in her cunny to the very base of his rampant cock. He took her roughly, not bothering to uncover her skirts from her face. Nelly could see the masses of golden hair she had set so carefully that very morning dragging on the floor as the mistress of the house wailed her pleasure at the brutal rogering she was receiving.

'Oh, oh, oh,' was all Annabelle could utter, each time the lusty man drove his weapon into her to the hilt. Nelly squatted and watched the hairy ball-bag swing and smack into her mistress's exposed backside. Then Sir Peter was shuddering mightily, and she could see his testicles contract, and pump again and again into the parted lips, until a white froth oozed forth.

Peter rose from his seat. Nelly looked at her mistress's disarray. Automatically, she bent to put her mouth to Miss Stone's drooling cunny. She was beginning to like the taste, she discovered, and wondered if she tasted the same.

'Not like that,' Sir Peter said. He reached for the two of them, and in a trice both women were completely naked. He stretched Annabelle out on the piano stool. The woman lay there, her eyes dreamy, her legs bare and her feet encased in fine white kidskin boots laced to mid-shin. Annabelle was breathing heavily. She watched as her husband pulled the willing maid to him and kissed her deeply, his fingers on the crack of her cunny. Then he held Nelly with one hand, while with the other he fumbled at a box on the escritoire. He held in his hand a sheaf of whalebone switches, fine white rods ending in feather smooth tassels. He allowed Annabelle to see them for a brief moment, then pulled Nelly to him, moving the serving girl's limbs about without a word. Nelly crouched over Annabelle's face, her own face seeming to project a single large question mark. Annabelle reached out with her mouth, breathing in the heady smells of the lustful servant's scent. Her thighs were quivering violently. This was a dream coming to life. Oh, how she adored her beloved Peter for arranging all this!

Nelly looked without comprehension at the switch Sir Peter had pressed into her hand. He stood behind her, his stiff manhood pressed against the flesh of her back.

'Beat her,' he whispered, one hand clutching at Nelly's swaying breast, the other groping for his wife's pale mound. He let off Nelly's breast when she did not comply, then gripped her wrist. With one smooth movement he lifted both their hands and brought the switch whistling down onto Annabelle's parted thighs.

Annabelle screamed, the sound muffled by Nelly's mound, and her tongue and mouth drove into the soft moist recesses. Nelly herself groaned, her own lust rising from the feel of the power in her hands, and the pleasure of the tongue beneath her. Gleefully she picked up the rhythm herself, and flicked the switch inexpertly onto the splayed flesh beneath her. Annabelle screamed again, her mouth full of curly hair and sweet, sweet flesh, her own thighs burning with pleasure.

'Pass your lips over her heated cunny from time to time, my dear,' Peter murmured, his finger stroking the dimple between her buttocks. 'Do you know what I am going to do now,' he continued, his finger denting the muscular vale with more pressure. Nelly nodded, her eyes closed, her fist rising and falling almost automatically. She knew, but she wanted him to tell her.

'I am going to fuck your arsehole, my dear,' he murmured, his fingers growing more insistent.

The distension of her bottom was not unpleasant, but she dreaded to feel the full raging thickness of his manhood.

'Yes, I am going to commit the sin of Sodom,' he said, and his finger left her bottom. 'And once I have done that, I shall also do it to the girl beneath you, and you will assist me.'

Nelly tensed herself, and her tenseness betrayed itself in her blows. Annabelle cried out wordlessly beneath her, her tongue and mouth digging deeply into her maid.

'Oh Lord, oh Lord,' Nelly whispered a litany. She struck the pale white flesh before her, her eyes glazing with the joy of inflicting such tortures on another's flesh. Instead of the searing pain she expected from his thickness crowding into her bottom, she felt the finger come back again. This time, however, it was coated with some kind of grease, and again it rubbed insidiously against her nervously tightening flesh. Soon, as her mistress continued lapping at her pussy, Nelly could feel her master's finger inserting itself into her. Unable to bear the pleasure, wanting to encourage the penetration even more, she bent forward. Annabelle's pink cunny was close to her mouth, and she hurriedly licked at the smooth expanse. Annabelle moaned again, her teeth nipping softly at Nelly's flesh, and Nelly knew that she had to be stern. Her teeth nipped into the overheated flesh, and Annabelle cried out once more. A second finger joined the first, and Nelly moved her ass backwards, staking herself onto the intruding digits. A third was inserted and the twirling of the three inside her bum caused Nelly to twist her hips in a frenzy, grinding them against her mistress's mouth while her own mouth bit and sucked at the inflamed tissues around the soft pink lips.

Peter, clad only in his shirt, crouched for a moment over the two entwined bodies, one dark the other pale. The picture was delightful, made all the more pleasant because he was soon to join the picture. He held his cock with one hand, his fingers still inserted deeply into the muscular clutching rear entry that was so helplessly exposed to his lust. Bending the shaft with an effort, he crouched lower and presented it to the greased entrance. His fingers had loosened the entry, and so he could pop in the tip of his prick without any effort. He held still for a moment, more to enjoy the sensation than to afford the woman time to adjust, and then he bent his knees and forced the shaft even deeper into her.

The clutch of her muscles at his organ was exquisite. His shaft slid into the greasy slick interior channel, grasped strongly on all sides by her lustful contortions. The maid's dark curls were buried between Annabelle's white thighs, but even so Peter managed to force his lips down on her, and she turned, her eyes moist, to kiss him deeply with Annabelle-pussy flavoured lips and tongue. They lay thus for a moment of lustful content, until Annabelle started moving restlessly under them. Nelly quieted her with a sharp slap to her golden pudenda, and then Sir Peter set to work to jam his cock deeply into his maid.

'Take that, you beautiful arse,' he shouted cheerfully as he rose and sank down again onto the two convulsing figures.

'Yes sir! Oh yes sir! Please ahhhh... oooh... fuck me!'

Annabelle added to the chorus as Nelly smacked her pussy again and again, between bites and long licks of the wet slit. 'Oh, please. Don't hit me. Stooop. Please. Ohhh yes, Nelly, do it again. Oh darling Peter, your cock is so beautiful. Fuck this bitch's ass. Oh fuck.'

'Oh you lovely arsed bitch!' he roared as he rose and dropped into the dark tight hole.

Nelly thought her head would burst with the pleasure of the scene. Her inner self was aflame, licked clean by Annabelle's by-now skilled mouth. Her rear passage was full of maleness, and the friction against the tender membranes was bringing her to a climax the intensity of which she had never known before. And every time she struck the woman beneath her, she felt a thrill of atavistic delight run through her frame. In short order the glow of pleasure was too great to bear.

'Oh, oooh, oooooohhh,' she cried. 'I'm coming... I'm speeeeeending!' The maid shrieked and clawed ravenously at the slit before her, her tongue digging as deeply as it could, her hands beating a rapid tattoo that raised a full flush on the soft inner thigh flesh. She quivered deeply, her anus contracting, and then collapsed on her mistress.

Sir Peter kept shafting at her, though his motions slowed down, allowing the maid to recover from her swoon. She turned her face towards him and kissed him shyly but passionately. He rose considerately from her, and helped her to her feet. Annabelle, her face laughing but contorted by unsatisfied lust, opened her legs wide, expecting to have her chance at John Thomas.

'No, my dear,' said Peter, allowing her to rise from the seat. 'Another treat awaits you.'

He indicated a large overstuffed wing chair with a straight back. 'Nelly, please seat yourself.'

The maid did as she was bid, settling herself comfortably, wondering what was next on the evenings list of amusements.

'Open your knees wide, Nelly,' said Sir Peter.

He turned to his wife, smiled, and seized the back of her neck, frowning hideously and twirling an imaginary handlebar moustache. As his own moustache was quite small and neat, it threw the women into gales of laughter, but they sobered when he rolled his eyes angrily. 'Is this how you obey your master?' he roared, and Annabelle jumped, even though she knew her dear Peter was merely play-acting.

'On your knees,' he commanded.

She fell promptly to her knees before Nelly's lap, and divining his intentions by the pressure on her neck, leaned forward.

'Lap that lovely cunny,' he said. 'That juicy woman's pussy.'

Hastily, and with feigned reluctance, Annabelle complied.

Seizing a bundle of birch twigs he had concealed behind his back, Peter lashed at the bare exposed bottom.

'Take that!' he roared. 'You have been a bad girl, cavorting with servants. Take that. And that!'

The twigs swished down musically on the soft skin, and Annabelle yelled, the sound only partly hidden by Nelly's thighs.

'Oh no sah,' she wailed in her best Southern accent, which she knew irritated Peter. 'Please don' beat me sah. Ah won' sin no moah. Ah promise yo'. Aaaaah!' she ended her words with a please as a particularly savage blow cut into her behind.

Peter danced about, cutting her here and there, now high, now low, until the birch bundle was in splinters. Fearing to pierce her lovely skin, he desisted. He looked at his handiwork. Annabelle's ass was covered with welts, all of them a deep pink, almost red colour. He gazed at his handiwork for a moment, then the heavy staff that rose before him recalled itself to his attention, and he advanced on the sore and lacerated behind, a cruel grin on his face.

There was no by-play with the fingers, no moistening of the nether hole this time, and Nelly saw what was coming. She gripped the blonde's head tightly between her knees, and leaning forward, pulled the pale pink buttocks apart. Softer, less muscular than her own, they yielded with less reluctance, until the vale between them was almost flat. Nestled in what had been a deep valley, the puckered entrance stood slightly everted, clenched tight, moistened by the juices that had dripped down on it before. The faint red stripes from the whalebone switch were clearly evident, crossing the distended mounds, framing the brownish hole, a deeper red against the broad flush caused by the birch.

Peter nodded his approval. He spat in the palm of his hand and wetted the tip of his cock. Holding it tightly in his fist, he brought it first to the moist slit, stroking it the length of the pink lips, then aimed it directly at the clenched bottom-hole. He pushed the tip slowly in, only enough to seat it properly.

'Ooooah,' Annabelle grunted at the pressure. She was breathing heavily, imprisoned, her face caught between the muscular columns of Nelly's limbs. She felt helpless, and the terror of the coming sensation was as exquisitely delicious as it was frightening. She could feel the broad male cockhead spear into her, and her anal muscles yielding painfully to the overwhelming male pressure.

For a moment measured in heartbeats Peter contemplated the scene. His bride's stretched-tight bum, and the tiny hole distended by the tip of John Thomas's nose. Gathering his concentration, feeling nothing except the exquisite pleasure of the tight resisting rear muscles, he thrust himself suddenly and brutally forward until his shaft disappeared halfway up Annabelle's pink bum.

The sudden insertion brought a loud series of screams from Annabelle's mouth. At first there was only pain, as the broad cockhead distended the hole past its natural width. The relief she felt as she was completely penetrated, and as the muscles closed around the thinner part of the shaft, brought with it the first intimations of pleasure, and she began to revel in the pain, yet, nonetheless, she screamed, howling in a Southern patois that she knew would fetch her man.

'Oah ma lawd. Oah God. Oh yes, fuck me dear Peter. Ah love that. It hurts deah. Oh it hurts. Fuck me up mah ass, honey. Ah love it…'

'Fuck and bugger you, my dear.' Peter's teeth were clenched with the effort not to pour his seed too soon, excited and infuriated by her accent, but the tightness of the rear entrance brought all his efforts to naught, and he could feel the juices rise in his stones. 'Oh darling, oh dearest,' he cried as a tidal wave of spunk issued from his balls and into the deepest darkest recesses of Annabelle's body. He cried out again, and she echoed his cry as his body collapsed onto hers and his weight forced her down onto the padded stool.

Annabelle felt the gush of sperm from her husband's cock inundate her burning insides. The warm male fluid lubricated the movement, and smoothed the passage of the male member up her tortured flesh. Her insides quivered in sympathy, and as his weight descended onto her naked back, her muscles clenched, strangling the male member with a grip that squeezed the last of his sperm into her insides. When her inner quivering had subsided, she turned her face to find his eyes gazing adoringly into hers, and his mouth conveniently close. Boldly, even wantonly, she stole a kiss, and they lay together for a while, luxuriating in their mutual pleasure.

Chapter Seven

Daisy watched Miss Stone with some apprehension. She stood modestly as she did so, her hands in front of her thighs. Miss Stone was a severe-looking blonde. Her eyes glittered as she considered Daisy. Beside her stood Nelly dressed in a starchy uniform with a rather short skirt. There was something almost familiar about the way Nelly stood, as if telling Daisy and the world that her position with Miss Stone was secure. Now Daisy could understand why Nelly was so reluctant to tell her about the job possibility. But she knew she could do it, she knew she was at least as good as her cousin.

'I imagine you have references from those places you say you worked at?' Annabelle asked. She looked carefully at the girl before her. She was slim and dark, much darker than Nelly, who confessed to being her cousin. Her features were neat and delicate. Annabelle shivered inside with anticipation. She *must* have this one. Surely Peter would like her too. Surely. She paused for a moment, not sure how to begin. This was the first time she had had to pander for her and Peter's tastes.

'I will pay you ten dollars a month,' she started. Daisy's black eyes widened with surprised pleasure. Ten dollars for a maid was a fortune. 'You will also, of course, sleep here. And be provided with clothes.'

'Yes'm,' Daisy responded automatically.

'We shall have to correct her pronunciation...' Annabelle said to Nelly. Daisy smiled. At ten dollars a month she'd speak any way they wanted.

'...I shall expect absolute obedient service and discretion,' Annabelle continued.

She was looking straight into Daisy's eyes, and Daisy knew that the choice of words was not idle. Ten dollars a month.... and what could happen to her, after all? For that price she'd even sleep with Miss Annabelle. She shook inside with laughter, the very idea of a Southern belle making love to her was ludicrous. The master undoubtedly would try something, if he could hide it from the wife, but that was the way of things... Maybe the wife and massa didn't get along so well, or maybe she just didn't care for nookie. Too bad for her. If the massa was anything of a looker, she wouldn't mind one little bit.

'You will have a bath every night, my husband is most particular,' Annabelle went on.

'Yes ma'am,' Daisy said. She was grateful for the order. In some of the houses she had worked in the owners had been as filthy as pigs, rarely washing or changing their underwear, notwithstanding their outward signs of gentility.

'...and change your clothes, including underclothes, whenever necessary. And if I hear you telling tales outside...'

The work was easy. It was afternoon by the time Daisy had finished her assigned labours, and even managed to polish some of the silver. She stretched tiredly. It wasn't too bad. Miss Annabelle came around to look at things, but after she had found that Daisy knew her way about a big house, she left her alone. And Nelly didn't seem to work too hard either, though there was a glint of something in her eyes every time she saw either Daisy or the missus. She still hadn't caught sight of the massa, and Daisy wondered what he was like. Would he want to drag her off into his favourite spot and fuck her right there and then? She shrugged mentally, adjusting the skirt of her somewhat brief uniform. Seemed like the missus didn't mind.

'Daisy?' Miss Annabelle was looking at her sharply. 'Finished already?'

Daisy jumped to her feet from the stool on which she was dozing. 'Yes'm.' She knew what was wanted, and gave a pretty curtsy.

Annabelle looked at her, head to foot, then strode away. 'Come with me,' she said over her shoulder. Daisy followed, sighing mentally. She had wanted to find some nook and catch forty winks. Annabelle strode ahead and flung open the door to the large indoor bath. It had been put in at Sir Peter's insistence, and Daisy admitted to herself that she had never seen a finer, nor larger one. She also groaned quietly. Cleaning this monster? Now? But her face betrayed nothing of her inner feelings. She looked carefully around as Annabelle went over to the side closet and extracted a large fluffy towel.

The bathroom was large, and needed to be, to accommodate the huge lion-footed bathtub. There were bronze taps for cold *and* hot water, and the bath could comfortably seat three.

'Sir Peter and I,' said Annabelle, allowing Daisy a moment to examine her surroundings, 'insist that our help be perfectly clean at all times. You shall have a bath now, and I shall supervise, to ensure that everything is done properly.'

Daisy noted a slight quickening of Miss Annabelle's breath, and a heightening of her colour, and wondered what it portended.

'Well ma'am,' she tried to protest, 'I'm sure I can have a bath—'

'No, that won't do,' interrupted Annabelle. 'It must be done to perfection, or Sir Peter will be most annoyed. Please get in.'

'Ah've got to... drop mah dress, ma'am,' Daisy said reluctantly. This was getting odder and odder.

'Of course,' Annabelle said. 'And please hang the items of your attire up properly.'

Daisy nervously squirmed out of her black dress, after struggling to untie the bow of her apron. She looked around for somewhere to hang the garment, and found a row of hooks high up on the wall. With an effort she reached for one of them and hung the dress.

Annabelle looked on as the new maid stripped. She could feel a weakness in her knees at the sight. The black dress came first, slipped over the maid's shoulders, pulled up over her head. At the sight of the knicker-less, beautifully smooth dark legs Annabelle had to pinch her own nipples roughly to stop herself from running over and sliding her hands up their delicious length. Her heart leaped to her mouth when Daisy stretched high to place the dress on the hook, which had been placed there in that position for precisely that reason. Her ass, uncovered by the brief lifting of her chemise, was muscular and well featured, the awkward stance heightening the tension of the muscles.

Daisy turned, as if she had sensed the eyes on her. She froze for a moment in the act of lifting her chemise. Annabelle looked at her, eyes almost glazed, and nodded at her to continue. She watched as the young girl reluctantly lifted her chemise. Her nipples and body were dark, far darker than Nelly's, and the hair under her armpits was a woolly forest that Annabelle would have loved to run her fingers through, and to rub her face in. Daisy's belly was rounded and muscular, and her waist slightly thick. As she pulled the chemise over her head, Annabelle could see the triangle of thick tight curls appear, and even the blacker lips of the maid's beautiful slit.

'We shall have to get you some petticoats,' Annabelle said, her lips and throat dry. 'Take off your stockings and shoes.' Peter had insisted the maids be properly shod, and now she appreciated why. The thin stockings in white combed cotton rose to Daisy's knees. They added a piquant flavour to the girl's skin. 'Then into the bath,' she added.

Uncomfortably, Daisy stepped into the water. The need to climb over the tall bath ledge afforded Annabelle a quick look between the maid's thighs. Her temples heated up and leaked perspiration. She watched Daisy settle herself gingerly in the water, which climbed to the level of her nipples. Wordlessly, she handed the young servant a bar of scented soap. As if in a dream she watched Daisy lather on her palms, and in the absence of a washcloth, start running her soapy hands over her body. When those same palms lifted the dark breasts, soaping the black nipples, Annabelle finally found her voice, though it was harsh and sounded strange to her ears. 'I shall do your back!' she announced imperiously.

Daisy looked up in alarm and surprise, and Annabelle, in her crinoline, pulled up the bath chair and grasped Daisy firmly by the shoulders. Her hands were trembling with lust, and in her mind's eye it was Daisy who was handling her so firmly. Soaping her hands, she ran them over the smoothly muscled back, and as her emotions got the better of her, scraped with her nails, only remarking that all the dirt had to be gotten out, as they were most particular in her household.

'Raise your arms,' Annabelle said in a hoarse whisper. Daisy, her eyes wide with wonder, and feeling emotions that did not seem proper, did as she was bid. Annabelle was greeted with the sight of her dark armpit, layered with the crisp froth of hair. The muscles that ran down and forward held up the curve of the maid's breast, and Annabelle's hand strayed, no longer under her control, towards the beauty she saw. Hastily she scrubbed at the concealed hair, with a hand on each side of the girl's body. Then her hands slid forward and scrubbed roughly at the girl's breasts. Daisy moved, as if in complaint at the slight roughness, but did not say anything.

Annabelle was now crouched uncomfortably by the side of the bath, and her hands went deeper, sinking into the water, rubbing at the gloriously smooth dark skin. 'Stand up, Daisy,' she said, her voice trembling with restrained passion. Daisy rose from the bath, streaming water. Annabelle hastily lathered her palms again. One of them went to the girl's belly, the other to her ass, and she began a rounded massaging motion. Then, throwing restraint to the wind, she soaped between Daisy's legs, taking special care that her fingers should taste every nook and cranny. Her fingertip brushed into the folds of Daisy's wet cunny, then parted her labia more deeply, as if accidentally. Daisy, speech struck, moved backwards, where Annabelle's other hand soaped the delicately clenched rear entrance.

Annabelle rubbed the soap between the young woman's thighs, her fingers prodding at the slit. Her eyes were on the young servant's, and Daisy let her gaze drop as a sigh escaped from her lips. Annabelle could no longer restrain herself. Her lips clamped down on the dark satiny hip, diamonded by water droplets, and her teeth sank into the sweet flesh. Daisy jumped in surprise, but the pressure of Annabelle's fingers on her pussy held her in place. Annabelle clamped her own thighs together, willing her jaws to close and not to cry out as the pleasure of the moment overwhelmed her. It was a tiny, almost unmemorable climax that Daisy's body offered up to her, but for the circumstances.

Annabelle rose, and with her voice remarkably steady, said to the other, 'Well, yo're... I mean, you are clean enough now. You may get dressed.'

Somewhat more enlightened than she had been before, Daisy obeyed her mistress.

Annabelle raced away from the bathroom in search of Nelly. The maid was folding the linen near the bedroom, and Annabelle grabbed her hand and towed her to the bedroom, where she flung herself on the bed, raising the hem of her soft dress as she did so. As she had become accustomed, she no longer wore drawers underneath, and found the result both comfortable and practical. As now.

'Beat me!' she almost screamed, raising her rear end off the bed and parting her buns with the palms of her hands. 'Oh Nelly, I do need it *sooooo*!'

Attuned by now to her mistress's needs, Nelly dropped the tablecloth she was holding. Her palm slapped sharply onto Annabelle's raised posterior. The slap sounded like a pistol shot, and the rattle of musketry soon followed it as Nelly rained blows on her mistress.

'Bitch, fuckin' bitch.' She was getting into the spirit. 'You want me to beat you? Here, take that,' and a palm splatted into the full pink roundness, painting it a fiery red. 'And that,' another blow on the companion mound. The hand rose and fell while Annabelle squirmed and moaned, begging for more.

Nelly could tell what was about to happen, and she waited until Annabelle was twisted into a knot, her ass high in the air. Her left hand darted forward and she captured the soft pink lips of her mistress's pussy in her fingers, then not without a struggle as the charming

Southern belle twisted about, she slipped two fingers into the moist and demanding pussy. Annabelle's cunt immediately gripped at the digital offering, and her insides clenched in a long and satisfactory orgasm. She subsided, panting heavily, while Nelly opened her bodice and fanned her sweating breasts. She was hot between her legs too, and in a moment she would be able to enjoy some relief herself, if Miss Annabelle's mood persisted.

Daisy, who had dried and dressed herself hurriedly, found the two of them together. Nelly's breasts were shiny with sweat, and she looked both dishevelled and excited as she rested on the large bed. Beside her, her white ass marked with pink blotches, lay the mistress of the house, her eyes slightly closed, her golden hair scattered across the counterpane, and her hand entwined in the dark one of her maid.

Annabelle looked up lazily as her new maid entered the room. 'Come here, Daisy,' she said. Her red lips glistened and her teeth sparkled in a happy smile. 'Take off your new dress, dear Daisy,' she said.

Daisy swallowed. She was not used to being addressed that way, neither in tone nor in content. But she knew that her new job depended on obeying the orders she received, no matter how peculiar, and she quickly unbuttoned and shed the borrowed dress that she'd so recently put back on.

Annabelle rolled over and rose to sit beside Nelly. 'What do you think, Nell? Is she beautiful?'

'Yes ma'am,' said Nelly, and her own eyes seemed to Daisy to possess a peculiar glint in them. 'She *sure* is.' Like Annabelle, Nelly sometimes lost her diction in moments of tension. 'Like a young panther.'

'More plump than a panther, I think,' Annabelle giggled. 'Would you like to kiss her?'

'Why Miss Annabelle, I've done that plenty of times...'

'Like this?' Annabelle queried mischievously, and her lips closed on Nelly's hungrily, her tongue probing the depths of the lingual orifice. 'Mmmm,' she said, and her tongue fluttered against Nelly's.

'Oh yes, Miss Annabelle,' responded Nelly, her eyes shining, and her hand probing at Annabelle's bodice. She squeezed the full melons, then rose to her feet and in one swift motion had slipped out of her maid's dress, the fabric pooling at her feet in a puddle of black and white. She stepped forward, ran her hands down Daisy's full flanks, and bent down slightly to kiss her. Daisy waited passively, curious to see what would happen. The warmth generated by her bath and Nelly's exertions on the bed brought even greater heat to the contact between them. She was conscious of the meshing of their bodies, of their soft breasts and bellies pushing against one another, of the wiry scratching of their intermingled pubic hairs as Nelly gently rubbed their mounds together.

Annabelle watched the motion with bright eyes, her tongue flicking out to wet her lips.

The two servants parted, and Nelly turned to Annabelle. 'That was truly wonderful,' she said.

'I want to watch you,' Annabelle answered. Her eyes were glittering.

Daisy and Nelly looked at her face, then at one another. They lay on the bed, Nelly with an anticipatory gleam, Daisy with some reluctance, but a shrug of submission. They kissed deeply, their arms around each other. Nelly pushed gently at Daisy until they were comfortable, Nelly on top. Then she started a sweet back and forth motion, scraping the curls of her mound against those of her cousin. Their tongues joined and Daisy daringly sucked at the pink digit that had invaded her mouth. Nelly stroked her flanks, and Daisy slid her fingers around the slimmer girl's ass until she could pull the buttocks open. Then with a free finger she explored the length of Nelly's deep valley.

'Ooohhh,' Nelly moaned as Daisy found the entrance to her inner core and slipped a finger inside. 'Yeah, do that baby,' and her tongue rewarded Daisy's mouth. 'Ohhhh baby, that' so *gooood*.' She dipped her head and licked at the prominent nipples, then laved them around with her tongue flat.

'I love that, I surely do,' moaned Daisy as the touch of Nelly's tongue set her nerve-ends firing.

They started moving faster, then rolled over on the bed to allow Daisy some time on top. Their fingers explored whatever they could reach, and their tongues never stopped wetting the skin, touching nipples, lips, tongue, shoulders, and any other place they could reach.

'Miss Annabelle, she soon join us,' whispered Nelly as her tongue probed Daisy's ear.

Daisy only moaned in reply, her stomach giving off tiny flutters, but she nodded in understanding.

Annabelle's nerves were shrieking as she watched the two dark bodies entwined on the bed. They were both sweating copiously and it gave their flesh a shine that was irresistible. Her hand stole to her dress, and before she knew it, she was as naked as her two maids. For a moment she contemplated ordering them to stop and do her, but then she knew that would not satisfy her. Instead, she crawled onto the bed, her eyes held mesmerically on the juncture of the two sets of shapely legs, where the maids' hands rhythmically dug into one another. She parted the legs roughly and exposed the two cunts. Daisy's four fingers were stuffed into Nelly's pussy, working in and out with slurping sounds. Nelly was using one single finger to thrum the glistening bud of Daisy's clitoris. Their eyes were closed and their mouths locked together as they squirmed and groaned.

Annabelle was drawn forward by the sight, and then her mouth covered Daisy's hand, licking hungrily at the moisture-covered fingers. Her tongue tried to shove the fingers aside, was rebuffed, and then found refuge as Daisy obligingly made room for the additional, oral, digit. Annabelle squealed as Nelly's knowledgeable fingers dug hard into her scalp, urging her on. Her tongue moved faster, licking at every inch of skin she could find, penetrating Nelly's willing anus and then moving to circle around Nelly's fingers as they pumped into Daisy's slit.

'Oh God! Do it, please do it. Go on! Don't stop!' Annabelle's voice was turning from one of command to one of pleading. 'Please Nelly, please help me. I need it!'

Daisy listened with slight bewilderment, as the wonder of another woman licking her hole swirled through her brain. She looked down to see Annabelle lapping frantically at *her* cunny; she, Daisy, the ex-slave and ex-teenage concubine. Her shoulders fell back onto the soft covers and she arched her hips to accommodate and enjoy the wonder.

'Please Nelly, Daisy. Do it to me. I have to have it,' Annabelle moaned between mouthfuls of Daisy's pussy.

Nelly leaped off the bed and reached swiftly for the red morocco box on the sidetable. She brought it back to the bed, then fumbled inside briefly while Annabelle's moans rose in pitch.

Daisy's eyes widened as the switch was thrust into her hands. She looked at Nelly in complete bewilderment.

'Please,' Annabelle was begging... begging *her*! 'Please Daisy. Please beat me. I love you. I want it. Here. The lash. No, use the dog whip. The whalebone...' Her pale hands were moving feverishly among the array in the box. 'I want it *so*... Uh, uh,' she cried out as she struck with the small lash at her own behind. Entranced, Daisy reached for the switch, her eyes on the pale buttock gradually reddening with darker stripes. She found the thin strip of whalebone, extracted from a stay. She lay on to the pale mound before her. Her enthusiasm rose as her fear that this was some sort of grotesque trial ebbed, and she struck away with a will.

'Take that... an' that!' she mimicked the master who used to beat her as a child.

'Yes, oh please, yes. Let me kiss your foot,' Annabelle whined and twisted about on the bed until she could reach her maid's toes. Gratefully she sucked them in while the lash struck again and again at her backside.

Daisy found that she was enjoying herself. She had not realised before that this switching business was not only to punish slaves, but because the masters enjoyed it. Now that she was not only free, but in the position of dishing it out, she was having tremendous fun. And between her legs she found a growing hunger. Barely daring to breathe she tugged at the golden hair at her feet. Annabelle eagerly followed, licking her way along the dark calves, to the knees, which she kissed with a passion while the switch rose and fell, reddening her behind. But it was clear to both of them that there was to be more. Daisy aimed her cuts more clearly, so that now they fell in the darker valley between Annabelle's two mounds. Annabelle squealed, a high-pitched sound in which pain and fright combined with delirious pleasure. Her mouth found Daisy's inner lips and she clung to them like a calf hanging on to an udder. Her lips moved, and as each blow was struck, she dug her tongue deeper into the humid recesses, moaning her desire and her pleasure. Daisy too was close to blowing her top. She clutched madly at her breasts, drawing long streaks, until Nelly, divining her need, lashed out with a leather belt at the blonde's exposed belly and hanging tits.

'Eeeeyhh' the blonde screamed as she was struck before and behind repeatedly. There was a cruel glint in Daisy's eyes as for the first time she got her own back for years of humiliation, but that was quickly overlaid with the growing tide of her lust as the wonderful tongue thrust deeply into her own cavern.

Daisy looked down. 'That's it missy, you bitch. Cunnylicker. Oaahh, so good. You're doin' good. Lick that pussy. Ah'm a cummin'. Ooooh, Ah'm hitting that sweet roll. Ooooh gawd. Lick me *goooood*,' she said in her commonest tones. She dropped the lash and pulled at the blonde tresses, trying to force Annabelle's tongue deeply into her as waves of passion spread in growing shocks through her belly.

Annabelle tasted the sudden salty flood of female juices that flowed around her tongue. She licked as furiously as she could, intent on absorbing the wondrous fluid. Her backside and belly were burning fiercely, and as she licked the last of Daisy's spending, she felt herself go as well. Her muscles contracted in delirious spasms that followed one another until she collapsed, totally spent, on the sodden counterpane.

Annabelle sprawled on the bed, swooning in the last spasms of pleasure. A sheen covered the join of her thighs, and the stripes on her breasts and belly and between her thighs tingled and burned pleasurably. She felt something between her lips and pulled out a dark wiry hair that had caught there. She touched herself delicately. This was the first time she had ever in her life been able to indulge her imagination. It had been perfect. Daisy stirred beside her.

Nelly, however, was nowhere to be seen. She had exclaimed something as Annabelle's head was still imprisoned between Daisy's thighs, and had rushed from the chamber. It took some moments for Nelly's departing words to register.

'Lordy, the massa is here.'

Still feeling somewhat shy about her recent activities, Annabelle rapidly pulled on a slip and ran down the stairs of the mansion to greet her husband.

Peter, his hat still on, was perched on the high stool that stood at the entrance. On her knees before him, Nelly had her face full. Her dark head was bobbing up and down in his lap. Annabelle rushed toward him. She flung herself into his arms just as the first waves of his pleasure started spurting into Nelly's hard-working mouth. Annabelle hugged him tightly as she cried, 'You are the most magnificent, most loving, most understanding of all husbands.'

He clasped her to him as his own passion subsided. Nelly withdrew her head, licking at the sperm that threatened her white apron front, and listened, bemused, as Annabelle recounted all she had done, faithfully and without any concealment. She had hurried downstairs to delay the master, and now it had proved to be unnecessary.

Peter kissed Annabelle lightly as he rose, she still cocooned in his strong arms. 'I am pleased with you, my dear. Not many women would have been bold enough, as you are, to snatch their happiness as they will. The mark of the true aristocrat.'

The town was very dark. Gas lighting had not yet arrived this far in the South. The cloaked figure marched along the boardwalks as if he owned the ground he was walking on, and none of the figures that were out in the rainy night dared dispute his possession. The figure snarled softly to itself when it stood before the grounds of a formerly grand mansion. A pale hand with long fingers stroked meditatively at a smooth cheek.

His enquiries had yielded a name – Heather Jakes – and an address in this crumbling white-painted pile. He waited patiently for the lit windows to darken. Only one, on the second floor, showed a chink of light when he moved. He scrambled over the wooden fence without being seen, then seizing a trellis, he hauled himself up to the second floor balcony. Heavy drapes obscured the windows. Using a clasp knife, he levered open one of the shutters and slipped inside the house, past the red damask curtains and into a dusty, unused room. As he crept across the floor he became conscious of a series of sounds, and he cocked his head to listen, before moving on.

The sounds emanated from the master bedroom, a room whose former opulence was indicated by its gilded reliefs and rather stained hangings.

A man, standing in his breeches and boots but without a coat or shirt, and a woman, kneeling before him on the floor and weeping loudly, were the only occupants. The woman was the one he had come to find. The intruder concealed himself behind the doorpost.

'Please Charlie, please not again…' she sobbed. Her cheap gingham housedress was shredded off one shoulder, and a full plump breast was bare, hanging enticingly towards the knot-carpeted floor.

'Why Heather, you are my *wife*, and you will do what *I* say,' insisted Charlie Jakes. He emphasised his words by shaking his wife's curls in his fist.

'But I can't… I can't,' wailed Heather. 'It is so disgusting!' She turned her head away.

'But I want it,' said Charlie furiously. 'All my friends

get it. *I* get it too, but not from *my wife*,' and he shook her again.

Letting her fall to the floor, he opened his riding breeches and exposed a semi-hard cock. 'Here you are!' he cried triumphantly. 'Suck it!'

'I can't,' she wailed again. 'You're drunk, Charles Jakes, and no gentleman, to insist on such a... a horrible action!'

'Hah!' he laughed, and his whole frame swayed. 'Disgusting? My cock disgusting? Here woman, take that!' He hauled her roughly up and threw her on to the bed. His hand slashed down on her fabric-covered butt, and she wailed convulsively.

Jakes swayed to his feet, his hands reaching for the front of his breeches. They fell and pooled down to his ankles. 'Don't you move now,' he said thickly. To emphasise his point he slapped the fabric-covered mounds before him once again. He staggered forward, hampered by his trousers, and fell on the soft mounds. Heather merely sobbed. His hips thrust against her, until he realised in his drunken haze, that there was an insuperable barrier. Hastily he tore off her drawers, flinging the lace-ruffled undergarment to the floor.

He pulled her legs apart, then positioned himself between them and thrust forward. Enraged at her passivity, her raised her knees to her chest, exposing the length of her buttocks and the hairy cleft, its thick lips squeezed into prominence between them.

'You're too dry!' he said angrily, as his half erect cock refused the post. He slapped her ass again and again and she shrieked, then he pushed himself backwards and spat onto her open thighs, spreading the saliva liberally with his tongue, trying to reach the mossy entrance with his teeth. Heather shrieked and tried to push him away.

'No Charlie, no! It's unnatural!'

'You're right!' he roared. 'You should be doing this to me. You gonna suck my cock!'

'No!' she said, shaking her head violently, burying it in the counterpane. 'Never!'

He slapped her rump again, then pulled away. 'Stay there!' he said. 'I need another drink. Don't you dare move!' He pummelled the proffered buttocks in emphasis, then he pulled up his breeches, and taking the candle, he staggered unwittingly towards the concealed observer.

Moving swiftly, the black-clad man spun into another doorway just along the landing. Charlie staggered by, then stumbled down the stairs. The intruder followed carefully and heard him pulling open cupboards, muttering about a drink. Then Charlie was at the front door, stumbling into the night, headed for a source of whiskey. Again following stealthily and peering through the almost-closed door, the stranger saw Charlie Jakes flop onto the swing-chair on the front porch. His instant and heavy snores indicated he would not be going anywhere for quite some time. The intruder considered the scene for a while, a plan growing in his mind. Jakes was asleep in a drunken stupor. Now was the time to act. But before he did... He grinned in the fitful moonlight, hidden by racing clouds. Before he attended to business, there was something else he needed. The stiff member in his trousers twitched in agreement.

Heather lay on the bed, clutching the counterpane, exposed from the waist down. her full thighs parted, glistening slightly with the moisture of Charlie's spittle. Her head was turned to one side, and although the lamps were now extinguished, in the dim moonlight he could see she was asleep.

Careful not to touch her with anything but his erect member, the thin man crouched over Heather's parted thighs. The tip of his cock penetrated between the limbs and searched through the mossy grove for the slick hole. It found the little mouth, and the man pushed forward slightly, enough to feel the pressure grow around his cock. Heather sighed in her sleep. He pushed deeper, feeling the tip of his cock slip between the lips with an almost audible clicking feel. He breathed heavily, easing himself forward until half his long shaft was inside her. Then he jogged his rump slowly, letting the shaft in and out. Heather started moving as she came awake from her dreams. She started to protest.

Pulling back slightly, the stranger slapped her buttocks as hard as he could. Heather subsided, murmuring, 'Please Charlie, don't do that!'

The man smiled in the dark above her. His pleasure started overwhelming him, and he moved in jerky, punishing strokes, trying to arouse her pleasure. Heather moved, moaning.

'Oh Charlie... hmmm. It don't hurt too much now.'

He grasped her hips, digging manicured fingers into her flanks. His ball bag swung against her raised rump. To encourage him, Heather clenched the sides of her slit, squeezing the punishing shaft as best as she could. She was rewarded by a muffled cry as spurt after spurt of his male milk filled her interior. Unusually, she found her husband did not let his entire drunken weight fall on her. Instead, the softening male member was withdrawn from her cunt and she heard him walk, staggering slightly, across the floor and out onto the landing.

Much later, as she was drifting off to sleep again, she heard the front door close. She did not hear the black-clad man wake her husband by the simple expedient of swilling out his own mouth with bourbon whiskey from his own flask, and breathing on him. Nor was she aware, that as they staggered in great bonhomie down the street, that black-clad stranger was quizzing her husband about her best friend.

Chapter Eight

Arm in arm the newlyweds walked up the stairs to the bedroom. They stopped momentarily to admire the sight of Daisy, still hazy from the residue of her spend, her legs spread, she was gazing silently about the room. At her master's unexpected entrance she scrambled about fitfully, trying to cover herself up.

'I say, gel, there's no need for that,' he said in lazy cultured tones. 'Rather like the sight, what?' His eyes gazed at her sardonically, and she relaxed enough to throw him an impish grin from the side of the bed.

'Lie right back, Daisy,' Annabelle was more sure of herself now. She turned to look at her husband as Daisy lay back on the bed, spreading her legs wide. At a gesture from Nelly, she started stroking her pussy, her palm flat on the mound, parting the little peppercorn curls.

Annabelle looked breathlessly at the spectacle, then turned to her husband. There was a growing lump in his trousers, and it was quite clear that the sight of Daisy's pleasure was affecting him strongly.

Annabelle slipped off her silk gown with alacrity. Beautifully naked, she strode to the bedside and lay down to examine Daisy's pussy once again.

She breathlessly examined the angle of the shapely spread legs. The moisture of their joining was visible, and a trickle ran down the slit and into the furrow of the dark girl's ass. It pooled slightly on the tiny clenched button between Daisy's buns. Annabelle's face dipped forward and her eyes closed. She sought out the pearly fluids, licking and sucking the long plump lips of the slit. Then she became more methodical, and her tongue probed from one end to the other. Inadvertently her tongue slipped and she found herself forcing her oral digit into the clenched lower orifice. For one moment, a moment only, she was horrified at what she was doing. Then she had to admit to herself that it had been her target from the beginning. Gently, but with increasing force, she speared her tongue into the clenched hole of Daisy's ass.

Daisy was at first surprised, then delighted by the new sensation. She writhed on the bed, wailing to show her pleasure, her hands unconsciously reaching for the other's head, her knees drawn back to her breasts to facilitate entry. For one moment she was shocked at her own boldness as she forced her mistress's tongue deeper into her ass, but then she gave herself in to pleasure as she realised that Annabelle, far from recoiling, was taking perverse delight in pleasing her rear hole.

'Tell me what to do!' Annabelle's voice was muffled. When Daisy did not immediately respond she commanded again, sharply, 'Come on. Tell me. Order me! Tell me what a bitch I am!'

'Fuck me bitch,' Daisy tried experimentally.

Annabelle's tongue delved even deeper into the puckered hole, and Daisy shuddered in her pleasure. She clutched once again at the soft hairs, and arched her back, conscious also of the male eyes that were examining the charming spectacle.

'Suck that asshole... let me have it,' Daisy ordered with more confidence. 'Come on, ream me out. Shove it into that black hole.' She wriggled her bum experimentally, and her mistress responded with deeper thrusts.

Annabelle was in heaven as her tongue explored Daisy's backside. She knew she had hidden this perversity from herself, and only circumstances had combined to allow her to express this desire. She beckoned hurriedly, and Nelly joined her on the bed. Annabelle, her curiosity not satisfied, pulled the other girl up beside her. She started by moistening her finger in the deep crack of Nelly's female parts. Then, brutally, she shoved her index finger into her maid's rear portal. Nelly squirmed until she became accustomed to the pressure, then gingerly started moving on the probing digit. Annabelle added a second finger, and Nelly jerked involuntarily, as did Daisy, whose rear portal was being probed by an exquisitely experimental tongue.

'Oh Lord,' Nelly breathed. 'Oh ma'am, that is so *gooood*.' The pain added a spice to her feelings, and she suddenly understood Annabelle's lust for pain with her sex. There were now three knowledgeable fingers in her pussy too, and she groaned with pleasure as Annabelle used her thumb to stroke the lips of her pussy.

The three women entwined on the bed afforded Peter a glorious sight. Annabelle's entire alabaster length was framed by Daisy's dark legs, and beside her lay the exquisite picture of Nelly, her legs parted, her eyes closed, murmuring her pleasure.

Annabelle raised her face to breathe. It glistened with the juices expended from Daisy's mucilaginous interior, and she was grinning triumphantly. She caught sight of her husband, his cock erect, his trousers down by his knees. Without a word she urged the other two up and over, until all three of them were on all fours, presenting their exquisite rumps to the air. Annabelle's pink mounds, still slightly streaked with pink from the lashing she had received, contrasted appealingly with the more sculpted dark asses of her maids.

His heart pounding, Peter examined the spectacle. 'I

say old girl,' he said in almost a whisper. 'Don't believe I've ever seen the like. I say! I must, yes really I must!' and he staggered forward, his usual calm shattered, as he tried to disentangle himself from his trousers.

'Not so fast,' Annabelle laughingly held him off, and the dark faces of the two maids peered at the half dressed man over their shoulders. 'Darling, you must take Daisy's remaining virginity. I will help you,' Annabelle begged as Peter examined the three backsides presented for his examination.

'Of course, my love. But…'

'It is all prepared,' whispered his blushing bride. She reached out a shapely arm and procured a small jar of scented pomade that she had intended for this very use. Kneeling behind Daisy, but making sure she did not obscure the operation, she had Nelly pull her cousin's sweet buns apart. Daisy's innermost beauties were thus displayed in all their delicacy. Down below was the pink gash, its surfaces barely peeking out, slick with her juices. The darker lips crinkled pleasingly into their oyster shape, and only barely hid the pink pearl of her clitoris. Above the slit, hidden slightly by enticing whorls of crisp, moisture bedewed hairs, they examined the tiny clenched bud into which Sir Peter was to insert his iron-hard machine. With long gestures, careful not to penetrate the hole too deeply and spoil its first time, Annabelle spread the unguent. The entrance glistened, beckoning enticingly, and Annabelle could not resist a deep, final penetration with her tongue.

Sir Peter, all but his shirt shed, strode up to his throne. For but a brief moment he crouched over the proffered bum. Nelly, her own concupiscence aroused by the sight, stroked his balls lightly with one hand then, with some effort, bent his pole until it was aimed downwards at the inviting target. The broad plum head of the cock rested for a time on the greased entrance to the chute. Then, with a swift lunge, Peter forced his way into the waiting orifice.

Daisy squealed as she felt the shaft spread the muscles of her rear. This was not the first time she had felt a man in there, but obviously it would have been impolitic to mention it. And besides, she had never had a white one there. She wondered what it looked like, and the mental vision sent a shudder down her spine that set the man above her to pushing furiously into her interior. She felt the entire length of the shaft, and the painful scrape of his curls at the skin of her crack seemed a relief compared to the pain of the initial insertion in her bowels.

'Ohhh, lawdy. Sah, yo're tearing me apart, sah!' she screamed in a mixture of genuine and pretended terror. 'Oweeeee, sah.'

Annabelle, touched by the real pain in the girl's face, crouched beside her and kissed her full lips with her own. She soothingly stroked the buggered girl's flanks, muttering endearments, her own excitement rampant.

Peter could not resist the opportunity, and his hand smacked the exposed pink bum with all his might.

'Oh yes, darling,' Annabelle groaned. 'Oh again, my love. Fuck this darling girl. Bugger her. Smack me again, my darling.' With each endearment, with each word, Peter's pulse raced. He started shafting into the demandingly tight hole with all his might, ordering Nelly with a muttered word to present herself to him as well. He clutched at the full bums to either side and before him. His hands wandered into their deepest recesses, and his body glistened with the sweat of his efforts. Every once in a while, as emotion overcame him, he slapped at his wife's pink mounds, rubbing his palms on her flesh.

Finally the crisis arrived. He seized Daisy's sweet soft sides, digging his fingers into her flesh. She hollowed with triumph, the pain completely forgotten as his rampant cock shafted its way into her without mercy. His movements became staccato and his breathing harsh. Daisy called out as waves of pleasure flooded her interior.

Annabelle, seeing the approaching crisis, had curled around under the writhing couple and applied her mouth fully to Daisy's erect clitoris. She sucked hard, and was rewarded by the twitching of her victim's inner muscles. The scent of Daisy's interior sent her to heaven, and her own fingers were inserted deeply into her own pussy, so that when Daisy's quivering started in earnest, Annabelle too gasped out in furious orgasm, her tongue and teeth digging deeply into the delicious hole.

Daisy's rear muscles contracted violently around Sir Peter's rampant root. He crushed her body beneath him trying to bury himself to the heart and soul of him. Through the haze of pleasure he could vaguely hear her squealing. He clutched her furiously, his cock reaching deeply into her interior. Nelly's face was peering at him appealingly, and he bent as far as he could, slipping his tongue into her mouth, licking her teeth and lips as jet after jet of boiling sperm erupted from his balls and was sucked greedily into the muscular orifice.

They collapsed onto the bed. The counterpane was wrinkled and damp in spots, and the four of them wriggled around to find comfortable positions. Annabelle kissed away the tears from Daisy's happy cheeks, and they all stroked and congratulated her on her fortitude. They fell asleep in the rucked bedclothes, their limbs still entwined.

Standing beneath a tree festooned with a beard of Spanish moss, a tall thin man watched the lights of the mansion go out. His hands nervously twined and parted as he tried to make up his mind to be bold, just this once. Instead, he retreated to his horse, tethered some way off, and rode back the way he had come.

Chapter Nine

Annabelle stretched as she awoke to the clatter of a tray. Nelly had slipped out of bed, and besides providing for their ablutions with hot towels in a moist Dutch oven – she was rather proud of her invention – had also procured some refreshments.

Daisy had vanished in the direction of the water closet, and had returned, dewy from her own ablutions. They ate together, not standing on ceremony, at Annabelle's urgings. From time to time she examined Daisy, and her eyes were glinting.

'Did you enjoy it?' she asked at last.

'Yes'm,' Daisy said, swallowing a spoonful of caviare, a food she had never imagined existed. 'I shore did.'

'Language!' mumbled Sir Peter. He was eating some of the caviare off Nelly's inner thigh, licking a trail of the shiny soft buckshot from her skin, one by one.

'Yes, of course dear. Daisy, you *must* try to speak properly,' Annabelle said, trying with difficulty to subdue her own accent. 'So you like being fucked in the ass?' She added crudely.

'Yes ma'am. Mas'... ah... I mean, Sir Peter's...'

'Cock,' supplied Annabelle helpfully.

'Yes ma'am – his cock, is so very lovely. An' I squirted all over the place...'

The rest of them laughed and Daisy blushed.

'Was it painful?'

'At first, ma'am, when he stuck it in ma...' she faltered again, and then continued, 'my ass. After that it weren't so bad. Then, ma'am, when you started... that was wonderful.'

'You mean, when I licked your cunny? That is the proper word for the female organ of pleasure, Daisy. Say it: cunt.'

'Yes ma'am,' said Daisy, catching on to the spirit of the thing. She had said cunt many times before, but never in such circumstances nor company. 'When you licked my cunt, it became a real good fuck. I likes it fine.'

'So do I,' said Annabelle, and her face was brilliant with anticipation. 'Darling Peter, can we retire to the rumpus room?'

Peter glanced at her and stretched lazily. She meant the cellar, where he had caused to be installed many playthings for their pleasure. Reaching for his embroidered dressing gown, he said, 'Of course we can, my dear.'

From behind a large tree dripping with Spanish moss, a man with a frown on his face watched the windows of the large white house. His hand, under the cloak he wore against the morning damp, was clutching the bulge in the front of his trousers. A dark slouch hat covered most of his features, but what could be seen was grim, and yet exultant. He stiffened somewhat when he saw the flash of white in the bedroom window. The rich red drapes were being withdrawn. It was a maid, in a black and white uniform. Her hands raised, she showed a pleasant stretching of the uniform. She looked straight at him, her mouth open in surprise. Though startled by her acute vision, the stranger was not flustered. He was a man of great resource. Holding up his free hand, he plainly showed the gold dollar piece he had hastily extracted from his fob pocket. For a brief moment the maid stood there undecided, then slowly vanished from the window. The lurker concealed himself to better effect, removed a small spyglass from under his cloak, and trained it on the upper window.

Soon he was rewarded by the flash of pink flesh as the mistress of the house went about her ablutions. The man smiled, his lips wet and hungry.

Annabelle could touch the floor with the tips of her shoes. She tried swinging on the silken ties that reached to the ceiling, and they supported her comfortably, and only a little painfully.

The sudden crack of the whip against her skin took her by surprise.

'Oh oh oh!' she screamed.

Peter raised his hand again, and Daisy brought the whip down on the silky pink buttocks once again. There was a grim and fervent expression on her face when she did it. She had been whipped once, and the shame and pain would remain with her for the rest of her life. Here was a chance to repay, even though the whip was not proper bull-hide but a weak substitute. She lashed repeatedly at the buttocks, careful to obey Sir Peter's whispered instructions. The naked figure before her writhed with the shock of each stroke, but the cries of pain and the twisting motions seemed to gratify, rather than hurt the victim. Out of the corner of her eye she saw that the Master's cock was hardening, and he suddenly took two steps in her direction and clutched at her naked teats, squeezing them hard. Roughly, he pushed her forward until the three of them, the bound woman, the maid, and the man, were clutched together. Still squeezing her breasts roughly with one hand, he clutched at Annabelle's pink-tipped mounds with the other.

'Oh yes,' shrieked the bound woman. 'Rub that wiry

mound into me. It feels *soooo* good.'

Knowing now what was expected, Daisy ground her wire-topped mound into the sensitive abraded skin of her mistress's behind. The whip was pulled from her hand and a shorter, more appropriate quirt was supplied by the ever-ready Nelly. As Sir Peter rubbed his semi-hard cock into the crack of her ass, she ground her own mound into the sensitive tissues before her, and her hand rose and fell with quick strokes, lashing the bound woman's flanks.

Annabelle screamed with real pain as her skin was abraded. But strong fingers were now searching out her pussy, and two mouths were sucking at her shoulders and throat while a third roved over her body. She was shivering from the lustful response brought by the nervous stimulation, and thought she would faint as worms of pleasure crawled under her skin, moistening her interior and bringing her to a pitch of lust.

'Oh, oh, oh I'm swooning,' Annabelle wailed.

Daisy found that the tiny pink buds of Annabelle's nipples had swollen to hard points and she pinched them as hard as she was able. 'Like that? Your titties really like that, hey? Come on baby, let it all out. Come on, kiss me. Let your titties enjoy themselves,' Daisy was screaming, deep in her own rut, conscious of the growing pole between her ass cheeks, wondering whether she was going to be penetrated again.

'Hit her!' roared Sir Peter, his forehead glistening with lust, his ass muscles outlined sharply as he crushed both figures to the satin-padded wall.

Annabelle screeched continuously, as the rough-haired twat of her maid and her no less rough whip hand sent sparks of pain through her system. 'Eeeeh, yes, more, more!' she exclaimed, forgetting all the niceties of her position. Peter turned around wildly, saw Nelly standing by doubtfully, and waved an urgent hand at the box. Nelly selected a new switch with alacrity, and handed it to him.

'No,' he gasped. 'Apply it to my bum, to me, to me!'

Nonplussed, she nevertheless complied and began lashing at his shapely, muscled, pale white buns. With each stroke a weal appeared on the white skin, and he jerked more furiously into the crack of Daisy's ass, without actually penetrating. His cock rose triumphantly between the luscious mounds, urged on by the jerking of his belly.

Annabelle was in heaven, the thrust of her maid's pussy onto her bruised and burning derriere raised her blood to a fever pitch. The excitement was transmitted to Daisy, who, letting out a wolf-like howl, discharged her interior juices onto her thighs. For a moment she slumped, unable to move, a puppet between the thrusts of Sir Peter and his spread-eagled bride.

Notwithstanding his own lust, Peter was the first to notice that the maid had swooned. He licked her ear and neck, then hastily disengaged and lowered her to the carpeted floor. Nelly cradled her heavily-breathing cousin's head in her lap, and Peter leapt to rescue his wife.

'Oh my dear love, why did you stop?'

He indicated Daisy's recumbent figure with a hand. 'Won't you help me revive her?' he asked.

Annabelle started looking around for the smelling salts, but Peter restrained her with a smile. 'There is a more delightful way,' he pronounced. His eyes were blazing, and he fell to the floor and parted the slick thighs. They fell on the young maid like going to a feast. Peter stuck his tongue as deeply as he could into the pink orifice, and twirled it around. A most delightful smell filled his nostrils, the smell of a woman well lubricated by erotic exercise. His wife contented herself at first with licking the residue of Daisy's powerful spend. Then she crowded out her husband, and they engaged in a duel over the pretty slit, now attending to the treasure beneath its dark hood, now delving deep into the inviting orifice, now sucking at the soft lips.

Nelly saw her cousin come into the throes of a second, then third spend almost as powerful as the first. Daisy clutched at her, her teeth digging deeply into the flesh of Nelly's hanging breasts that overhung her face. Nelly cried out with the flash of unexpected pain which seemed, somehow, to have translated itself to warmth in her groin. She bent over, cupped Daisy's mouth in her own, and they kissed deeply just as the third climax hit the recumbent girl.

They lay together for some while, swimming in a sea of bliss.

Peter looked down and saw the state of his penis. He gave it an admonitory shake, as if to prepare it for battle, and then he seized his wife. With much giggling and mock struggle, and Nelly's willing aid, with Daisy looking on, he finally managed to lock Annabelle into another one of the clever contrivances he had made especially by a carpenter in New Orleans. It was a wide square frame across one side of which ran a padded bar at about hip height. Bolted securely to the floor, another two uprights held by a horizontal bar held attachments for cuffs, made of padded silk. Other similar rings could be attached to a bar that ran at foot level, and could be raised or lowered, according to preference, the victim thus suspended in a variety of interesting and charming poses at will.

'Oh, sir,' she giggled in mock alarm. 'What on earth do you intend?'

He laughed, twirling his moustache and falling into the

spirit of the game. 'A spirited filly, what? You shall have you're just deserts, never fear.'

'Oh, la sir, you are committing the greatest indignities on my person!'

'And worse is yet to come, my dear. Ha ha!'

'Pray sir, oh no, do not tie my limbs to the strange device!'

'Make them tight, Nelly old thing. Her wrists up here – there, that's the ticket. Ankles down there, too. Oh, that was a mighty kick. Here, this ought to serve you a remembrance,' and his hand splatted against the pink glowing posterior.

'Oh sir, such violence against my person is surely unwarranted!'

'Ha, ha, is that what you think? Punishment is what you need – proper discipline!' and he smacked her quivering bottom half a dozen additional times.

He stood back to admire his efforts. Annabelle was displayed to charming effect. Her hands rested on the gripping bar before her, held there by the silken manacles. Her bum was prominently displayed, and spread wide by the width of her stance, as her ankles were tied to the base posts of the bar. Her breasts hung down like large fruit, and her body was covered with a sheen of perspiration. Between her legs all three of her admirers could see the golden-haired purse, bisected by its delicious looking slit from which her delicate inner lips, pink as coral, peeped shyly.

'Whip her a bit, both of you, to warm her up,' ordered Sir Peter, breathing heavily.

'Oh, no, oh, they are killing me!' shrieked Annabelle.

'That's it, Daisy, one after the other. First me n' then you,' said Nelly, her muscles quivering and her shoulders rising and falling. She was the only one who had not been satisfied, and she wondered what her master had in store for her.

'I do like this,' said Daisy breathlessly as her arm swept down again. 'Now *that* was good one. Did you see her jump?'

'Eeeyahhhh! Oh please, squeeze my cunny, lick me, do somethingggggg!' Annabelle begged.

'Her cooze is so damned wet,' cried Nelly. 'Ah gotta fuck… I jes gotta!' In her excitement she forgot the elocution so thoroughly drilled into her.

'And so you shall!' cried Sir Peter. He grasped Nelly by the waist and passed something around it. With a quick movement she found a hard object pressing between the lips of her vagina, and as she moved, the artificial phallus swayed before her, tickling at her sensitive clitoris, and held by a broad ribbon around her waist.

'Oh sir,' Nelly breathed. 'This feels so good, but surely I would prefer your cock in me?'

'Ha hah,' he laughed, but not cruelly. 'And that you shall have, my dear. But first, we must help poor Lady Stone, must we not. Step forward, my dear.'

The rain of blows that had been sending storms of fire from her behind suddenly stopped, and Annabelle, not wishing to spoil the surprise, did not turn to look. A hard warm object probed at the entrance to her slit, and she gradually subsided against the pressure as the delicious member probed at her sensitised membranes. The long slide into her flooded salacious interior felt like a trip to heaven. She was somewhat surprised that the cock did not feel as Peter's usually did, but did not open her eyes so as not to spoil her own fun. And rather than the swirling grind against her buns which usually characterised Peter's thrusts, the delicious shaft was almost immediately withdrawn.

'Oh, please put it in again! Oh please, my darling, please. Ooooh... yes, shaft me all the way, like that. No, don' take it out all the way!' She shuddered with the attempt to hold the cock in her inner recesses.

Nelly eyed the shuddering moaning figure tied across the bar before her. Sir Peter stood behind her now, their bodies touching at every point, and she could feel the heat from his body as well as the hardness that jutted from his hips. It was warmer and alive, unlike the one that jutted from hers, but suddenly she felt herself to be as powerful as a man. She bent forward, and for a moment parted the soft buttocks even wider than they had been. Grasping her dildo firmly, her hand guided by his, she aimed it at the tiny puckered hole. The moisture-lubricated dildo slid into Annabelle's anus, parting the muscles easily. Just then, once she was fully seated inside, she felt Sir Peter fumbling at her own rear portal. His greased cock slid easily into her, and she leaned her face back to accept his kiss, moaning as deeply as the victim before her.

'Together, eh Nelly?' Sir Peter licked her ear fondly. He rammed down on her with his full force, and her artificial penis was thrust deeply between Annabelle's waiting white buttocks.

Annabelle screamed at the sudden power of the stroke. She imagined it felt as it would have felt if a stallion had mounted her.

'Oooooooh,' she whimpered. 'Oh mygo... O lordy... ohhhhmigod!' As the long shaft penetrated her to the roots and Nelly's wiry bush ground into her soft lacerated bum she gibbered incoherently. 'Oh, in mah ass. Oh, he's fuckin' mah ever-lovin' ass. It hurts... it hurts so *good*. Oooahhhh!' She opened her eyes and turned her face to be kissed, only to find that the face closest to her was that of her maid, and *she* was being kissed by Annabelle's own husband! For a moment the pain was accelerated by her jealousy, and then another powerful thrust nailed her to the bar. 'Oh yes, oh fuck me! Oh bugger. Kiss me, oh how delicious,' she shrieked. 'Mmmm, oh both your tongues together. Oh yesss. Daisy, Daisy dear,' she was crying out. 'My cunny, baby, get my cunt!' And the willing maid obliged, ducking under the moving bodes and using her lips and the squeezing of her powerful fingers on Annabelle's available orifice, until with a scream the beautiful blonde collapsed insensate with pleasure on the restraining framework.

With a final thrust, Sir Peter's cock started spraying Nelly's insides with his sperm. 'Oh... I'm spending,' he cried. With a violent and painful motion he tore himself from Nelly's clutching asshole and squeezed himself to her back, bedewing her ebony skin with milky white drops. Nelly screeched at the disappointment of the sudden departure, but her own frame shook as sandwiched between her master and her mistress, she quivered to an orgasm touched off by the spray of boiling spunk that coated her ass and lower back.

Chapter Ten

The weather was ghastly, and while Peter was away – invited by a neighbour on a shooting trip – Annabelle was cooped up in the house because of the rain. She wanted some excitement, and her hand automatically stole to her lap, as she wondered what Peter was up to. In her dreams he was rogering a beautiful willing woman of large breasts and a demanding pussy, the maid of his friend's, and at the fantasy she felt her own juices starting to run. Her tiny pink tongue slipped out between her pearly teeth and licked at her cherry lips. She came to a sudden decision: she would call in one of the maids and enjoy herself.

Daisy arrived promptly at the bell. As she had been instructed to do when no one but members of the household were present, she wore little but a sheer shift that reached midway to her knees, and black stockings.

'Yes'm?' she asked formally, but there was no mistaking the welcoming smile on her mistress's face, nor the lascivious tongue that licked at her full lower lip. Without another word Daisy slipped out of the conservatory, on the glass of which fat raindrops drummed and obscured the garden, and returned with the morocco-leather box.

Annabelle examined the contents, then shook her head. 'No, I don't want to know. Let it be a surprise.' She rolled languidly over on the stuffed sofa, and her magnificently proportioned bum jutted out as she dreamily contemplated the soggy world outside.

Daisy ran the selection of instruments over with an

experienced eye, then selected one which she thought might be a good opener. With no man about the house for the next three days, who knew what Miss Annabelle would be up to?

The light tawse flashed through the air and slurped at Annabelle's backside. She jumped with a squeal.

'Oh… yes. Oh please.'

'Here it comes, you bitch,' Daisy said through clenched teeth, and she began whipping the proffered rounded moons with relish.

'Oh, more, much more. Lay into me darling. Call me names… Ohhhhhh!' Annabelle's ennui had vanished. She wriggled in mock protest at the blows, while her fingers dug deep into the treasure between her thighs. She began rocking backwards as her fingers sought out the core of her womanhood. Daisy responded by whipping harder, the lashes whistling through the air before they landed, scattering sparks of pain on Annabelle's behind.

Nelly, attracted by the hollering, entered the conservatory. Peeking under her armpit, Annabelle admired the beauty of her personal maid, clad as the other was in a sheer shift of a beautiful violet colour and matching stockings.

'Oh Nelly,' she moaned, 'Oh Nelly. Please, please help me!'

Nelly knew immediately what her mistress wanted. She approached the chaise with rapid steps, then grasped Annabelle's beautiful blonde tresses and yanked them savagely to her.

'You'll do as I say!?' she demanded with a theatrical hiss.

'Oh yes, oh yes. Anything you say dear. I'll do anything, *oh*, that stung,' and she jumped as the tawse struck her wobbling behind again.

'Lick it!' Nelly demanded, hauling the willing lips down towards her belly. Annabelle found herself snuggled up against the maid's rounded muscular belly. Her own tongue peeped out as Nelly growled wordlessly at her delay, and she licked at the perfect oval dimple on Nelly's stomach. Nelly moved the muscles in a lazy circle, and Annabelle liberally lathered the skin with her saliva, squealing rhythmically as the tawse struck her upended moons.

Pushing down on the blonde tresses, Nelly parted her legs and raised one foot onto the back of the chaise lounge. She clutched at Annabelle's head and forced her lips onto the mound of black curls that graced the lower part of her belly. 'Suck my snatch, you bitch,' she snarled, forcing herself against the helpless mouth.

'Unghh... it's so good,' Annabelle moaned indistinctly, her mouth muffled by Nelly's muff. 'Ooooh, my bum's on fire. Oh yes, let me have it.'

With one hand on her victim's head, Nelly grasped a full porcelain breast with her other and squeezed brutally. Tears rose in Annabelle's eyes, and she whimpered at the new sensation. Most of her body was aflame now, and she could barely control her actions. 'Oh, oh yes... yes... yes...' she mumbled over and over. Her insides were awash with pleasure and her tongue and hands sought out the delicious interior presented so alluringly to her mouth. She slurped loudly at Nelly's juices, inhaling the lips and tiny pearl as one would an oyster. Her frame quivered at the combined stimulation of the hands on her breast and the straps on her behind.

'Change the instrument,' Nelly said quietly to Daisy through Annabelle's loud moans. The other girl obeyed with alacrity. Her left hand sought among the instruments in the box until she came up with a thin wooden paddle.

Made of flexible and light willow-wood, it nonetheless carried a sharply different sting than the tawse. Without losing any of her rhythm, Daisy smacked down with the paddle.

'Oh eyaaaah!' Annabelle wailed, jumping at the sudden sensation. Daisy dropped the tawse, switched hands, then bent over Annabelle. Her free hand reached for the soft valley between the reddening bum cheeks. She pushed questing fingers into the two exposed orifices, and Annabelle groaned again.

'Oh yes, I needed that. Oh darling. Please do it again. Rub my little boatman. Twist it. Pinch my lips. Yes darling. Oooooh yes.' She jogged her rump back to impale herself on the questing digits.

Nelly felt Annabelle move, and to remind the blonde of her obligations, she started smacking her hanging breasts.

Splat! *Splat*!

The flat of her palms landed full on the fleshy fruit, first to one side and then to the other. Nelly herself felt that she needed some relief, and she even knew what form that relief would take. But not right now; not when Miss Annabelle was so happily confused and so delirious with pleasure. Instead, she raised her stockinged foot and dug her toes strongly into her mistresses exposed ribs. Annabelle screamed anew as the weave abraded her delicate skin.

'You're going to have to lick that,' Nelly said, slapping Annabelle's exposed breasts and forcing her mouth onto her crotch again.

'Mmmph! Yesss!' screamed Annabelle, her cries muffled by Nelly's lower belly. The maid released her, and stripped off the stocking. Balanced on one foot, she rested the other on the back of the padded seat.

'Lick them,' she ordered. Daisy, her interest aroused, kept up her methodical slapping of Annabelle's behind. Annabelle turned her head and encountered the pink and brown toes. First she ran her tongue over the surface of the foot, and then dipped between the toes, showering them with her saliva. Finally she sucked in each toe in turn, while Nelly rocked herself to a climax, jamming her fingers deeply up her own nether hole.

Suddenly Nelly pulled away from Annabelle. Daisy froze in mid-motion as she saw Nelly's fixed expression and glaring eyes. She dipped into the box and emerged with two godemiches. With jerky, almost nervous movements, she tied one around Daisy's waist. One horn of the V-shaped ivory phallus slid up Daisy's sopping cunny. The plumper maid's eyes rolled into her head, and she gasped as the insertion reached into her deepest recesses. Her face still set, Nelly steered Daisy to the chaise lounge, and placed her there on her back. The ivory contrasted neatly with the darker colour of her natural limbs, and she peered between her breasts, repressing an uncertain giggle.

Nelly seized Annabelle's neck in a vice. 'You wanna screw?' she asked, her face only inches away from the frightened Southern belle's. 'You want a fuck, whore? I'll give you a fuck,' she snarled, and the tone was only partly in jest. She grasped Annabelle's neck with one hand, while the other dug painfully into the soft rump so conveniently to hand. Her mouth clamped down onto the perfect white, sweat-salty shoulder and bit down, and she manhandled Annabelle to a crouch over the waiting phallus.

Annabelle was startled when Nelly pulled away from her suddenly. She wanted to order her back to work, but was distracted by the stinging pain in her buttocks. Peering over her shoulder, she watched impatiently, but with greater understanding, as she saw Nelly dress Daisy for battle. She knew what was to come when Daisy disported herself supine beside her, and the menace in Nelly's voice was so palpable that she trembled inside with an incredible frissón of fear and lust. The dildo was hard, smooth, and inviting, and without further ado, she relaxed her ham muscles and allowed herself to sink dreamily onto Daisy's spurious erection. The ivory penis penetrated her with a delicious slowness, and her eyelids dropped as the shivers of rising lust percolated through her aching buttocks and her deliciously warmed groin. She leaned forward dreamily to kiss Daisy deeply, and for a brief moment their tongues played together like two goldfish in a pond. Then she peered over her shoulder, her lust bedewing her insides with the beginnings of the fountain of her pleasure, as she and Daisy watched Nelly prepare herself. Nelly grinned at them both for a brief moment, but there seemed to be an element of hidden cruelty in her fine features. She armed herself with a further godemiche, and tied it into place. Annabelle's heart pounded in anticipatory delight at the sight, as well as at the anticipatory gleam in Nelly's eyes. Whatever came, she knew, would be exquisite. Nelly strode over to the two on the lounge, her mock phallus swaying before her. She parted Annabelle's buttocks, and studied the joining between the two women. Annabelle relaxed her rectal muscles in preparation for the penetration, and Nelly mounted the sofa behind her.

Annabelle cried out at the first feel of Nelly's penetrating thrust. 'Oh my Lord... Oh, it's so tight!' she squealed in anguish as the elephant tusk-cock inched forward. 'Oh, oh, oh. Oh please, it hurts so. Oh, I've never... please, oh please!'

Nelly laughed in imitation of Sir Peter. 'How do you

like having two cocks up you, eh? That pussy will take anything, even two cocks. Even two field-hand cocks! Hah ha!' Her laughter accompanied a vigorous thrusting motion of her loins as she pumped frantically into the blonde's pussy. Then she raised a hand and slashed it down onto Annabelle's exposed ass. 'Hah ha! How do you like that? Another one, eh, for being such a whore? You like cocks, eh? Take more of this one.' Her movements and gyrations over Annabelle's body brought the Southern belle close to a swoon. Annabelle was calling out in a choked voice, and Nelly grasped her hair once more, and forced her mouth over the blonde's cherry lips.

'Now I'll fill your mouth too, bitch,' she growled, and stuck her tongue deeply into her mistress's mouth.

Beneath them, Daisy squealed in pleasure as Annabelle's movements, transmitted to her quim by the godemiche, brought her close to a climax. Screaming together, their mouths alternating their kisses between them, and their bodies joined at a single point, they drove onwards to a thundering climax. Wave after wave of pure pleasure swallowed all three women, and they eventually collapsed in a tangled sweaty, juicy heap on the embroidered covering of the chaise, which creaked under their combined weights and movement.

Chapter Eleven

'Dear Nelly,' Annabelle said, cuddling up to her maid's sweaty form. 'Is my husband very good in bed? Compared to other men, that is.'

The question took Nelly by complete surprise. 'Why, I'm sure I can't tell…'

'Surely you've had a few? You said "even a field hand's cock" a while ago,' Annabelle pointed out, looking her maid in the eye but blushing deeply. 'Do tell me.'

Nelly was blushing too! Annabelle stared at her maid and confidant in amazement. 'Why, no ma'am, I ain't never fucked with another man. I ain't never fucked with no man but Sir Peter.' In her confusion and embarrassment she reverted to the language uses of her childhood.

'You mean you were a virgin when he met you?' asked Annabelle excitedly. At her maid's nod, she hugged her fiercely. 'Why, we really *are* as close as sisters. And what about you, Daisy?'

Daisy had been wiping and returning the instruments to their case. 'I done fucked plenty of men, ma'am. And their ain't no real difference between them, leastaways in the dark.' She flashed a grin. 'Though you sure better not tell *them* that!'

The three women giggled aloud, then Annabelle's face took on a thoughtful look.

'I'd like to… to fuck someone… from the lower orders.' She blushed slightly. 'I *really must* do it.' She turned an imploring look on Daisy. 'How…?'

Daisy considered it gravely, while Nelly tried to warn

her with her eyes. If Sir Peter heard of this... but Daisy resolutely ignored the glances.

'There's young Duke, he do work in the garden,' she essayed doubtfully.

'No!' Nelly was firm. She knew what consequences might arise from *that*. The scandal might cause her to lose her job, and worse, not to mention what might happen to Miss Annabelle. 'Got to be someone who will *never* know and can't tell neither!'

'I'll think of something, never fear,' Daisy said rebelliously. Nelly eyed her with disapproval, but conceded, under pressure, that they could be careful.

The following morning Annabelle was driven into town. She attended to her shopping, finding a particularly attractive range of silks she was interested in. What a difference, being married to a rich husband, wishing to please! Then she headed to Heather's house, thinking to pay a call, her sweet figure moving smoothly through the crowd.

'Annabelle, darling Annabelle!'

She turned to find herself facing Heather, her round face aglow. She had just stepped out of Mrs Mawbry's teahouse, accompanied by two men. Annabelle's face fell somewhat. She was not taken with Charles Jakes, her friend's husband. Then her eyes lit on the other figure. He was tall and thin, imposing in a genteel, yet slightly foreign way. He reminded her of someone, though search her mind as quickly as she could, she could not name the resemblance.

'Dear, Charles' friend, Mr Wildfire,' Heather quickly introduced the strange man.

'Enchanted, ma'am,' he said, his tall form bowing over her extended hand. He squeezed the hand slightly longer than politeness called for, and his eyes were frankly admiring.

'My friend, Miss Annabelle Stone,' Heather said hurriedly. 'Lady Stone, I should say. She is married to a countryman of yours, one of your aristocrats, I should say.'

'Why, you must be English!' Annabelle exclaimed as she looked back at his grave mien. Heather and her husband Charles had obviously been out for a stroll, and Annabelle immediately acquiesced to a brief promenade. Mr Wildfire extended his arm. 'Allow me, Lady Stone,' he said gracefully. 'I would be most happy to hear from you about my fellow countryman...'

Annabelle gratefully accepted the proffered arm. Such a tale she would have to tell Peter when he got back! In her joy at meeting her friend, she failed to notice the looks exchanged between Mr Wildfire and the person who had stood unnoticed behind her.

'Please take the packages to my parents' house,' Annabelle said gaily over her shoulder to Daisy. 'I shall join them there directly.'

'Yes ma'am,' Daisy said huskily through dry lips. She looked once more at the retreating form of Mr Wildfire and her heart thumped uneasily in her ribcage. Even the feel of gold coins underneath her skirt failed to squash her unease.

On the second day of Peter's absence, once Annabelle and Daisy had returned from town, Daisy excused herself for a brief time. She gave Annabelle a saucy look, and such was the communication between the women, that nothing needed to be said. Only Nelly kept her apprehensions to herself.

Daisy returned from the brief expedition, her face

flushed by more than exertion.

'I found one!' she cried gladly to Annabelle, who, together with Nelly, was busy concocting an apple pie.

'Oh, good,' said Nelly. 'Hand me some of them raisins then.'

'No, a man. I found one for Miss Annabelle. He's a new wheelwright working for Master Jeremiah Crook. An' he is *magnificent*!' She clapped her hands, she was so pleased with herself. 'And,' she added, her eyes twinkling, 'he is going to move on later this week to St. Louis, 'cause he's got a job waiting for him there!'

The three women exchanged glances, and even Nelly was convinced, albeit doubtfully, of the course of action they planned.

The cellar had been kept deliberately dark, and Daisy had to clink the two quarters in her hands to keep the man's confidence. Annabelle appeared fearfully in the gloom, holding a shrouded lantern. She had prepared herself to the extent of disrobing all but her petticoats, and she was trembling from fear and excitement.

'Has he been properly washed and blindfolded?' She asked nervously.

'Yes, miss,' Daisy replied in a whisper. 'He's magnificent, isn't he?'

'His name is Isaac,' contributed Nelly. They were all speaking in whispers as a precaution against being recognised, though Isaac had willingly agreed to the conditions the unknown servant girl had imposed before offering him his recompense.

Annabelle shivered excitedly, then nodded her agreement. In the light of the lantern, Nelly was showing the man off while she excited him in readiness for her mistress. His dark body was muscular, almost blocky with huge muscles that crawled beneath a plum dark skin, a tremendous contrast to Peter's slim elegance. His cock was enormous, curving out over a flat muscular belly. Below it swung a large dark bag. His nervousness and fear had vanished as soon as he felt the touch of a female hand on his dungarees, and when Nelly had kissed the tip of his cock, it had lost no time in extending itself to its utmost, like a rattler emerging from winter hibernation. The cock shaft was almost black, but the head, peeking out in fiery glory, was deep red. The black hood that covered his face, leaving room for only his nose and tongue, lent a dangerous air to his maleness.

Breathlessly, Annabelle slipped out of her petticoat. She knelt over the hard cock, for one moment licking the fiery tip. It jerked and a tiny drop of transparent fluid formed at its tip. Nelly reluctantly released the huge shaft, and Annabelle grasped it firmly with her hands. When he reached for her she slapped his hands away forcefully, and stroked the shaft. It was silky to the touch, warm, and hard... so hard. Her mouth covered the broad head, and her tongue washed the tiny drop of transparent fluid – Peter called it his gun oil – and sucked the salty morsel down. Then she opened her mouth as wide as she was able, and sucked the lively member deep in between her jaws. The man's hips moved in response, and Nelly was forced to grip his hips to keep Annabelle from ingesting more than she could bear. She moved her head, feeling the tip against her palate, then pressing down with her tongue, now pushing it against one cheek, now against another.

Tiring of her lingual amusement, she rose and examined the shiny, wet cock, then she knelt on all fours on the sofa, knowing fully what she was about to do. With the aid of her willing assistants, the young man mounted behind her, one foot on the floor, the other resting on the sofa. Pulling the shaft at her, Annabelle aimed the tip to her greased rear entrance. The perversity of the action almost overwhelmed her, and she found it hard to refrain from crying out as the tip nosed at her portal. Then she pulled mercilessly at the shaft, knowing the pain would come, anticipating it as part of her pleasure. As soon as the tip was lodged in her, she gave him one final tug, then braced herself against the armrest, knowing what was to come, peering over her shoulder at the thick join between her soft rounded ass and his muscular belly. She was grateful for her forethought in rubbing her behind with pomade. Nonetheless, his driving shaft was to elicit a surprised and pained cry from her.

Isaac, divining by the sharp tug and male instinct what was needed, drove forward with his considerable strength. Annabelle shrieked as the long shaft penetrated her vitals. She felt behind her, stopping him forcefully from moving out again. The long shaft was nested in her to the roots. The full bag swung beneath her own buttocks. She could hear his harsh breathing behind her. She ran her fingers around the distension in her rear hole. She was stretched tightly, and the pain was a burning, yet familiar sensation in her butt. As he started to move she dug her nails into his belly, drawing blood. He desisted, though the tension remained in his stance. She pulled forward herself, giving herself some relief at the expense of pleasure, then drove herself back again, impaling her ass on the massive intruder. Slowly, then with growing confidence, she started to move, shafting herself with growing speed on the member that sprouted from her fundament.

'Oh man, oh man, such a pussy... I ain't never felt so good in my life,' he cried. 'Yo' Southern gals sho' knows how to treat a man. Why, ah could stay here all mah life.

Oh fuck, that is so tight. Ain't she a virgin? I ain't nevah fucked a virgin. Oh my...' Groans and weeping sounds issued from the mask as the pleasure started reaching the man.

Suddenly his massive frame was jerking, and Annabelle furiously realised that she had brought him to a climax well before she was ready. She turned to rebuke the man, when there was a rush of motion. Nelly was at her side, her hands at the join of their bodies, doing something. The man cried out and Nelly whispered into his ear. He panted heavily, then knelt as before without moving, though the tension in his muscles had sagged considerably.

Nelly knelt on the carpet near her mistress's head. 'I hit him at the base of his prick,' she whispered, giggling. 'He's too fast, though I think he can do it several times.'

Annabelle held out her lips gratefully for a kiss, which Nelly obligingly reciprocated. Annabelle moved more slowly this time, fearful of losing the wonderful shaft before she was ready. The pain was diminishing rapidly. 'Get between my legs,' she gasped. 'Now, quickly.'

Nelly obeyed with alacrity, sliding under Annabelle's body, her head between the pallid beauty's knees. She could see the juicy pink lips clearly now. Above them the soft flesh was distended around the massive shaft, but the beautiful cunt lips were empty. Hastily she applied her lips to Annabelle's slit, and drank in the nectar of her mistress's pleasure.

'Beat me now!' Annabelle pleaded, and when no response was forthcoming, she lashed her hand out and struck wildly at her lovers. Daisy hurriedly struck out with the flat of her hand against Annabelle's distended mounds. Then she took the labourer's callused hand and showed him what needed to be done. Surprised, but not reluctant, he slapped heartily at the jiggling flesh before him.

'Harder, oh harder!' Annabelle cried. The muscular man hit her quivering buttocks again and again as his massive cock drove into her depths.

With brute strength, Annabelle pulled and pinched Daisy before her, forcing her to lean her belly uncomfortably over the sofa's armrest. Her tongue found the girl's erect clit and sucked and nibbled as the pain and pleasure mingled in her backside. In her passion she used her teeth freely, and Daisy had her work cut out in trying to restrain her young mistress. Annabelle's lace-gloved hand worked away at the two sweet holes before her, Nelly's below and Daisy's above. The lips, framed in black, were so delicious as the inner pink was revealed. She closed her eyes, drinking in the pleasure, and her own skin quivered with pleasure as Isaac drove his ravaging pole into her innards and his leather strap flashed down on her again and again.

She climaxed in a flush of pain mixed with pleasure. Her insides contracted around the male shaft and the female tongue between her legs, and her own lips clamped around Daisy's sopping hole. Flashes of delight racked her frame, and she was but dimly conscious of the massive flood of spunk that flooded into her interior, and even squirted back onto the woolly black belly-hairs of its erstwhile owner.

Together they collapsed in a pile, from which Nelly extracted herself with difficulty.

Chapter Twelve

'Why, darling Annabelle,' Heather said sweetly. 'I haven't seen you in weeks. Not since we met in town, in fact. Married life must agree with you.'

Annabelle blushed obligingly, and Heather laughed, twitching her fan and looking pointedly at her friend's lap. 'Why, darling... we all had to go through it.'

'You sound as if it is a duty, instead of the most delicious pleasure there is for humankind...'

Heather looked at her soberly. 'Pleasure? I imagine there is some for the man, but for the woman? Hardly much, and so soon over.'

Annabelle could hardly hide the pity in her eyes, and she hugged her friend to hide her surprise.

'Why Heather dear, you mean...'

'Let us not talk of it,' Heather cried in annoyance. 'It is just one of the crosses womankind must bear. I am just so glad there are whores for my Charles to go to. They at least are paid for their suffering and inconvenience.'

'But darling,' Annabelle could not bear to leave it be. 'It is the most wonderful thing that ever happened to me. Why,' she blushed, 'Peter and I are most thrilled with one another. And such joy he gives me with his...' she suddenly realised that she was trespassing on the polite usage of society, and stopped.

Heather was still looking at her as if she expected her friend to continue. She delicately touched her gloved hand to her lips and looked out of the window. 'It is not so between Charles and myself. My person is his to

Great Northern Publishing

The home of quality publishing in Yorkshire

PO Box 202, Scarborough, North Yorkshire YO11 3GE
Telephone and Fax: 01723 581329

PUBLISHERS ~ BOOKSELLERS ~ DESIGN & PRINT SERVICES

CREDIT CARD RECEIPT

Please find attached the credit/debit card receipt for your recent order of goods or services purchased from Great Northern Publishing.

Important Note: some credit card companies abbreviate our company name on their credit and debit card statements. You should be aware of this when checking your card statement as this has caused some confusion with customers. We only use our company name when processing orders and subscriptions, and you will not see details of your order or subscription on your card statement.

We value your custom.
Thank you for your order.

E-mail: books@greatnorthernpublishing.co.uk
Website: www.greatnorthernpublishing.co.uk

ENTERPRISE AWARD 1998 - 2000

command of course, but I lie there until it is all over, and I am free to sleep in five minutes.'

'Five minutes?!' Annabelle interjected, unable to contain herself. 'Surely more than that? Surely more than when you were first married?'

It was Heather's turn to look surprised. 'No, of course not. What woman could stand a man puffing and huffing over her for more than five minutes with that little worm drilling her in...' She blushed, realising that she too had said more than was proper.

'So why don't you get on him?' asked Annabelle. Heather's revelations were amazing her and she was beyond shock at the perversity her friend was expressing.

'But... but... it is not possible, dear. The organs of generation were made for a...' Heather stopped, at a loss for words, then, remembering this was her best and oldest friend, and a married woman to boot, she continued, '...made for use in only that one way.' She was startled out of her self-absorption by Annabelle's hearty laugh. Offended, she stopped speaking and stared out of the window, her face and neck red.

Annabelle stopped her laughter immediately. 'But darling,' she said, the Southern accent returning to her with her strong emotion. She had been trying to copy Peter's drawl. 'There are many ways for the act of generation. Why, Peter and I have done it in this very chair, with me perched on him, and...' She suddenly recollected that Heather was sunk in misery, and did not complete the sentence.

'And?' Heather prompted, her eyes alight.

Surprised, Annabelle continued. 'And on the dining room table, and standing against a wall... a "knee trembler", darling Peter calls it. And oh, dozens of other ways. And all of them so wonderful. Not, mind you, that some of them are not more wonderful than others.'

'I wish my life were like yours,' Heather said sadly. 'The only pleasure I get out of his person is when he is a bit drunk.'

'Drunk? How can he be of any use to you at all then?'

'Why, he becomes most violent then. He almost thrashed the horse boy to death some time ago. And some of that... well, I've learned to enjoy.' She blushed again, and again looked out of the window. Annabelle was moved by the curve of her friend's neck, so well framed by the auburn curls. She touched Heather's throat delicately.

'What does he do?' Her lips were close to her friend's ear and her breath stirred the curls gently. So much like Nelly's curls, she thought, in all but colour. A tingling started rising in her loins at the thought, and for a moment she wished Heather would shorten her visit and she would be free to command Nelly or Daisy to attend to her needs. Maybe she would try some birch twigs this time. She had been reading a travel novel set in Russia, something Peter had brought her.

'He beats me too, when he's drunk,' Heather whispered, and Annabelle's blood ran cold at the thought of this delicate creature being mauled by her brute of a husband.

'I do so love it when he uses the whip,' Heather confided. Her eyes were glittering with some suppressed hunger. 'Though he don't use it as frequently. It's the terrible prices for cotton these days. And the servants are getting uppity...' She sighed, then asked with suppressed excitement, 'Does Peter beat you?' She cast sidelong glances at Annabelle, and her lips were moist. 'But I haven't heard of all those other things...'

'Why, darling Heather, I love it myself,' Annabelle looked shyly at Heather out of the corner of her eye, considering telling Heather the full details of her peculiar pleasure. But caution reasserted itself. 'He does indeed beat me. Most lovingly too, and certainly not in his cups!'

A sudden idea came to fruition in Annabelle's mind. 'Would you perhaps like to observe us?' she asked. Then in growing excitement, 'Tonight. Send a message you are staying for the night, and then... I'll smuggle you into our room through my dressing room, and stir him up...'

There were only the three of them for dinner. Peter accepted the presence of the unexpected guest with complete equanimity. The conversation was as light as the wines, and Peter sent the fair company into gales of laughter as he described some of the grosser peculiarities of the English landed aristocracy.

'Lah, Sir Peter, I do believe y'all are pulling our legs, sir!' shrieked Heather.

'Just call me Peter,' he begged, his eyes on the white expanse of her bosom. 'I would certainly love to!'

She laughed back at him, her eyes dancing, a blush of anticipation on her cheeks. Annabelle saw the by-play, but said nothing, except to wink at Heather when Peter's eyes were turned to call one of the maids.

The ladies had departed, and Peter, after seeing to the doors and wishing for the tenth time that he had a proper butler to do that for him, ascended to the connubial chamber. His bride was waiting, dressed in her usual bedclothes of a semi-transparent silk gown, a red one this time, over which she wore a floor length embroidered Chinese housecoat. Both items were open to the waist, and Peter could see the tops of the pink areolae, which so delightfully beckoned to their centre, peeping at him. He flung off his clothing and rushed to her side, grasping at her waiting figure.

To his surprise, his blushing bride pushed him off furiously.

'You are in love with her!' Annabelle stormed.

Peter stared at her with his mouth agape. 'I say old girl, steady on!'

'That's it!' she said tearfully. 'You think I'm old!' and she pouted tearfully.

'No, no, I say, you're not old by any means—'

'You think I'm too young to have married you!' she wailed, and tears ran down her cheeks. 'Oh, oh, oh. I shall have to return to my mother. It's her, my best friend that you love, a sophisticated woman rather than my poor little country self!' and the tears turned to a torrent.

'Of course not!' Peter snorted. 'Merely because I paid her a compliment—'

'You had your eyes on her the entire evening,' she insisted.

'Merely because I looked at her? She's a demn fine figure of a woman,' he said, drawing Annabelle to his side. 'And I wouldn't mind a gallop with her. But that's all. Remember our agreement.'

Annabelle sniffed and nodded. 'Yes I do. But you'll no longer love me.'

'Darling!' He said, in obvious agitation. 'How can you say such a thing? I've galloped Daisy and Annabelle, with you in attendance! That only made me love *you* the more—'

'Then show me,' she interrupted again. 'Here… right now. All the ways you can.'

Heather peered wide-eyed as Peter took Annabelle in his arms. Then he was on his knees before her, his body hidden under her nightdress.

Moving slowly so as not to dislodge him, conscious of the hidden audience, Annabelle dropped the housecoat and raised her nightdress over her head. Heather cast but a glance at the taut full breasts crowned with their rosy nipples, and at the perfectly rounded belly. Her eyes were riveted to the sleek male head. Peter's eyes were closed and he was rooting and snuffling between his wife's thighs. Her silky blonde triangle was moist with the movements of his tongue. His excitement was obvious as he threw her, legs apart, onto the bed. He sucked at her erect little clitoris, his mouth using every trick at his command to satisfy her. Still she persisted in her subdued snuffling, while her laughing face was turned to the door of her dressing room behind which Heather sat on a comfortable chair provided for the purpose.

Annabelle persisted, trying to resist her inclination to cry out in pleasure, 'You love her, not me. You never lick my cunny like that, you must have learned it from her!'

Peter's reply was muffled by his wife's bush. He extricated himself with difficulty, and addressed her most severely. 'My dear Annabelle, if you persist in this I shall be forced to take steps!'

She buried her face in her hands and her body quivered. 'Oh Mama! He's threatening me! Oh how can I be so miserable!'

Peter rose to his feet, his face like thunder. In two rapid steps he had extracted a thin switch from the ever-ready red leather box. He seized Annabelle by the ankles and swiftly flipped her over. Her pale buttocks, still marred faintly by the weals of previous beatings, excited his gaze. He stared at the quivering mounds in fascination, while the litany of abandonment still careened from his wife's lips. Then he raised the whip and brought it down forcefully on his target.

Heather had found her friend's excitement bizarre at first, but soon was caught up in the game, just as they had plotted as little girls. She had helped move the chair to the dressing room door, and upon Annabelle's sly suggestion, had made herself comfortable as she peered through the crack of the half open door. Annabelle's night attire had been a revelation to her. She herself slept in a heavy flannel nightgown, as every proper matron should, "to ward off the night's chill", even though nights in summer were enough to cause a mule to sweat. And for the first time in her life she actually saw an adult woman's body, as Annabelle slipped gaily out of her clothes, giggling hugely, and then draped herself in translucent silk.

'Oh, I shall make him *so* mad,' Annabelle had giggled. 'Oh, he shall beat me and beat me.'

'Do you... do you, ah... always wear that to bed, dearest Annabelle?' Heather tried to avoid looking at her friend's body; it made her so uncomfortable, though she could not say why.

'No, of course not,' Annabelle giggled again. 'Usually I wear nothing at all, or only a pair of stockings... Maybe I should? But no, dear Peter would only tear them off...'

Heather shrank silently into the chair as Peter had walked into the room. The way he looked at his wife, his eyes hungrily examining her semi-clad body, was a revelation to Heather. Her eyes glued to the opening, she watched as Peter's head actually dropped between her friend's legs. She had never seen the like before, nor had she ever seen a woman's organ, her own included, opened so wide. She tried to suppress the feeling that stole over her at the sight of her friend's beautiful slit, a pink flower bud surrounded by golden fuzz, but when she caught sight of Sir Peter's tongue busily flipping into the inviting hole, she could barely contain herself. Eyes glued to the door, one hand stole under her dress between her petticoats. She had removed her hoops before Sir Peter had arrived, again upon Annabelle's suggestion, because they creaked and interfered with freedom of movement. Now she found greater freedom as her hand started stroking the juncture of her legs.

She heard the discussion by the bedside, and was hardly surprised when Sir Peter brought forth the lash, though she trembled an instant for poor Annabelle, before she recalled that Annabelle had said she enjoyed it too. It gave Heather Jakes some consolation to know that not only she suffered from that awful vice, but in this case, voluntarily!

'Oh, ah, Peter dear,' Annabelle moaned on the bed as the long rod came crashing down. Her bum moved, wriggling on the bed, and Heather was treated to another view of her friend's full purse, its entire pink length exposed to her gaze.

'Oh yes, oh yes... That is so *gooood*.' Annabelle's self-control had apparently completely broken, and she was no longer able to sustain the jealous wife role. Sir Peter, the frown on his face replaced with an indulgent smile, raised his hand again and swiftly cut several times into his bride's delectable white behind.

'Oh! Ahhh! It hurts so! Oh Peter dear! Harder, harder... Hit my ass!' Annabelle cried.

The movements of Heather's hand became rougher, and she actually, for the first time in her life, penetrated her quim with her own fingers. Her other hand joined the first, pinching brutally at the thicker outer lips, and with a rush she realised that for the first time in her life she was experiencing something of the pleasures of the body.

Sir Peter fell on Annabelle and his tongue lapped

hungrily at her prominently raised ass. 'Oh darling, dearest,' he groaned.

'Beat me some more,' his wife implored. 'I've been a bad girl, really sir…'

Sir Peter leapt to his feet. He rapidly approached Heather's hiding place, and she shrunk back, fearful of discovery. Instead, however, he stopped by the chest of drawers, pulled them open, and extracted a handful of silk stockings. They lay in his hands in a torrent of colours, which Heather, who had seen only pink, black, and white stockings, could barely imagine, let alone see someone wearing. Fire reds, glittering blues, and a lemon yellow cascaded from his hands.

He seized Annabelle quickly, and soon had her spread-eagled before him, hands and feet tied to the bedposts. Heather now had the opportunity to examine her friend's profile. As Sir Peter rooted about in the box, Annabelle raised her head and winked in the direction of the dressing room.

The instrument Sir Peter flourished looked not unlike a feather duster. At the end of a flexible rod was a wild medley of coloured cloth strips. He twirled it expertly, and strode to the bed. For an instant Heather could see him full on, as he turned, and she noted with faint alarm the size of the organ that jutted out from below his belly.

He raised the duster over his head and brought it down onto Annabelle's exposed mound.

'Ahhh!' she shrieked.

He hastily bent down, and Heather Jakes saw that he was running his tongue deeply into his wife's gaping slit. Then he raised his head and brought the instrument down again, this time onto the tiny peak of her nearest nipple. He was standing at Annabelle's head, and so Heather could see the strike of the punishing instrument, the quiver that ran through Sir Peter's reddened instrument, and the nipple which immediately engorged and rose like a pink cherry. Curiously enough, she noted, the strange whip left no marks on the perfect snowy hillock. Sir Peter's head was there again, his tongue flicking out and twiddling the red nubbin. He raised his hand again.

'Ahhhh!' Annabelle shrieked again. 'Oh my darling,' she gasped as his tongue laved the assaulted flesh. He continued his activities, until there was not an inch of Annabelle's hidden parts that had not tasted both the whip and his tongue. Heather could see that his massive instrument was trembling violently as he climbed onto the bed, and delivered a final lash straight between her friend's legs. The beautiful Southern belle screamed once again, her hips arching off the bed to meet her husband's descending lips and tongue. Ass in the air, he buried his face deeply between her parted legs and Heather could hear her groans of gratification. Then, after the quivering in her loins had subsided, a quivering which looked to Heather's inexperienced eye as if it was entirely uncontrolled, he pulled back and kissed his wife's lips. Annabelle, roused from her swoon, responded passionately to the kiss, her tongue darting into Peter's mouth, then withdrawing like a coquette.

There was unaccustomed wetness between her legs, and Heather thought she would faint at the sight of her friend. She peered down, and when she raised her eyes once again, found them opening wide with horror. She herself had experienced the terrible trial that awaited her friend, and now she had to watch silently in anguish as Annabelle suffered the same fate.

Sir Peter had pulled back from his wife's erupting spend as the last quivers in her belly quieted down. He kissed her deeply, then whispered, 'My darling, there is something we have never tried that we should show our guest.'

Annabelle's laughing eyes and rising flush told him that he had guessed correctly.

'Anything, dear heart,' she said, able to enunciate clearly as he liked her to do, now that the vortex of pleasure had died down somewhat.

'I wish to insert myself fully into your mouth and fuck your throat.'

'Oh yes, dearest,' she replied, all afire. 'We have never done that before.'

'I shall be most careful,' he said. 'Strike me lightly with your free hand if you feel the least discomfort,' and he rapidly loosened the hand hidden from Heather's view.

Squatting over her pillow, her head tilted back, he inserted his member deeply into her mouth. Annabelle breathed carefully, yet with difficulty through her nose. Soon, as she felt more comfortable with the monster installed in her mouth, she managed subtly to wriggle herself upwards, like a snake engulfing a lizard. Slowly, her muscles relaxed until she found herself with the tip of his cock lodged firmly in the back of her throat. With infinite caution, as the horror-stricken Heather watched from the shadows, Sir Peter began fucking Annabelle's throat. As he moved he could feel the pleasurable yet slightly painful scrape of her teeth on the root of his prick. His movements speeded up imperceptibly, and aided by the touch of Annabelle's busy tongue on the length of the shaft, and her clever use of her lips, he soon found himself pulsing. Hurriedly, yet still infinitely carefully, he pulled back just a little.

'Mmmm!' Sir Peter groaned mightily, and a gush of seed spurted from the tip of his overstrained member and down his wife's throat. The touch of the elixir soothed the outraged membranes and she gulped as greedily as she could at his libation.

Heather watched in horrified fascination as pearly rivulets of the disgusting male substance rolled down Annabelle's cheeks, one almost reaching her ear. She seemed to be delighting in catching as much as she could with her tongue, and Heather could not understand her friend's pleased, even excited expression. She remained frozen in her seat, as Sir Peter blew out the bedside lamps, and only when she sensed the quiet breathing of two people in deep slumber, could she make her escape to her own room.

'Did you know she was there, darling?' Asked Annabelle, once the stealthy footsteps had faded away, and she could hear the sound of a door being closed quietly.

'Well, my love, I guessed as soon as I saw you winking at the dressing room door. But I didn't give the game away, did I?'

'Oh, darling Peter, you are the best husband in the entire world!' She hugged him fiercely, her soft breasts squashing against his chest.

'Well anyway,' she confided thoughtfully, 'there's something about Heather. Yes,' she nodded at her husband's quizzically raised eyebrows, 'she only likes it if she's beaten. She told me her husband does that. Sometimes—'

'Beaten?' he interrupted. 'I say, what a cad.'

'Well, yes dear, he *is*. But that part is the only part she likes.'

At length they looked at one another in the moonlit dimness. Then her eyes dropped away. 'I really much prefer servants,' she said. 'But if she didn't know... and if I could... if I could whip her a little... it certainly would be exciting... very exciting.' Her eyes shone with lust.

'We could entice her here,' he suggested tentatively. 'But she must not know it is us, for that would surely ruin your friendship. How would we do it?'

'A ball!' she cried in excitement. 'With blackface minstrels. We could...'

They hastily fell to making plans in which Heather Jakes figured prominently. And personally.

In her guestroom, Heather stroked her swollen clitoris. Her hips responded with alacrity, and for the first time in her life she masturbated herself to sleep, thinking of Peter's thick cock as it spurted again and again into Annabelle's delighted mouth and throat. Then she imagined Annabelle's face changing to her own and she climaxed with feelings of rapture and guilt intermixed as she imagined Peter's face hovering over her, and his tongue penetrating into her vaginal opening. That image was overlaid by the distorted face of her husband, his hand raised with his quirt in it, raining blows onto her rump, then falling sodden drunk onto the floor. If only he would continue the act to its logical conclusions! But in real life he never did, and when sober, he was almost too correct to have her.

Chapter Thirteen

'Darling, such a wonderful idea,' Heather said gaily as she examined the garden over her fan. 'And entertainment too. This is really *quite* like the old days, before the war.'

'Heather,' Annabelle said distractedly, then with growing excitement. 'How about playing a joke?'

'Oh yes, dear friend,' she enthused. 'Such fun, just like when we were girls!'

'Let's go and borrow some of that blackface stuff from the minstrels. I've got an idea…'

They eyed one another, and could barely contain their laughter. Annabelle had procured two of the uniforms used by the hired servants. White breeches and stockings were complimented by yellow and black striped vests over paler yellow shirts. They also had gaily coloured ties, and large caps to hide their hair beneath.

Unknown to Heather, these costumes had been expressly designed by Annabelle herself to further her plans. She looked at her friend critically. Heather Jakes was only a year or two older than her. She had a slim, almost boyish figure, graced by flat flanks and belly, which allowed her to pass far more easily as a boy than the more voluptuously constructed Annabelle. Her breasts were slightly larger than her own, though they hung lower on her chest, so they had had to strap the waistcoat in tightly. All in all, in the dark they could easily pass as black male waiters. They giggled again conspiratorially, and strode forth.

Mingling with the guests, each holding a tray of snacks,

they were privy to the kinds of confidences people do not usually share with their equals.

'Wha' Cunnel, ah believe that he ain't really an aristocrat,' one Southern gentleman was saying to a crony, as he looked enviously around while engulfing a piece of roast. 'Wha, mah cousin George? He says that you kin' *buy* them titles…'

'Mah deah Miss Puddly, ah hain't seen yo' in a month o' Sundays,' one middle-aged gossip was eliciting confidences from a slightly younger edition of herself. 'Is anything the mattah? Whay, yo' can confide in *me*, mah deah. Is it Pinkney again? After the servant gals no doubt. It's all because of the war, deah.'

'Heah boy, another of them mint juleps, and don' mind about no mint, hah hah,' a florid man in a white suit placed an empty tumbler on Heather's tray. She scurried to obey, exchanging winks with Annabelle as their paths crossed, and arriving in time to hear the end of a salacious story about a neighbour whom she had *never* suspected of being so depraved. All in all, though, she decided after a while, being a servant was too much hard work and not as much fun as being served, and she went off in search of Annabelle.

'Dear Annabelle,' she whispered in a corner of the garden, near a table piled high with plates and silverware for the guests' refreshments. 'I do think I have had enough. Let us retire and return to our true natures.'

'In a moment, Heather dear,' said Annabelle, glancing covertly at her watch. She was relieved to see that though she had forgotten her timing in the excitement of the fancy-dress she had assumed, Heather's boredom had kept things on track.

As if to punctuate her words, there was a sudden explosion, and the large lanterns that had been placed about the garden were blown out by the servants. Heather screamed and jumped at the noise, and the table holding silverware was knocked about, some of the silver falling to the ground. As the lurid light of the fireworks glared overhead, and the band played "Dixie", Heather knelt to pick up the silverware.

'Come on, hurry,' there was a flush of excitement in Annabelle's voice as she tugged at her friend's shoulder. 'We can get away now and make a grand entrance.'

Absently, neatly as always, Heather put the spoons into her waistcoat pocket, intending to return them to the kitchen, and was dragged hurriedly in the direction of the mansion hall.

In the darkness, confused by the changing coloured lights outside, Heather lost Annabelle. Nonetheless, knowing her way from her previous visit, she made her way confidently towards the staircase and the bedroom she had been allotted.

'I say, who are you?' The sharp voice brought Heather spinning round in a panic. It was Sir Peter. He seized the supposed serving boy by the waistcoat shoulder, and examined her in the shifting dimness under one raised eyebrow.

'I can't remember having employed you for tonight,' he said quizzically.

His ears caught a faint chinking sound. Quick as a snake he had his hand in her waistcoat pocket. She twisted away, trying to release herself, and managed to pull away but for the folds of her waistcoat that went over her head and trapped her in place. The master of the house took a firmer grip on her waistband and held on, while he explored the recesses of her pocket.

'Well boy, so you're trying to steal the silver, eh?' Sir Peter's voice came at her from the muffling folds of the fabric that had been thrown over her head. She tried to call out her name and beg for mercy, then realised that would be even more embarrassing.

'You'll have to be whipped, damme,' his voice continued, and Heather shivered with dreadful anticipation. 'Let us see if there's something else,' he said, and his hands moved familiarly over her body.

Her position clarified before her eyes in horrific detail. If she said nothing, she would be whipped and thrown out, but could resume her normal attire and even return to the party. On the other hand, if Sir Peter discovered her deception... why, land's sakes, what would he think? What would all of society think. So she stood as still as she could, while Sir Peter ran his hands thoroughly over her person, in vain pursuit of more fruits of her supposed pilfering. Finding none, her twirled her around and marched her off, her head still hooded by her gaily-coloured waistcoat. The cellar door, previously locked, was conveniently near, and in a trice she had been manhandled down the stairs and over to the punishment bench. It was a broad, padded bench modelled on the piano bench upstairs. There were rings attached to each sturdy leg, and a step ran along each side to facilitate its use. Sir Peter had commissioned it along with the rest of the curious and entertaining furniture of their exercise room, which was also well-supplied with copies of some of Sir Peter's more expensive toys, supplemented by simple natural materials gathered in the countryside, such as green birch twigs and leather whips.

'Nothing to say, eh boy?' Sir Peter's voice broke in on her shock. 'Well, that's the spirit then. But of course, you can't avoid your just deserts!' and he tied her securely face down onto the bench. Her head hung down one side, and she prayed her cap would not come off and disclose her chestnut curls. Her thighs straddled the width of the bench, not uncomfortably – the padding helped there – and her ankles had been secured to the bench's ornate lion's feet.

She heard Sir Peter step around her, as if to admire his handiwork in the dim light of the candle he had lit earlier.

'Well young 'un, the time has come, eh? Expiation of sins, and all that, as the Head at college used to say. The hand, I think.' Her position too awkward to see what was happening, she resigned herself to her fate, vowing that no betraying feminine sound should emerge from her lips.

Sir Peter grasped the small of her back, above the fleshy swell of her buttocks. A sudden hard slap smacked into her raised behind.

'Humph,' she groaned, her lips clenched. He raised his hand and brought it down on her behind again and again. Tears came to her eyes as her ass flamed into a hot burn. His pace was even, and he did not miss an inch of skin, spacing his smacks evenly about her soft tensed mounds.

'Humphhhh!' she gasped as a particularly hard blow stung the base of her ass. Suddenly she was conscious of the dimly realised fact that there was an item of essential nature to her disguise that she did not, could not have. And while she grunted at another blow she thanked her stars that Sir Peter did not try flogging her bum naked, as many a master had been wont to do before the damnyankees had spoiled it all.

'Peter dear, are you down there?' Annabelle's clear voice, properly enunciating the consonants as Peter insisted she do, floated down the stairwell.

'Yes, my dear. Domestic duties, don't y'know? A little of the servant problem, I'm afraid.'

'Well Peter, you simply *cannot* leave your guests alone. You must come up on the instant, and leave the servant for the meantime. Is it a whipping? Oh, and have you seen Heather?'

'My dearest, of course. How silly of me, I quite forgot. And no, my darling, I haven't seen Heather, just this little blackamoor I am whipping. Game boy, what?' His voice started fading as he made his way up from the cellar. 'Not a peep out of him. Haven't finished of course. Have to send someone down to attend to it, whom do you think?' His voice faded, and Heather was left alone in the cellar, to the light of the single candle. The dim light and the position of her own neck did little to illuminate her about her surroundings, and she let her head slump, even going off into a doze...

Heather was awakened rudely by the feel of a hot wire slashing across her mounds. She almost squealed in surprise and agony, and she had the vague memory of the sound of a whip.

'Hmmm,' a grating voice she did not recognise, but which was definitely *not* that of Sir Peter, sounded hoarsely. 'Much better if you're trouserless,' the voice said, in a parody of Sir Peter's usual drawl.

Heather tried to struggle, knowing the result of disclosing her true nature under her tight pantaloons, but to no avail. Her tight breeches were soon pulled off her backside, then pooled about her ankles, and she realised with dread that the unknown tormentor had come equipped with scissors or a knife.

'Hmmm, a dozen of the best, Sir Peter said,' breathed the voice, and Heather shuddered in fear.

The whip came down on her bare backside and she squealed with muffled terror. 'Ahhhh...' was all she could say, intent on hiding her true nature, hoping that in the dark it would not be exposed.

Another blow, and she squealed, higher this time, then

bit her lip. Her tormentor took no notice of her grunts and screams, landing regular stripes on her quivering behind, without let. Heather's buns were touched with a burning haze. Yet she found a rarely experienced wetness in the tight little chink between her legs, and she moved her thighs uneasily. A glow had been lit in the depth of her belly. With every blow her imagination conjured up lascivious scenes. A faceless man, his male member extended, approaching her across a candlelit floor of a great ballroom, men and women cheering him on. The sight of a vagina opened and glistening. Her own legs locked around thrusting hips. Sir Peter's face peering up at her from between her legs while his long glistening tongue extended into her. In her mind's ears she could still hear the terrible words that her best friend Annabelle had said, words she thought the innocent Annabelle could hardly know, and she repeated them to herself with each blow as the images paraded before her. 'Fuck!' she cried out in her imagination. 'Fuck! Quim! Cunt! Prick!' And she sank into a swoon.

She came to as the candlelight shifted, and Heather knew that her secret would soon be out, as the pleased master of her punishment inspected the results of the whip's actions. The light moved slowly from side to side.

'Damme, it's a woman,' the hoarse voice said, then coughed into a cupped hand. A palm slapped down on Heather's heated behind.

Annabelle examined her friend's lacerated bum keenly by the light of the candle. She herself had stripped to her shift, to allow her freedom of movement, and she was sweating copiously. Heather's tight bum was neatly marked with reddish stripes, all more or less evenly spaced, as Peter had told her she should. Heather had not said a word, though her shoulders and behind were still quivering and, glory of glories, Annabelle could see the entire length of the valley between Heather's sweat-bedecked shining globes. Happily, she stretched out her hand and ran it down between her friend's buns.

'Hmmmph,' Heather snorted indistinctly, the rule of silence she had made binding her still.

Unable to contain herself, Annabelle bent quickly forward and ran her tongue the length of the beautiful crack, from its beginning beneath Heather's now-prominent spine, along the musky rear hole, down to the honeyed interior of the channel walls, and as deeply as she could into that channel.

Annabelle first amused herself by playing with the lovely length of hair-covered pussy that ran from the ass until it was hid by the bench. Heather's hips were full, and in a few years she could be fat, but now, at nineteen, she was truly voluptuous, and Annabelle intended to amuse herself with every part. She moistened the hairs, then, her palm almost flat, squeezed and kneaded the furry flesh. Her free hand roved over Heather's delicious body, now shaking a quivering buttock slightly, now squeezing a breast squashed flat by the bench, now tickling the girl's armpits or ribs.

Soon Annabelle found she was as randy as her victim, and knew something had to be done. First she looked about desperately for Peter, or Nelly, anyone to help her with her torment. In their absence in the cellar, she resorted to her husband's magical box. Rooting about in it, she found an instrument she had never tried before. It was a large double dildo, carved at an angle, of some hard dark wood. Realistic knobs and veins had been carved on each end. She giggled silently as she extracted it, and with a delicate sigh, inserted one end into her own hungry orifice, and tied it in place around her waist with the provided ribbons. As she walked back to where Heather's supine form reclined on the padded bench, she giggled once again at the strange weight wagging before her hips. And to think men had to wear this thing day in and day out!

Then she caught sight of Heather's twitching behind again, the long puffy slit, the bare bum marked with the stripes of her lust, and the shy puckered entrance. She forgot her controlled mannerisms, almost called out to Heather aloud, and fell to her knees before the proffered morsel. No morsel, indeed, but a complete meal, as she attacked the dim cavern's of Heather's privates with her mouth and tongue.

'I must have it,' she muttered to herself, as her mouth dove deep between the prominent mounds and into the waiting cavern.

'Oaaaahh... humphhh...' came from Heather's obstinately closed mouth.

Slobbering and licking, Annabelle pushed her face deeply into her friend. Her nose nuzzled against the humid fragrant little bud, and she happily pushed in against the muscular resistance. Her lips sucked in the prominent lips, then released them again only to chase them with her tongue. She moved her head up and down, the better to festoon her face with the trails of moisture and the delicious smell that emerged from her friend's privates.

Heather thought she would go mad as the strange man's face nuzzled into her secret recesses. She had never dreamed anyone would do this thing in that filthy part of herself that she hid from every eye. Now there was a tingling and the rising of nervous excitement in her that she found impossible to contain. Notwithstanding her bonds, she began rocking backwards, trying, if only with the movements of her rear, to show her unknown assailant what she wanted. The delicious tongue slipped into her orifice and out again, and with each insertion, she felt the tide of her pleasure rising, until, she could not longer contain herself.

'Oh my Lord...' Heather sobbed. 'Please, please... Do it to me, give me all of it.'

The stranger happily obliged. Her stinging buttocks were pulled widely apart, and the knowledgeable tongue sank deeply into her, touching every membrane.

Finally Heather could contain herself no longer. An incessant and uncontrolled wail emerged from her throat. Waves of overwhelming pleasure, like nothing she had ever felt before, boiled out of her stomach. She could feel the walls of her vagina contracting, and a flow of her juices sluiced down to inundate the invading face in her behind. Rather than drawing back as she had expected, the tongue lapped wildly at her outpourings, and as she subsided slowly with diminishing jerks of her bottom, she felt it even climb up and push its way past her guardian muscles, entering and laving her tight little anal bud.

Annabelle rose from behind Heather, her face shiny with her friend's liquids. The raging fire in her pussy had grown to unbearable proportions, and she knew she had to do something or die. For a moment she toyed with the thought of presenting herself to Heather, but that would spoil all the fun. Then she was conscious of the weight of the dildo pulling at her waist, and the pressure of the other end in her inflamed cunt. She crouched over Heather's inviting behind, aimed the wooden shaft with one hand, and pushed herself inexorably forward into Heather's slick entrance. With the other hand she held a smaller ivory dildo, for which she had special plans.

Heather grunted anxiously as she felt the first dildo penetrate her sore, pearl-bedewed slit. Annabelle crouched over her friend's supine figure, taking pleasure in the perfect skin as much as in the complete helplessness. She wanted to clutch the smooth back to her, to smother Heather's helpless figure, but had to restrain herself in order to keep her full breasts from giving the game away. Then she drew back. Heather breathed a sigh of mingled relief and regret, and Annabelle aimed the second dildo at the tiny puckered hole between her friend's full ass mounds.

The bound girl screamed with outrage as she felt the member penetrate her in what she had thought was to be used only for another thing. A quick smack on her inflamed behind quieted her expressions of outrage. Then the thin dildo was penetrating past the guardian muscles and into her little hole. She bit her lip in anticipation of the pain, but the stranger had so lavishly lubricated her behind with her tongue, that the expected pain never came. Instead, she felt penetrated by two glowing pillars of pleasure. Once again she oscillated her buttocks, unable to control her desire to have more and more of the pleasure-giving shafts ensconce themselves into her behind.

Annabelle waited until she saw that Heather was not only not resisting any more, but actively encouraging the double invasion, and she started moving with greater speed and strength, aping the actions of her dear husband as he applied his real member to her. Her fingers clutched at her friend's back, drawing small beads of blood, and subsequently, she found a better purchase clutching the reins of Heather's hips as they both rocked towards a climax.

'Unhh… unhh… unhh…' was the only sound Annabelle could make, while under her, Heather unconsciously muttered endearments and encouragement to her unknown lover. With a final thrust, and with a clutching grip that scored deep marks on Heather's hips, Annabelle felt her own juices descend, flowing along the shaft to meet Heather's. The two women screamed almost in unison, heedless of the guests in the mansion.

At long last Annabelle withdrew from her friend. She inspected the damage. Heather's asshole was still slightly open, a dark and inviting hole. Her nether hole drooled from Heather's offerings, glistening in the candlelight, and the plenteous hairs around the two orifices glittered with moisture like diamonds. Swiftly, Annabelle gathered her clothes for a hasty toilet, and vanished up the stairs, to report her adventures to Peter and have him rescue the prisoner.

Relaxed in a delirious haze, Heather waited for recovery...

'Did you have a good time, Heather?' Annabelle asked her friend. 'I lost sight of you when the lights blew out.'

Heather shivered at the remembered pleasure. She knew Annabelle would never forgive her if she told her what had happened, and with Annabelle's new husband as well! So she merely smiled and said, 'I had a wonderful time, my darling friend.' Then realised she meant every word of what she had said.

Chapter Fourteen

'My dear, how charming you look...' There was an undertone of venom in Chastity Brown's tone, Annabelle was perfectly certain of that. Mr Brown and her Daddy were talking business, and why he had to talk business with Yankees from Boston, of all people, was well beyond her. Chastity was a tall bosomy female, with a dark face now turning reddish from the sun. She was *so* careless of the Southern sunshine, Annabelle thought. Hard on the heels of that thought her dear Mamma said, 'My dear Mrs Brown, you really should cover up more. Your skin is getting so... so dark.'

Indeed, now that she noticed it, Chastity Brown's skin did have an undertone of perhaps a darker ancestry...?

Mamma sighed. The damnyankees were everywhere, and one could hardly avoid them. The Brown's had descended on her while Annabelle was away in her new house. They had an introduction from a friend in Charlottesville, and one of course could not refuse, particularly in these hard times. Annabelle had found the woman to be insufferable. She had, in her rudeness, actually made reference to the war! And if that was not enough, was constantly comparing the wonders of the South to that grey metropolis she had come from, and not in flattering terms either. The water was bad, there were mosquitoes, the men spat, why, she had even dared to criticise Annabelle's dress as being at one and the same time "too showy" and "rather simple"! And the dress in question was one of her favourites, an exquisite creation that Peter had ordered some months before as soon as he had seen her for the first time. This last remark set her mind onto unaccustomed paths, and before long she found herself staring thoughtfully at Mrs Brown, while she awaited the sound of the carriage that was due to take her home.

'My dear Miss Brown,' Annabelle put on her most sincere tone, fluttering her eyelashes and oozing Southern charm. 'You and dear Mr Brown just must come and visit us at home. We lie just outside town, about a mile from dear Mama. Perhaps you would care to stay the night? Sir Peter would just love to meet Mr Brown.' That, she knew, was a gross calumny on her husband's character, but she knew he would support her in her necessary deceit for such a worthwhile cause.

Brown raised his head suddenly from the conversation he was having with Annabelle's dear papa about the price of manufactured goods. '*Sir* Peter?' he said in surprise and interest.

'Oh yes, didn't I mention it?' said Annabelle, with exaggerated innocence. 'My dearest Peter is a real aristocrat. Terribly old family in England.'

'Why but he's so democratic,' said Annabelle's mother, beaming with pride. 'No one in the family calls him Sir Peter at home, of course.'

'Why, I really had no idea,' said Charity Brown. A smidgen of envy, well concealed, soured her voice just a little.

'Won't you please allow your wife to come and visit us, sir?' Annabelle asked, her hands clasped in supplication before her.

'Why, my dear Mrs... or shouldn't that be *Lady* Stone?' he asked smarmily.

'Why sir, you're among friends here,' Annabelle replied.

'Just call me Annabelle. You will allow her to come?'

Purposely misunderstanding her words, the gleam of anticipated social, if not economic profit in his eyes, Mr Brown said, 'Why, we'd be delighted. Shall we fix a date?'

Annabelle was in a storm compounded of rage and delight when she got home in the late afternoon.

'...And the minx and her disgusting damnyankee husband are coming tomorrow,' she concluded in triumph. 'I wondered, oh Peter dear, it would be such a triumph if you could not think of some way we could have her?'

Peter smiled indulgently, then teased her gently. 'Why my pet, I do believe that since dearest Heather your horizons have broadened.'

She blushed, and he kissed her lovingly on the lips. Peter thought for a moment, and then said, 'I have an idea. After dinner...'

Dinner was superb, spoiled by only two things: Mr Brown's insistence that a little bit of cigar smoke could do no harm to man nor beast, and consequent puffing throughout dinner, and his constant boastful discourse on the development of Boston City and his part in it.

'...Why sir, you have no *idea* of the industry involved. We will soon rival London for size. And as for industry, well sir, I can tell you we are on our *way*. Yessir, we are just *driving along*.' He took another pull at his cigar in satisfaction.

Annabelle took advantage of the break in the monologue and rose, saying pointedly to Chastity Brown, who had spoken of little but how better suited Annabelle and "her dear Sir" would be in Boston, where she could show them to all the right people, 'I believe we ladies should retire and leave the men to their whiskey and cigars. Chastity, slightly bewildered but willing to follow aristocratic custom, as Peter had risen and courteously held out her chair, departed with her to the recesses of the house.

Peter rang the bell and Daisy entered, bearing a tray with a decanter of good bourbon and a humidor of excellent Havanas. Peter poured both men a generous portion. Brown's eyes were on the serving maid as she cleared away the dishes. Nelly entered, and Brown stroked her figure with his eyes, even hidden under the layers of dress she wore. She bobbed a curtsy to Sir Peter and whispered something in his ear.

He took a sip of his whiskey, lit Brown's cigar, and said, 'Terribly sorry old man. There's a minor matter come up. Have to see to it myself, you know. Awfully rude of me, I know, but could I leave you to yourself for about half an hour?'

Brown nodded expansively, and gulped at the fiery liquid in his glass. The smoky flavour worked its way down his gullet, and the good meal had made him somnolent. He would not mind a quick forty winks in the comfortable armchair he was ensconced in.

Peter refilled Brown's glass and departed.

He hurried through the house. Nelly at his side, Daisy, who had slipped through the kitchen door, joined them as they quietly walked to the conservatory where Annabelle had decreed the first act of the drama was to begin.

Chastity Brown had just brushed some crumbs of the excellent shortcake she had consumed, when Nelly stood by her side, brush and dustpan at the ready. She bent over as if to whisk at Chastity's lap with her brush. In a trice she had seized the other woman's hands. Daisy, who had slipped up behind her, tucked a folded napkin into her mouth. In seconds the two maids had Chastity bound hand and foot. They stepped back, only slightly dishevelled, the surprise had been so complete.

On the sofa, Mrs Chastity Brown rolled about, her mouth working frantically but without result, her eyes wide with surprise and terror.

Annabelle laughed, a tinkling light sound in the room. 'My dear Chastity... for I believe that is your Christian name? Well, my dear Chastity, no damnyankee is going to insult me in my own home. *Boston* indeed!'

'Mmmpphh... mmmpphhhh!' was the woman's only response.

'Take her down,' Annabelle ordered her maids, and they picked Chastity up and frog-marched her down to the door to the cellars.

The cellar itself was extensive. Its original use as a wine cellar was augmented by the special equipment Peter had placed there on the occasion of Heather Jakes' edification. Part of the cellar near the stairs had become very cosy. Heavy hangings kept out the cold and damp, and the original bench had been augmented by curious articles of furniture which been procured by liberally paying a local joiner. The two maids seated the struggling Mrs Brown in a chair and allowed her a look around. It was clear that she had no comprehension of what was about to happen to her.

'Oh, Peter dear,' said Annabelle, standing with her husband and watching the three figures disappear down the stairwell. 'This is going to be *such* fun.'

He smiled, turned to her and kissed her deeply, then started undoing the bows at her shoulders.

She slipped away from him, laughing. 'Lah, sir. I have a better use for your vigour right now. You must do me a service first. I shall prepare myself. Do go down and keep our guest company. I shan't be but a moment.' She turned swiftly away, while Peter obeyed and descended to the cellar.

'This, my dear Chastity, is called a dildo,' said Peter. 'It is of curious make, in that it is studded with little insets of amber. Part of a punishment set I bought in Africa, don't y'know. The Arabs use them when they are tired of a woman and want some rest.' His voice was as courteous as ever, as he explained the various implements in sight in measured tones. He had done little more than talk, though he had been familiar enough to take off his coat, and Chastity wondered what it was he wanted from her.

Annabelle descended the stairs. Peter looked up at her in admiration. Her white gloves and button boots gleamed freshly. Her hat was a vision of pink muslin and lace. Between them she wore nothing but her skin. He rushed at her, panting fretfully. 'I must have you, darling Annabelle. Now. Look!' He pointed to the rising lump in his smooth breeches, and Annabelle playfully tweaked the massive bulge. He held her gloved hand there a while, struggling at the same time with his flies, and the monstrous erection sprang free into her hand.

'Now!' he repeated, forcing her to her knees.

She obediently bent down, kissing the object that was as instrumental in her pleasure as in his. 'Please, dear heart.' She smiled so prettily his heart melted, as did some of his erection. 'Not just now, please? I promise a greater pleasure...'

Chastity Brown looked on apprehensively as the naked vision approached her. Annabelle looked the older woman over critically, from foot to head, smiling slightly all the while, then turned to her maids. 'I would think she should be more comfortable, my dears. Those stays must be killing her. Do untie her,' and she stepped back.

Charity breathed a breath of relief. At last to be free of these ropes! She would give this disgusting Southerner and her effete husband a word or two, for frightening her with this silly trick!

Then, powerful and inescapable as two panthers, the two maids were upon her. Before she could collect her wits, they had unbuttoned her dress, exposing the underclothes beneath. She started struggling, muttering inarticulate cries into the immaculate handkerchief that filled her mouth. Her wriggling and squirming was as nothing to the two maids who had been taught well by Annabelle in the arts of dressing a lady. She was rolled on her side to let her corsets be unlaced, then back again to undo and slip off her camisole. It had been a hot day, hotter than she was accustomed to, so Chastity Brown had not worn drawers. She shrieked, or tried to, as the two maids touched her more intimate parts, but there was no escape.

Annabelle and Peter, arm in arm, watched the spectacle with interest. When Chastity was naked but for her stockings, Nelly turned a silent question on Annabelle.

'It is rather hot,' Annabelle said judiciously. 'I believe she will be more comfortable completely naked. And dear Nelly, do not hesitate to enjoy your work!'

Nelly flashed an understanding grin at her mistress. 'Be quiet, you!' she said ferociously, and aimed a slap at the heavier woman's thigh. The pain was slight, but the surprise and indignity brought a shriek and renewed wriggling from the bound figure. Nelly grinned again, and deliberately grabbed at the scant dark fuzz that adorned Chastity's prominent Mound of Venus. Daisy, taking the hint from her cousin, seized one of the flattened soft breasts and squeezed it so that the brownish nipple stood out brazenly.

Chastity moaned and tried to struggle out of the two maids' grip. Ignoring her, they started to explore her body with a thoroughness that had never occurred on that particular landscape before. Daisy's other hand smacked brutally against the erect morsel in her hand. Chastity Brown shrieked soundlessly into the handkerchief in her mouth, but she shrieked even more when Daisy bent her perfect dark neck and lapped at the poor distraught nipple, delicately nibbling at the morsel with her perfect white teeth. She pulled back for a moment, her eyes fully on Mrs Brown's, then set to work with both hands, squeezing the rather flabby mounds deliberately, mashing them against the woman's panting ribcage, then holding the nipples high with pinching fingers. She shook them about, examining the ripples in the soft flesh, and finally lowered her mouth to bite not too gently at the palpitating mounds.

Chastity shrieked anew as she felt inquisitive fingers explore that place where no one had ever explored before. Even her husband did little more than shove himself into her. Now slim, knowledgeable, delicate fingers were parting her labia, as Nelly explored the nether regions. She shrieked and arched her hips in protest, trying to twist them away when the fingers approached that forbidden little nubbin of flesh which lay at the front of what she privately called her naughty nook. The fingers withdrew the little standing piece from its shading hood, and rolled it between them. Chastity's frenzied attempt to escape converted almost without her knowledge nor consent into a lengthy, leisurely twist of the hips as her body betrayed her and sought to prolong the contact.

'Slap her! Hard!' was Annabelle's succinct command. The two young women lashed out at their bound captive. Daisy concentrated her blows on the full fuzz-topped mound, and the clenched thighs, while Nelly slapped again and again at the woman's rounded belly and quivering breasts.

'Will you be good?' snarled Nelly into her victim's face.

'Unhhhn nnnnno…' was all they could make out, and the slapping resumed once again.

'My dear Chastity, have you had many men?' Annabelle's curiosity, and her desire to exploit the unusual circumstances, had the better of her.

Chastity Brown looked at her in horror. The matter-of-fact tone and the attempt to strip her of the remainder of what she thought of as her dignity, was the last straw. *No, no, it's none of your affair!* was what she tried to say. But all that came out from behind the gag was a mumbled, strained, 'Nnnnn... Nongyubzzz!'

But Annabelle persisted, the feathers in her hat swaying over the trembling victim, while her tormentors idly stroked their preferred parts.

'I asked you dear, how many have you had? And I *will* have an answer!'

Chastity shook her head heavily.

Annabelle's lips firmed, and she looked at her maids. 'Five stripes,' she said.

Chastity, understanding the helplessness of her position, wildly pushed at her captors with all her might. In the struggle she and Daisy fell to the floor. Enraged, the maid raised her hand to rain blows down on the obstreperous woman.

Annabelle stopped her with a gesture, and a word to Mrs Brown. 'Five stripes from each of us,' she said. 'Daisy, the brush please.'

Daisy rose to her feet and soon brought a large ivory-handled wide-bodied hairbrush to her mistress. On the floor, Chastity watched the approach of the instrument with horror in her eyes.

'I imagine she will want to resist,' Annabelle said thoughtfully. 'I do not want to tie her down yet, and I do so want to feel her skin. Darling, may I?' She raised her eyes to Peter who was looking on indulgently, his cock erect and almost panting in company with its master. He stopped stroking his wife's perfect naked bum, and urged her on wordlessly, a glint of mischief in his eyes.

The three women pounced on their bound victim as one, and when the dust had settled, Mrs Chastity Brown found herself face down over Annabelle's perfect lap, heels and shoulders held down by the two glowing maids.

Peter looked on, entranced at the stunning picture the four women presented. They looked, he thought, like one of the more attractive Italian set pieces. Annabelle's beautifully naked form was slightly obscured by the constantly moving body, slightly darker in hue, of her prisoner. The pretty hat his wife wore nodded perfectly over the scene, and the two maids, crouched over the prisoner's extremities, provided perfect frames to the central images. For a few brief moments, Annabelle allowed Mrs Brown to realise the helplessness of her position, while her hands roved over the woman's exposed flesh. She stuck a curious finger into Chastity's vulnerable cunny, noting that it was still dry, notwithstanding the maids' ministrations. With her left hand she felt between their bodies, squeezing the pendant breasts. Then she reached for the brush.

'My darling Chastity, I am now going to smack some obedience into you. *If* you behave yourself, I shall only use the bristle side once, then the back of the brush. Otherwise, dear, it's bristles all the way.'

She raised the brush swiftly, and brought it down onto the fat buttocks before her. Chastity, notwithstanding her bonds and the strength of the girls who held her down, jumped like an eel.

'Yeaaaagh!' she screamed, a sound that could be heard clearly through the gag. 'Nnnnn. Nnnnn!' Tears were leaking down her cheeks and dripping onto the sofa. The second blow, the one she dreaded, was slow in coming, and in the interim she had a chance to realise, to her surprise, that the blow, painful as it had been, was also raising uncomfortably lustful feelings that she would have liked, modestly, to banish from her consciousness.

'And now for the back. Do stay quite still, my dear Chastity.' The brush rose and came down fast, the smooth ivory back smacking smoothly against the reddened flesh, marked with tiny brighter pinpricks.

Had she had time to think, Chastity Brown would undoubtedly have held still. But the humiliation of her posture, and the unaccustomed pain from the previous blow, were her undoing. She screeched loudly and once again attempted to evade her tormentors. 'Oooooooh! Ydastards!' she screamed as she tried to extricate herself.

'Why, you sure do carry on, Miss Brown!' Annabelle looked down cruelly at her victim. The brush rose again and descended, bristles down once more.

Chastity shrieked and attempted to escape throughout the entire five. She gave a sigh of relief when the last one was done, having forgotten the rest of her sentence.

Annabelle motioned to Daisy, and passed her the brush. 'You were the insulted party, Daisy dear, you be the first.'

Daisy flashed a smile at her mistress. The ivory handled instrument rose in her hand, but before she could bring it down, she heard Annabelle say, 'Bristles down, dear,' and hurriedly shifted her grip. She hit once, twice, with ferocious accuracy. Having had time to study the situation, she knew precisely what she was going to do. Each measured stroke of her powerful arm hit on a different place. First one buttock, then the other, then higher up, and the final insult being a blow to the middle, as low as she could get.

Chastity screamed once more, though her strength and resistance were wearing out. The last blow had scraped the sensitive tissues between her legs, and she wriggled and writhed in her bonds most satisfyingly.

'Oh, Peter dear,' Annabelle turned her flushed and delighted face to her husband. 'She does wriggle so! I can feel her bush against my thigh and it is *so* delicious! Nelly, you must have a go.'

Nelly and Daisy changed places, but by the second blow, delivered in a timed manner, Chastity was trembling as she tried not to arouse the ire of the woman upon whose lap she was lying, and who held her immediate fate in her hand.

'Will you tell me now, dear?'

For a moment Chastity gazed at her tormentor with glazed eyes, as the carpet she had been deposited on at Annabelle's feet, pricked uncomfortably into her lacerated bottom.

'How many men have you fucked?'

Chastity looked at her uncomprehendingly, and Annabelle took pity on her, remembering her own days of verbal innocence.

'How many men have put their manhood in that…' she nudged Chastity's prominent mound with the soft toe of her kidskin boot. 'You will tell me, right?'

Chastity nodded hastily, and the two maids giggled.

'More than ten?'

Chastity shook her head.

'More than five?'

She shook her head once more, sniffling damply.

'One?'

She nodded hastily.

'Well, well, well. And women?'

Chastity looked at Annabelle in horror, and then at the other two girls in the room while she shook her head and tried to wriggle away.

'No dear, that will do you no good,' said Annabelle, in her exaggerated drawl. 'I think that your damnyankee impudence comes from not having had enough. So in the spirit of sisterhood for which the South is known, I am going to rectify the problem. An' if you need some encouraging, why I'll supply it.' She motioned with her eye, and the ever-attentive Nelly brought forth the silk-tasselled tawse which Annabelle ran slowly through her fingers. 'Now,' she continued, 'we are going to loose them ankles, and you are going to lie there like a good little girl while my girls show you a thing or two.'

Hastily the three women set to work, and in a trice had bound Chastity Brown supine on her back to the special, heavy padded bench Peter had procured for the furnishing of their little scene. Her hands were tied beneath the bench, and her feet tied to the floor to convenient knobs on the furniture's legs, so that her legs were well parted.

'Now my dears, you may mount her,' Annabelle said. And she motioned to Daisy to remove the gag. 'If you make a sound, I shall have you whipped with a horsewhip!' Annabelle cautioned, and Chastity knew that was not an empty threat.

Nelly promptly dropped between Chastity's parted legs. Her wiry pubic hairs rubbed onto the other woman's softer, wider mound as their hairs mingled. Nelly sighed in satisfaction and she clutched at Chastity Brown's breasts, then sucked on them like a hungry babe.

All this time her mound was rubbing furiously at her

victim's, and to her surprise, Chastity found that she was responding! Something she had never before experienced was happening between her legs. Liquid was moistening her channel, as sometimes happened when Brown took his once-monthly pleasure of her. Only this time it went on and on. When the serving girl brought her lips to hers, she kissed back without a thought, and even when the demanding tongue invaded between her lips, she did not dare protest, and soon that too became pleasurable.

Nelly slipped her hands around Chastity's full hams and began kneading her buttocks, pulling the other woman to her mound. Chastity started gasping, feeling, for the first time in her life, the rise of female pleasure. Soon she was responding with all her might to Nelly's thrusts. Her bound hands found their way around the other's dark neck, and she offered her lips to be kissed and sucked again and again, finally, as her climax approached and her movements became less and less controlled, even daring to stick her tongue into the grinning delectable mouth.

Peter watched the two women on the bench. His John Thomas was so hard it felt almost painful. The taut buttocks jogged unmercifully onto the older woman, and he needed to put himself into something to relieve the pressure. Finally the muscular movement of the buttocks was too much for him to bear. He crouched over Nelly, his cock in his hand, waiting for the opportunity to stoop like an eagle and impale the bound woman.

'Darling, please don't waste yourself. There is a special pleasure reserved just for you in a moment. In the meantime, why don't you work some of your nervous tension off in me?'

He turned in a flash and seated himself on the sofa, pulling his wife to him, and peering over her shoulder as she impaled herself on his rigid prick. Sighing in satisfaction, yet careful not to spend, he poked his wife with vigour while they watched the scene before them.

The climax arrived for both women simultaneously. Nelly's form straightened on her victim's, and she thrust her tongue deeply into Chastity's mouth while her mound scraped powerfully on the other's soft pussy. The sudden movements, and the tremors that followed, were too much for Chastity's newly awakened sensibilities. She arched herself off the bench, trying and barely succeeding in controlling her cry as shivers of lust coursed through her body.

Barely had she recovered from her first spend, the very first she had ever experienced, when Nelly rose dutifully to her feet, to allow her cousin to take her place. A glance at her mistress showed that she was bobbing on Sir Peter's prick, the long shaft, reddened by lust, emerging from between her legs, then disappearing once more.

Sir Peter caught her eyes and motioned above their heads. She understood immediately, glancing at the clock on the newly installed mantelpiece. Only fifteen minutes had passed, but Master Brown might be turning fretful. She hastily donned her outfit once more, and slipped up the stairs.

Daisy had not been idle during this exchange. At first she had placed herself as Nelly had, and began a long, languorous stroking that made the heavyset woman beneath her respond with a deep moan and another arching of her body. Looking down at the closed eyes and wide open mouth, another desire took hold of her. She rose, and Chastity's eyes opened in unconscious protest. Then they protested more as Daisy arranged herself with her knees straddling her head. Sudden certainty bloomed in her mind, and she gathered her breath to shout.

Annabelle tore herself from her husband's embrace and

fell to the floor at Chastity's head. 'Would you like to feel this?' she hissed, flourishing the tawse. Chastity's eyes went round with fear, but the idea... the very idea... a servant, a member of the lower classes... about to put it on her *face*!

'Daisy, hold her legs and slide forward a moment, my dear.'

Daisy hurriedly obeyed her mistress, and Chastity barely had time to recover from her horror at what was expected of her, when Annabelle raised the tawse slowly over her head. The tassels danced merrily, and for a moment Annabelle regretted she had not chosen the leather tawse. Then, when her victim had had time to absorb the idea, she brought it down on Mrs Brown's pulpy breasts, her hand flat on the Bostonian's mouth.

'Eeeeyahhhhhhhh!' Chastity squealed. It felt as if thousands of wires had dug into her sensitive flesh. Her squeal went on and on, and then she found the words. 'No...' she mumbled. 'No more. I'll do what she wants! Please, I'll do what she wants! No more!'

Annabelle removed her hand, then bent and kissed the sobbing woman gently on her lips. 'You will enjoy it, I promise,' she said.

Daisy rearranged herself on Chastity's face. 'You lick it proper, Miss Brown, and we both go to heaven,' and she bent forward to part Chastity Brown's pouting cunt lips. The outer lips were fleshy and full, and the inner lips were thinner and curled like a leaf of lettuce, and now covered with the sheen of love juices Chastity had extruded. Curious at the appendage, Daisy peeled back the hood at the tip of the slit while Chastity gave a moan and unconsciously jogged her hips towards the searching fingers. Her clitoris was a tiny, shiny button hidden under its mantle.

Daisy smiled a broad smile and said over her shoulder, after grinning at her audience, 'You just do what I do, Miss Brown, you hear?'

Chastity grunted something and Daisy pinched the clitoris, at which the woman under her gave a shriek and a quick, 'Yes, oh yes!' as Daisy lowered her head and sucked in the shiny clitoral nub. She waited for a second while Chastity fumbled at her own opening, and licked the swelling lovingly when Chastity managed to find the right part.

The two females set to work on a complicated game of follow-the-leader, with Chastity striving to emulate her tormentor as best she could. When she was dilatory, Daisy pinched her most sensitive tissues, and Chastity Brown hurried to satisfy her. Daisy started jogging her bum onto the other woman's face. Her eyes became dreamy and she sighed through her actions. Beneath her, Mrs Brown, as affected by the continuous laving of her vaginal tissues, raised her loins to meet the thrusts of the maid's active tongue.

The climax was upon them, and both strained at one another, pushing their mouths deeply into the juncture of the other's legs. Daisy stabbed her tongue deeply into Mrs Brown, and Peter, who had moved so he could see Chastity's face better, saw that she was emulating the maid as best as she could, and that her actions were far less forced than they had been before.

A copious flood of salty-sweet juices inundated Chastity Brown's face. She sobbed with a mixture of despair and triumph as her own vaginal libations showered down and wet Daisy's hungry tongue and active lips. Sighing deeply, the two females swooned in one another's arms.

At a signal from the impatient Annabelle, Daisy roused herself from the plump figure she had been reclining upon.

Standing magnificently naked, her lips and chin slick with a mixture of her saliva and Mrs Brown's exudations, she smiled beatifically at her employers and said politely to the bound Chastity, 'Thank you, Mrs Brown,' and scampered into her clothing and up the stairs.

Annabelle stroked Chastity's smooth belly with her gloved hands. Then she squeezed the generous breasts, pushing up the nipples and displaying them for Peter's admiring glare. Chastity hollered in renewed anguish as she recovered her senses from the storm of her tribadic encounter, partly at the shame and partly at the pain.

'Why dear, you really must know more about gloves,' Annabelle said consolingly. She wandered over to the sidetable, and Chastity, fascinated despite her position, watched the undulation of the smooth pink bottom with fascination.

'Why, a well bred Southern girl would *never* appear in public without her gloves.' She examined her gloved hands held out before her, and smiled secretly. They were of beautiful lacework, and she had had them made for a ball, but they would do nicely. 'I really must show you how nice they are, dear Mrs Brown.'

Peter hurried to her side and poured her a small glass of cordial. 'Why thank you, Peter dear.' She wandered, glass in hand, back to Chastity, who watched the approach apprehensively.

'Until now, dear Chastity – I may call you Chastity, as we are well acquainted by now – you have been what I would call, superficially fucked. Yes, I believe that's what I would call it. In other words, you have not *really* put that organ between your legs to its proper usage. Now we are going to change all that.'

She strode over until she stood between the horrified Boston Yankee's parted thighs. Slowly she lowered her gloved hands until they both rested on the supine woman's prominent Mound of Venus. First she rubbed her gloved hand along the top of the mound, twining her lace-clad fingers in the scant brown hairs. Mrs Brown twisted slightly and tried to close her legs, and Annabelle had to restrain her with a sharp slap on the squishy exposed female flower.

'Ah, oh please Mrs Stone – Lady Stone!' she hastily corrected her error. 'That does hurt so!'

Annabelle smiled impishly. 'Did you like the girls?' she asked.

Mrs Brown blushed and her throat heaved as she tried to frame an answer that would satisfy her tormentor. Annabelle struck her playfully on her mound again.

'No shilly-shallying, dear Mrs Brown. Did you like the girls?' she repeated.

Mrs Brown nodded mutely.

'I don' think a heard that. Did you like that bit of girl-play?'

'Yes, yes... I did,' confessed the defeated Yankee.

'Well, ain't that dandy. Now, I think we really should explore this delightful little ol' beaver, my dear.' Suiting action to words, she shoved a stiff lace-covered index finger as deeply as she could into the hefty woman's slick cunt.

Chastity Brown shrieked at the sudden penetration, as the tiny knots that made up the best Flanders lace Peter could buy, scraped at her sensitised interior, sending a thrilling, not altogether displeasing, but utterly unexpected sensation to her brain.

'You see,' Annabelle said, as Chastity shrieked once again as her beautiful hostess agitated the digit in her pussy, then added another, 'the lace is so soft to the hand, but it is rather ratchety when you place it somewhere else.'

Her fingers sawed back and forth against Chastity's soft slit, eliciting another shriek. Annabelle played with the woman's pussy, as Daisy had done before her. Her motions were hard and driving rather than loving, and, notwithstanding the rising tide of pleasure, Chastity's breeding forced her to beg that she stop.

'You will obey ma wishes, won't you darling?'

'Oh yes, Lady Stone,' the woman panted. 'Oh, I'll do anything, please, just lay off…'

'Lay off where?' Annabelle's wide open eyes and innocent expression were the perfect picture of ignorance.

'My…' Chastity gulped, finding it hard to say the word as Annabelle had found it hard not so many days before. 'My cunt…' she sobbed.

'Well, ma dear. I was only doing my poor best to keep you entertained. But if there's nothing I can do for you, there sure is something *you* can do for little ol' me,' and she smiled down triumphantly at her victim.

To none of her audience's surprise, she seated herself over Chastity Brown's homely face. 'Do use your tongue, my dear,' she said in her normal tones.

Peter could not help but admire his wife who moved from one role to another, from the down-country girl to the proper lady, in one second, dressed in nothing but boots and feathered hat. Obediently, and a testament to Annabelle's tutorial powers, Mrs Brown immediately began to lap and suck at the perfect pink slit that offered itself to her face.

'She's doing it, oh my dear Peter. She's licking my cunny,' and to express her excitement more forcefully, Lady Stone rubbed her crotch more deeply onto Chastity Brown's heavily bedewed face.

Peter was breathing deeply, his cock erect in his hand, his eyes glued to the charming sight before him. He knew he could not restrain himself for very much longer, and was about to throw himself onto one or the other of his charming and busy companions, when his wife spoke again.

'Fuck me now, darling,' Annabelle said, judging the time just right. 'Here, go all the way.' She raised one leg elegantly over Chastity's chest, exposing her exquisite pink cunny to her husband's gaze. Peter approached with alacrity, his huge cock jutting out before him. She moistened the tip unnecessarily with her tongue, bowing forward so that her breasts hung temptingly besides Chastity's face. Then the thick shaft was pistoning deeply into her body, parting the perfect pursed lips of her pussy until he sank inside her to the balls. He pulled out slightly, then, his lust inflamed by the sights he had seen, rammed back in again with a corkscrew motion that drove its recipient almost wild with delight.

'My dear Mrs Brown,' drawled Annabelle. 'Please don't let the sight of our amatory connubial bliss distract you from your duties,' and the young bride leaned forward once again, from the embrace of her husband, and pinched her victim viciously at the tip of her clitoral hood. Chastity Brown would have shrieked once again but that her mouth was busily occupied with sucking and licking the joined and rapidly moving members of the young couple.

It was not long before Peter could contain himself no longer. He cried out and bit his bride's shoulder while a flood of seminal fluid rose from his jewel bag and rushed along his livid prick to irrigate and soothe his wife's raging membranes. Annabelle too, once she felt her husband's discharged, obliged with a heavy sigh, a wriggle of her bum, and a discharge of her own which mingled both fluids in a heavenly explosion of scent and movements.

'Oh, Peter dear,' she cooed, 'this was *soooo* delicious.

So good. Oh my darling.'

'Yes my love. So good and so tender you are my bride. Darling, yes, yes...' and they swooned together onto Chastity Brown's passive body.

Peter withdrew from Annabelle's gluey cunt once they had recovered somewhat. His wife rose from her crouch over Chastity's face, and examined her victim's physiognomy thoroughly. She noted with approval the lowered, sated eyelids, and the face upon which the various discharges had left a sticky residue. She slipped off her glove and held Peter's member for inspection. It was softening, but still large and impressive.

'When engaged in domestic duties, in the confines of her house, a Southern lady *does* take off her gloves,' she said mischievously to Chastity. 'Oh look. Poor thing, it is both tired and somewhat... soiled with use. I do hope you don't mind preparing and purifying it before my darling Peter presents it to you, my dear?'

Chastity shuddered and tried to turn away, but Annabelle held her head. She watched in trepidation as Peter obligingly brought his cock closer to her mouth, then laid the sticky member full on her lips.

Annabelle produced a thin switch and lightly stroked the juncture of Chastity's thighs with it. 'To encourage you in your duties, my dear.' Her voice hardened suddenly. 'I want you to know that this article is strictly mine. And I would greatly appreciate, *greatly* appreciate, getting it back in good and usable condition. Or else I'll be forced to use this,' and suddenly the switch rose high in the air and came down, swishing across Chastity Brown's ample belly. She shrieked and struggled against her bonds, her back arching against the padded leather, but to no avail.

'Open your mouth,' Annabelle said.

All hope gone, the Boston woman obeyed. The broad

purple head slid slowly into her mouth, banging against the opposite cheek. Hastily she set to work to suck and lick it clean. At first she found the taste, or perhaps it was the presence in her mouth of the male member, utterly revolting. As she licked and cleaned however, she discovered the marvellous power women held over the generative organs of men, as Peter's cock swelled in response to her ministrations. By the time it had risen to its hardest proportions, she was more anxious than afraid, wondering what that instrument was to be used for, half fearful it was to be used on her, half afraid it was not.

At his wife's gesture, Peter pulled back from the gulping, inexperienced mouth. Annabelle inspected it carefully, and when satisfied, she urged Peter around the bench. He positioned himself carefully, then lunged forward into Chastity's waiting hole.

Mrs Chastity Brown sighed from the bottom of her chest. The massive penetration was not only not painful, but, she suddenly realised, it was precisely what she needed.

'Oh, oh, oh,' she mumbled, but these were not cries of fright nor denial, but of encouragement and appreciation.

Peter set to with a will, and without any attempt at gentleness. It was a topping good fuck that he was in mind for, a true rogering, and no damn love involved. His wife saw and approved, and to encourage the couple, she drew a slender switch and lashed unmercifully at Chastity's exposed breasts. To her surprise, Peter motioned at her without staying his thrusts, and she included his muscular pumping buttocks among the recipients of her hand. Faster and faster he rammed, and Chastity's moans and cries merged into one long howl of desire and pleasure as she felt herself fucked properly for the first time.

'Oh my God… I'm… I'm… Ah ahhhh…!' she called out in a hoarse voice.

'Spending, eh?' gasped Peter. 'Are you spending, eh? Yes? Is that what you want?'

'Yeeees! I'm spending… oh!' and the Boston matron clutched the man to her with her thighs, and clipped at the tip of his cock with her inner muscles while her bound hands struggled against her restraints and the thin lash cracked onto exposed skin.

Peter lay on the plump form for some time, allowing his John Thomas the opportunity to soak fully in the juices that had accumulated in Mrs Brown's cavity. Eventually, when it had completely softened, he rose from the woman's spent body. She had passed away in a quiet faint, though a tiny smile at the corner of her snoring mouth indicated that the swoon came not from an excess of bile, but rather from an excess of pleasure.

Though her victim was senseless, Annabelle whispered excitedly into her husband's ear. He smiled gravely, and after carrying out his ablutions in the corner set off for the task with good porcelain fittings, he assisted his wife in carrying out their plan. Fully dressed, his hair and moustache impeccably arrayed, he essayed up to the room where Mr Brown awaited. Passing up he glanced at the clock. The entire affair had taken no more than the promised half hour.

Chapter Fifteen

Mr Brown of Boston was quietly smoking his cigar and drinking his brandy. He had been very somnolent when left by his host, and had gladly dropped off into a quick nap. The maid had come into the room quietly, but moving about, clearing up the brandy snifter he had dropped, had brought him awake.

He watched the girl move about, and a stirring began in his pants. He had rarely seen a woman in service so stately looking, so self-possessed, nor so beautiful as this one, and he longed to have her under him. He moved uneasily in his seat, hoping that whatever his host was engaged in, would take some time.

'Will there be anything else, sir?' she asked.

'Yeah girlie, bring me another one of these apple brandies.'

She poured the liquor, handed him the glass, and turned to go. Mr. Brown's hand moved of its own volition, and he stroked the prominent buttocks. The maid ignored the gesture. Inflamed, Brown leaped to his feet. He took two rapid steps and threw his arms around the girl. His hands came up full of soft mounds of vibrant flesh. He nuzzled at her neck, and shoved his crotch at her firm backside—

Brown came to be seated in the chair. There was puffiness about his eyes that meant someone had dealt him a powerful buffet. Vaguely he remembered the maid, remembered something shiny in the air above his head, the sight caught from the corner of his eyes. The maid was standing demurely by the door, her back to the wall, and her quizzical eyes on him. The heavy silver tray on which she had brought his glass was on a small table. Brown moved uneasily, struggling to rise to his feet to try and repeat his seduction, when he heard his host's footsteps in the doorway. Hastily he sat back down, attempting to appear engrossed in the pictures hung about the room. His head was whirling dizzily.

'So sorry old boy, to have kept you so long. Nelly!' he said sharply, and Mr Brown looked up guiltily, hoping the girl would not peach on him. She was a damn fine looking bit of baggage but! In Boston he would have had her soon enough. A bit of pressure, the offer of some money, why, a quarter would do it... and she'd be his. But here in this damn heat he had to keep up appearances. And with this damn Limey too. At least he got the women out of the way. Maybe there be some sort of entertainment between the men, eh? He wondered how he could go about suggesting a bit of quiet fun with the slave girls... ah, coloured girls. 'Bring us some more of the Armagnac, if you please,' completed Sir Peter.

She hurried to comply, and Brown accepted another large glass of odd-flavoured brandy that the Limey insisted was fifty-year-old apple brandy, and gulped it down. It went down smoothly enough, as did the smoke of the excellent cigar his host offered from a silver humidor.

'I say, old man,' Sir Peter confided over the smoke. 'Now that the ladies are gone, I wonder if... er... well, you know.'

'Speak on old man,' the bluff Yankee had adopted Peter's drawl and some of his speech mannerisms. It was obvious that Peter had made a hit.

'Actually, I'm in a most damnable position you know. Only recently married and all that. That's why I had to leave you by yourself for so long. Duty, y'know. Lord of the manor and all that.'

Brown grinned. 'Yes. Very lucky man…'

'Well, y'see, it's this maid we have. Seems she has displeased Lady Stone. Terribly displeased, y'know how women can be.'

'Well, get rid of her then. It's not as if you own the girl.'

Peter shook his head. 'That is precisely what I can't do, y'know. Put the fear of hell in them, that's what I've got to do. If I'd send her away, why, in three days Lady Stone would be sending me off to fetch her! Only one can do the ironing proper and crisp, *she* says.'

Brown licked his lips. 'The whip. That's the ticket. You know, in old colony times in Massachusetts, well, let me tell you sir, the servants never got above themselves. Never! Stocks and whips – that's the answer!'

'I say, what a jolly good idea, old man. Problem is, of course, I'd have to whip her backside naked, y'know. Old college tradition an' all. Can't do it. Wife would be awfully upset; husband seeing maid's naked backside.'

Brown gulped and his face turned a brighter shade of red. 'Y'aint… er… y'aint thinking of letting her go without punishment, are you?'

'Of course not.' Peter sipped at his brandy. 'But I ain't relishing the prospect.'

'Perhaps I could assist you in some way?' Brown was practically slavering at the thought.

'Wouldn't, er, Mrs Brown object?'

Brown winked grossly at Peter. 'Don't have to know – know what I mean?'

Peter smiled. 'Why, that's wonderful. Actually, just to ensure there are no problems later, I mean, your reputation an' all, I'll have her stocked and bound for you. All you'll have to do is, well, I'll leave that to you of course… that is, if you'll agree, old man?'

Brown beamed at Peter, his eyes practically bulging out of his head. He ran a finger around his collar. 'Excellent…!' he managed to pant. 'Excellent…!'

Peter put down his glass. 'Can you amuse yourself dear fellow while I see to the preparations?'

Brown brought a trembling hand to his lips and gulped his Armagnac.

His host was back in minutes that seemed like hours to the agitated Yankee. He felt the pressure in his tight pants, and was relieved that his host appeared not to notice his priapic condition.

'Are you sure you won't mind?' Peter asked solicitously. 'You know how these things are. A little bit of a delay creates apprehension and sharpens the punishment, but too much… And of course it must be without a word, purely mechanical. I'm afraid I'm completely worn out afterwards, and Lady Stone is so demanding these days…'

'Of course!' Brown said heartily. 'Only too glad to oblige.'

'The… er… instruments, are hanging on the wall. Don't bother to deal with the afters, old man. All taken care of. And she won't even recognise the difference.'

Brown made his way diffidently down the stairs to the lower levels of the mansion. He had been an ardent supporter of the North in the war, but that had nothing to do with his feelings for the slaves. And the prospect of… well, of being a real master, enticed him thoroughly. The punishment room was dark, barely lit by two lanterns, but Brown was far too excited to go back up to get another. There was much to be done, and he licked his lips heavily.

The erring servant was a rather heavy-set woman. She was tied to a padded bench. Her knees were held in the air by straps that led to the side. Her fat, sparsely-haired mound was exposed to his gaze, as was the entire length of her thick thighs and heavy buttocks. Her face was covered, and the sack had been brought down over her rather heavy breasts, which flopped to the sides.

On a rack against the wall were organised some leather lashes, a dog whip, a whalebone lash, and several sheaves of birch rods. He approached the woman cautiously. It would not do for her to recognise him, perhaps point him out in public… he shrank at the prospect. He tried to raise the black silk bag, but a complicated series of tapes had been tied to keep his features, and incidentally hers, anonymous. For a moment he regretted it. He loved having his cock sucked, and Chastity so infrequently agreed to do so. On the other hand, this one was completely exposed. He gazed long and thoroughly at her uncovered body. He had never seen a woman naked before. Chastity, of course, always wore a heavy nightgown to bed, and his few experiences with whores had been hurried affairs in the dimness of their cribs. There was something else, too, he had wanted to do, but never tried…

But first, to follow instructions.

The whalebone whip was flexible and springy. He drew it lightly over the woman's buttocks, and she quivered, mumbling something beneath the hood. His eyes lit hypnotically on the bulging cunny. The lash rose in his hands.

The whalebone whip moved flexibly through the air and whistled down on her exposed thighs. Brown was hardly an expert, and so he missed his mark which was the fleshy part of her ass, hitting her higher up the thigh.

'Unghh… don'… stop!' she mumbled through what must have been a gag, clearly in fright and pain.

Brown grinned in delight and raised the lash once again, bringing it down more accurately on the now no-longer pristine flesh. Another weal appeared beside the other. Brown trembled with the pleasure of the sound of the strike, and the responding muffled cry of anguish. His hand crept to his groin and he struggled to release the buttons while he flailed away at the exposed bum, occasionally hitting the prominent mound.

'Oooooooaaaah,' the muffled sob came again and again. 'Yieeeee!' she cried as a particularly sharp blow stung her soft mound.

Brown's cock was in full erection, and he released its throbbing length. One hand on the shaft, the other on the lash, he beat every inch of exposed flesh. She cried out again and again 'Yieeeee... Ommmmggddd...!' and the sounds inflamed his lust to a greater pitch.

He stopped for a breather, then realised that for the first time in his life he could gratify any wish he had. He hastily crouched between the newly striped thighs, and examined the cunt held so deliciously for his inspection. He regretted that the only light was fixed to the wall, casting a pale glow, and Sir Peter had forgotten to leave the candle. He gripped the full lips and pulled in opposite directions, exposing the raw, slippery-looking interior. It was smooth and inviting, and the passageway into the delicious interior wafted a lust-provoking aroma to his inflamed senses. His cock was throbbing painfully, and he was able to hear the hot blood pounding in his ears at the sight of the helpless female flesh.

His trousers were down to his ankles in a flash. The welts on her bum excited him to a frenzy. He crouched between her spread legs, mumbling to her, and shafting his cock furiously. In a trice the broad head, glowing a deep purple, was nudging at the entrance to the sweet hole. He pushed with all his might and was rewarded with the feel of the length of his shaft penetrating deeply into the smooth and well-lubricated channel.

'Ohhhhhhh,' she mumbled beneath her gag as she felt his pubis grinding against her own.

'You like that, don't you, you bitch?' he muttered. 'Such a lovely fuck you are. Ah, ah, take that, and that,' and his fat rump jogged against her with as much power as he could must. He seized a breast in each hand and twisted them cruelly to the sides, admiring the tension on the skin. Chastity never allowed him that much liberty, not that he would have thought of demanding it of a respectable Boston matron.

'Unnnhhh,' the prisoner replied.

'Oh yes, what a lovely fuck. You have such a lovely tight quim. I could fuck you forever,' and trying to suit action to words, he shafted her merrily, muttering as many gross words as he knew. The pressure against the shaft of his prick grew and grew. He felt his balls start to contract, then the idea that this woman was truly *helpless* before him made him pull back, struggling for control. He panted heavily, weighing the results of his actions and deciding, finally, that he would finally do it. The servant would hardly have anything to say against him, and if she did, he would claim it was just her way of getting back at him.

He rose from the supine form, holding his cock and rubbing it frenetically. Then lowering over her, he grasped and separated her thighs to their widest gape. Below the reddened split was a little puckered hole. He stared at it for a while, then brutally shoved his thick thumb into the tight orifice of her ass. The servant screamed something incomprehensible into her gag. She writhed furiously, and he quieted her with three quick lashes from the dog whip.

His thumb was buried to the webbing in her rectum, and he twisted it about in a frenzy of pleasure. The sensation threatened to overcome him. He aimed his turgid cock, and roughly pushed into the tight spidery opening. Again she squealed something, but he was too enraptured at the feeling to notice. The hood of his cock slipped fully into her anus, and he bent to see the vision – one he had imagined before but never seen. Then his need rose in him, and he moved his hips. The long shaft disappeared into the flesh until the curls at his belly obscured the opening. He pulled back, and the ring of muscle seemed reluctant to let him go, raising a ridge around his full cock. With great will, he set to work to bugger the servant.

'Oh yesss,' he cried, as his crisis rose. 'Ah, ah, such a tight little hole. Cornholing is good for you, you bitch,' and his hands clawed at her breasts, her thighs, her belly, as his spunk started spilling out. First in tiny drops, then in a rush that washed away his very innards, he spent inside her bottom hole, howling almost insensibly at the pleasure. His howls were echoed by the muffled wailing of the errant servant.

At last, exhausted and delighted by his activities, Brown collapsed on the woman's ample bosom. He lay there, sucking at her nipple, his hands roving over her bum for a while. Then, without a word or a further look, he rose, rearranged his clothing, and furtively climbed the stairs.

Exhausted and undone, Chastity heard her husband's heavy footsteps recede to the house above. A side door into the cellar opened and she heard two female figures beside her. Lips were applied soothingly to her breasts and to her slit, and she trembled again, involuntarily. She was too exhausted to care now if they would take her again. Then her bonds were loosened and deft hands rubbed her body with damp scented towels, taking particular care with her tender groin and breasts. She was lulled to sleep, barely conscious of being lifted and carried, of having her nightdress slipped over her head, of being laid into bed.

Later, when Brown came into the room in his nightshirt, she was conscious enough to wonder whether he intended to do those things to her once again, realised that she was too exhausted to object, then surprised herself by wishing he would do them anyway; later, when she was conscious and able to feel every sparkle of the delicious sensation. She fell asleep on that thought, her hand comfortingly between her legs.

Chapter Sixteen

'How do you do, my dear Mrs Jakes.'

Heather turned at the voice. It was that odious friend of Charlie's. There was a strange glint in his eyes.

'I'm afraid sir that my husband is not at home.'

'Quite all right, my dear,' he said, unconcerned. 'It is *you* I have come to see.'

Heather looked around in confusion. There was little left of the money that the Jakes had made by selling cotton before the war, but she tried to maintain at least the reception room in proper order. The two servants, freed slaves who had elected to remain with Jakes, hardly meant a grand establishment. Like the rest of the South the former mansion was run down, and now the stupid servant had gone off to chat with the cook. There was no help at hand.

'Very well, sir, though this is most improper,' she said in her coldest voice.

'Of course,' he smiled, and his pale face was bisected by a cruel grin. 'Do you know you have the most charming cunny?'

Heather's jaw dropped. 'Ah... Ah...'

'I tupped you most deliciously several nights ago. You have chestnut hair on your cunny, and a small scar near the base of your belly. Inflicted by your husband, I daresay?' He raised a hand to stem her protesting stuttering. 'I wonder, should I tell your husband?'

'He...' she squeaked. 'He will kill you!'

'I have fought seventeen duels,' Wildfire said calmly.

'I've also been in several military actions. I rather think not. In any case, the rest of Savannah will undoubtedly *love* to hear the reason for the duel.'

'You utter devil,' she burst out, rising from her seat.

'Shall I tell your husband?' Wildfire asked again.

'It wasn't my fault,' Heather stormed, blushing, and throwing herself back into the armchair. 'Oh, oh, why am I always the subject of such savage rapine? First Charles, then you, then Sir Pet—' she caught herself in mid-sentence at the realisation that she had let the cat out of the bag.

The effect of her words on Wildfire was extraordinary. His pale face blanched so white it looked like bone, then flushed a brilliant scarlet.

'The dog!' he groaned. 'The utter despicable hound! Again he is there before me.' He ground his teeth in fury and his hands reached for Heather's shoulders. Bringing his face close to hers he muttered through clenched teeth, 'You shall lie back and make yourself available to me on the instant. Or else I shall assuredly tell the whole town of your activities!'

She gasped and struggled in his grip, then uttering a piteous moan, she sank backwards onto the chair, parting her legs.

'Make yourself ready,' he repeated, still snarling.

Hastily she pulled up her skirts, displaying her fine legs, the curl-enhanced juncture of her thighs, her swelling inner lips. He stooped and applied eager lips to her bulging cunny.

Heather gasped at the sensation. Charlie had tried that, but he was too drunk to touch her core. Sir Peter had caused her enjoyment. Now Wildfire was subjecting her to the same indignity. His teeth closed on her sensitive post and Heather yelped with the familiar pain of teeth on her flesh. Outrage, pain, and pleasure rose in her in equal measures.

Her fist pounded on his broadcloth-covered shoulders. 'Oaaah,' she groaned as his tongue bored into her. Flashes of pleasure mixed with the pain from his teeth racked her frame.

Wildfire rose from her. His lips and chin glistened with her juices, and the furious look was still on his face.

'I must be where he has not been,' he shouted. His eyes set on her parted thighs, on the glistening surfaces of her pussy. 'Yes,' he said. 'Yes I shall. I shall have you unnaturally, then at least shall my need be slaked for a while.'

Heather winced inside. Remembering the unknown man who had fucked her at Annabelle's party, and his unexpected attentions to the darker hole between her buttocks, she started to correct his misapprehension, then realised it might lead to worse punishment.

'The beast,' he groaned. Heather looked upon him without comprehension as he seized her knees and tore them wider apart, pulled her bottom forward on the chair, then slid his rough palms up her legs. Holding her thighs apart with his hands, he directed the tip of his shaft to the lower, still virginal hole. With a groan and a thrust he felt the clenched muscles part and the nose of his cock was lodged inside.

Heather cried out as she felt the unnatural entry into her asshole. She tried to clench the muscles, to resist the invader, but to no avail. His fingers dug into her extended thighs, and thrills of rough pleasure ran down her frame. The wide head of the knob barged against the inner tissues, and she cried out until silenced by the vibration of his tongue in the cavern of her wet mouth. Through the pain of her extended thighs she could feel the slap of the thick padded bag at the base of his cock as it slapped against her tailbone. Squirming, she tried to dislodge him from inside her, but only succeeded in exciting him to further wild thrusts. He pulled back and glared down at her tear-streaked face.

'Ahhh, you hurt me so!' she exclaimed, trying to eject his member.

With a wild cry he plunged down on her again, his hands clutching at her soft flesh. Then he pulled back abruptly, the tip of his cock popping out from her hole, leaving it gaping moistly.

He sank down on her belly. Spurts of white juice gushed over the rounded hillock, turning the curl-topped motte to a swamp of earthy-smelling liquids. They both sighed as he pumped heavily at her, and Heather's raised feet fell to the floor.

'Now,' he said with satisfaction, examining her ruinous glutinous state, 'you will do as I say. And soon, soon, I shall be ready.'

She turned away from the gloating in his voice, not even concerned when he twisted her damp pubic hairs viciously.

Several miles away, Annabelle clenched her thighs in exultation. Between them she could feel the hairy flanks of her beloved husband, and another part of him was inserted well inside her own body. Peter withdrew the length of his prick from his wife's hungry slit. His teeth nipped delicately at her pale cherry nipples and they flushed with red.

'Oooh yes, my darling,' she sighed. Her eyes were closed and Peter stole a glance the length of their sweating bodies. So delicious, he thought, fucking buck naked, something rarely to be achieved in cold England. He could see the shaft that seemed to sprout from between her legs, then urged on by the bite of her nails on his back, he thrust home once again until he could feel the squish of their damp hairs meeting. He clasped her soft buttock mounds to his loins, and wriggled about furiously. Annabelle thrust her questing tongue into his mouth, humming deeply, searching to lick his teeth, duelling with his tongue, while she clutched at his grinding body with her hips, and dug long pink grooves in the milky skin of his shoulders.

'Ahhh, I'm coming,' he roared, and bit down on her exposed lips. 'Yes my dear... oooh.'

The grinding of his hips, and the plenteous supply of milk-white seed that splashed into her insides brought about Annabelle's climax as well. She wailed, high and loud through his clamping lips, and her nails drew blood in a pattern over his back, while her own hips quivered with the strain.

They lay clasped in a warm embrace, their flesh quivering until Peter sought to withdraw from her warm interior.

'Not so fast, my friend,' Annabelle laughed up at him, then swiftly rolled them both over until she was sitting. Her breasts hung down over his face, and she lasciviously moved her shoulders to and fro so that they slapped delicately against his face. Her hand slid down behind her until she was grasping the base of his softening stem. Clenching her inner muscles as much as she could, and jogging her rump delicately while pinching the base of his cock soon brought him back into a hardened readiness, which she knew would soon change to a full-blown rigid stem.

To ensure their pleasure she called out over her shoulder. 'Daisy dear, would you please?' and indicated the still slowly stiffening manhood. Daisy, who had been watching the antics on the bed, a supply of refreshments by her side, hurried to comply. She parted the man's hairy thighs, and her face disappeared between them. Her tongue flat and moist, she began lapping the exposed length of cock, adding slight nips to the skin of the shaft and the bag beneath. Experience over the past weeks of her employment had taught her that there were other things she could do as well. With the finger of one hand she massaged the base of the bag, rubbing against the hidden root, while her other hand pinched together the exposed lips of her mistress's cunny.

Annabelle bent forward and kissed her husband long and lovingly. He responded in kind, his hands playing now with her dangling breasts, now with her jogging rump, now stroking Daisy's crisp curls.

'Darling, I have been thinking,' Annabelle breathed. 'I am worried about poor dear Heather.'

Peter groaned in reply as she jogged her soft rump over his loins to emphasise her point. 'You... ahhh... want to fuck her again?'

'Oh yes darling,' she enthused, not stopping her movements. 'Yes I do, and so do you, my randy lover,' and she tweaked one of his nipples forcefully. 'But I am really *worried*. She seemed so dispirited when I spoke to her. That drunken husband of hers...'

'I say, old girl,' Peter was beginning to see where she was headed. 'Can't interfere between a man and his wife...'

'But Peter darling, the man's a rake and a wastrel, and he chases all the servants besides.'

He thrust suddenly into her, arching his hips, and smiled. 'Well, so do I,' he said, and his hands went down to stroke Daisy's busy head.

'Yes my dear, and that is precisely the point,' Annabelle's voice was hoarser now, and she gasped as she spoke. Daisy increased the pressure of her tongue, sharing it between master and mistress. 'Because... ahh... *you*... ahh... also... give me... what I...' she emphasised each word with a grinding of her ass onto the mound of his pubis. Her face was flushed and her eyes were closing, and Peter suddenly grasped one buttock viciously with his hand, while he slapped it as hard as he could. The sudden sound of the slaps and the burning feel they engendered sent Annabelle into a paroxysm of delight. Her lips wrinkled back and her hands clutched at his muscular chest, pulling at the scant chest hairs. Daisy, knowing Annabelle's climax was near, bit deeply into the bare ass over her. Her hands slapped at the jiggling moist skin, bringing out red marks against the pale flesh.

'What I want... oooh,' Annabelle whimpered and her whole body contracted in the throes of her climax.

When she had recovered somewhat, and after Peter had lovingly wiped her privates with the warmed scented cloth he had Daisy prepare as she usually did, Annabelle continued pursuing her train of thought.

'You see, darling, there is a difference. I *want* you to beat me, particularly when Daisy or Nelly are doing so to.' She blushed slightly, still unsure of the propriety of her own particular desires. 'But Charles? Why, he only beats her when he's drunk, and then he fucks her as quickly as possible. I thought...' she blushed prettily again, 'I thought a brief course of instruction might mend his manners.'

Daisy's face had been hardening as she heard all this. 'I'm sorry Miss Annabelle, but did you mean Master Charlie Jakes?' she finally blurted.

'Why, yes I do, Daisy dear.'

'He's a bad 'un, and no mistake,' Daisy said, her eyes blazing. 'Why, there's not a servant girl in miles he hasn't tried to force himself on to.'

'I say, what a cad,' uttered Peter. His eyes glinted dangerously. 'Don't tell me he did you as well.'

'He sure did try,' Daisy snorted. 'Why, he chased me with his horse, that was before I come to work for you Miss Annabelle. And when he was here at the party, why he sure did try again, but he was too drunk to catch me.' Her breasts, under the rich velveteen of her dress, rose and fell with barely contained passion.

Peter's face was set in stone. 'Why the cad,' he burst out again. 'The absolute cad! I shall horsewhip him from here to Atlanta! I shall have him hounded from the clubs. I say! Trying it on in a man's own home.'

'That's right, my dear,' his wife soothed. 'And I have just the means – our delightful sanctuary downstairs has not been used for a full two weeks now – and a plan.' She snuggled back into his arms, calming his outrage with a few kisses.

'Rather a bounder, I must say,' Wildfire's voice was low, and his face serious. Even the empty bottle of bourbon he and Charlie had been imbibing from did not seem to disturb his gravity. Charlie bent closer as Wildfire continued sadly. 'Yes, rather a bounder. Cheats on his wife you know.' He shook his head sadly. 'And with the servants, too!'

Charlie felt a stiffness in his trousers. This was a new aspect of the oh so dandified Sir Peter. And the serving girls too. He grinned expectantly.

'Y'know,' Wildfire continued with drunken gravity, 'bounder even boasted he had tupped, yes tupped, his wife's best friend. Imagine that! Wouldn't hear her name.

No I would not, sir! He wanted to tell me too, described her, scar on the... er... lower abdomen an' all. Total cad.' Wildfire subsided and poured himself another drink, apparently oblivious of Charlie's stricken look.

The young Southerner staggered to his feet. 'Gotta go,' he whispered. His body straightened painfully. 'Gotta go. Take care of a matter. Back soon.' He staggered off, muttering about his pistols, absently clutching the bottle of whisky. He did not see the sharp look Wildfire gave his departing back.

Charlie Jakes was feeling as mean as a sack full of wildcats. He had a brace of pistols tucked in his belt. He had searched for the bitch Heather, and not finding her, had consoled himself with the remainder of the whisky – almost a quarter of the bottle – while he hunted out his pistols. Well, he'd teach her. She was no better, no, she was worse, than a bitch, and she didn't even give him the satisfaction of crying out properly when he beat her. The thought of the beating, of his lash splitting into soft skin, caused an inevitable reaction, and as he rode he rubbed his semi-erect prong against the cantle.

He turned down the lane that would lead him in the direction of the Stone estate and a movement caught his eye. In an alley two women were standing, their arms around one another's waist. They looked vaguely familiar, but to Charlie's sodden brain the only matter of importance was that they were female. And saucy. And possibly available. And definitely unprotected. He looked quickly around. It was dark, but for the glowing moon. The two women were absorbed in one another. Women! Doing what was rightly done by a man. The fires of righteous indignation glowed in his breast, along with the sour mash he had imbibed. Stealthily he lit from his

horse, and taking his riding crop, he crept into th...
The two bitches were still there, walking away from...
their heads close together. Charlie slavered at the s...
and crept after them as silently as he could. They turn...
at the alley mouth, the woods behind them, and glanced
at him. Seeing him coming, they did not do the expected
and run. Instead they smiled broadly, tauntingly at him.

'Why, ain't that the little peckerhead Jakes?' one of them said.

'Yeah, can't get it up without a leash,' the other affirmed.

For a moment, Charlie Jakes wondered about their strange behaviour. His reputation was such that most women ran if they met him in a dark alley. But those two bitches were laughing at him! At him!

He rushed forward, a veil of red before his eyes, his whip flailing. He failed to notice the rope stretched between the two fences on either side, nor did he know where the sack that enveloped him suddenly, had come from. And a blow on his alcohol-mazed head ended his thinking for the while.

He came to in darkness. He was lying on something hard that creaked under his weight, and his wrists and ankles were tied apart. Charlie tried to struggle, but the bonds that held him to the board were too strong.

'Who's thea?' he called out. He was angry, very angry, and he could think of nothing but the need to punish whomever was responsible for this practical joke.

A giggle, very feminine, answered his query.

'Why, Master Charles,' an unfamiliar voice said. 'I'm your teacher.'

'Get me out of here you bitch,' he growled, 'or I'll have you skinned.'

'Why, such a temper,' another female voice said. 'Allow

me to introduce ourselves. I am Miss Whip,' continued the voice, and a long strand of leather trailed over Charlie's stomach. He suddenly realised he was tied prone, and completely naked, and he shivered. 'And this is Miss Splat,' a wooden paddle smacked very lightly onto the skin of his thighs. 'And here is Miss Rope.' A loop of cord dropped out of the dark and curled around his flaccid cock. Charlie yelped and his hips bucked into the air.

'Well now,' crooned another female voice. 'I guess this little ol' soft thing ought to be encouraged to grow...' The loop of cord was wound several times around his member. Charlie, nightmares of retaliation for his treatment of young women flooding his mind, screamed in terror.

'You'll keep your mouth just like that,' another voice sang into his ear, exaggerating his own heavily-accented speech.

Charlie was conscious of two smooth pillars of skin sliding over his ears on both sides. A humid smell, completely unfamiliar to him, bathed his face in a miasma that was both frightening, and horribly desirable. He had no yearning to find out what it was. A firm hand gripped his still soft cock.

The dark pink interior hovered over his face, and Charlie nervously licked his lips. Quick as a flash, Nelly exploited the opportunity and brought her cousin's cunt down on the open mouth. Before the Southern gentleman had time to react he found his mouth smothered with the humid female scents of a woman in lust. And before he could react even further, the warm muff was snatched from his baring teeth.

'Now you're gettin' the idee,' the commanding female voice said. Suddenly there was a burning stripe across his thighs, and an adept hand was milking the flapping length of his cock.

'Oww, you bitch!' he screamed in earnest.

'Why, such love names,' the other voice said. There was another brisk swishing sound and a second burning stripe joined the first.

'I think we ought to ensure his... readiness,' said Annabelle from the shadows, a glint in her eye. She searched the ever-present morocco box, and extracted a length of rough raffia twine. Sir Peter had explained its use to her, one of the souvenirs of his travels in Africa.

The length of twine was wound around and around Master Charlie's rather thin shaft, keeping it erect and firm, yet forbidding any untoward incidents on his part. Nelly giggled as she saw the reddening head. Unable to control herself, she bent forward, her breast's brushing against Charlie's bound arm, and nipped the glowing plum. He squealed high and loud, and to soothe him she ran her tongue over the bulbous head. A transparent drop of pre-come silvered the little eye.

'Why, the poor baby, he's cryin' so!' Nelly exclaimed, and laved the tip once again.

'Let go of me,' the terrified man shouted.

'I do declare, he does make such a noise,' exclaimed Nelly with annoyance. She looked up at Annabelle, who in the heat of the exhibition, and enjoined to silence, had shed her outer clothing. Dressed in nothing but a thin shift that barely covered the tops of her thighs, she was a ravishing sight. Nelly saw the discarded garments and started looking around. Their victim screamed again as Daisy let the quirt fall across his thighs.

'A shoelace,' whispered Nelly. Sir Peter, his own delirious excitement at the women's undress palpably in evidence, divined her meaning. Wordlessly he knelt down, and handed her his bootlace. The product of a public school, he thought he knew what she was about. Slowly and thoughtfully, while she sipped delicately at the tip of the bright red cock before her, she folded the shoelace precisely in half.

'You, jelly-roll,' she hissed. 'I am going to teach you how to be nice to a lady.'

Charlie only muttered a curse. Daisy, intrigued by her cousin's actions, bent closer to look, and Annabelle craned over her maid's smooth shoulder. Nelly dramatically raised her lace and brought it down on the erect shaft. The blow was quick and soft, but against the twine-wrapped erection it burned like fire.

'Oh no! Oh no!' screamed Master Charlie. 'Please, please, don' do that again.'

Nelly hurriedly applied her mouth to the sensitive tip, rolling it about on her tongue, squeezing it against her palate.

'Ohhhh,' Master Charlie moaned.

Nelly pulled her head back and brought her hand down. The lace lashed against the erect shaft, and Charlie screamed once again.

This time, when she appended her tongue to the shaft, slathering it with the moisture from her mouth, he was far more responsive. She raised her head slightly and brought the lash down again. Charlie squealed in pain, but his cock rose to greater heights as he waited for the soothing balm of tongue-work that followed each punishing stroke. Nelly did nothing, only bringing her mouth close enough for him to feel her breath. He shoved his cock forward, determined, even in his blindfolded state, to force himself into the soothing mouth. Instead the sensitive underside was lashed again and again. Even with the protection of the twine twisted around it, he felt the blazing pain and squealed once more.

'Oh no, oh my! Please… I'm begging you… please no more!'

The minute he said "please" Nelly applied her mouth to the tip of his cock. And as soon as he started thrusting with his loins, her soothing lips were withdrawn.

'Come on, you bitch…!' he started to say, forgetting his position. The lace descended once again onto his rampant member and the final word tailed off into a high-pitched squeal.

'Like a real hog,' Daisy quipped.

'Yeah, this little pecker is a hog for punishment,' Nelly answered.

'Please,' Charlie moaned. 'Please don't hit me. I'm begging you.'

Again she applied her lips and he lay quiescent, a violent trembling evident in his thighs, as she suckled at his stem. Daisy, a huge grin on her mouth, motioned to her cousin that she too would like some of the nectar. Nelly pulled back, but when Daisy applied her lips and the cock was fully seated, she smacked with the lace once again.

'Oooahhhh,' Master Charlie cried out. 'Why are you doing that to me?' he whined.

'It sure don't matter at all what you do, Charlie Jakes. It's what *I* do what counts, right?'

'Let me go, or else—' he tried to sound menacing once again, but the swish of the lace through the air cut him off in mid-sentence. Nelly directed her cousin to more vigorous efforts, and Daisy's head moved back and forth, her tongue pressing on the soft flesh, lapping at the swollen shaft between the strands of thigh, then moved back to allow the lash to descend.

Charlie Jakes screamed then, as his hips began pumping at the delicious sensation of the mouth, coupled with the intense fire of the strokes.

'Ah can't… ah can't hang on,' he cried, his hips arching against the restraints. His shaft began pulsing, and the bag beneath his cock contracted. Swift as a falcon, Nelly swooped on the base of his cock, and with brutal force dug her thumb into the fleshy zone behind the ball-bag. Charlie whimpered, and his pulsing died down.

'Now, Master Charlie, are you going to behave yourself?' Nelly asked.

'Yes'm,' he agreed weakly. 'Please ma'am, could you, I mean would you be kind enough to…'

'To what, Charlie?' Daisy asked.

'To suck my cock, ma'am, begging your pardon…' he cringed, expecting a blow.

'Why Charlie, what an awful thing to say to a proper lady like myself,' Nelly said in a thoughtful mode. 'I might, but you will have to earn the privilege,' she said.

'Yes'm,' he blabbered. 'Anything you say ma'am.'

Nelly bent close to his ear and whispered, 'Would you like to lick my cunny? It's nice and wet.'

'Your… your pussy. Ah…' Nelly enticingly trailed the bootlace lash across his chest, down to his erection that Daisy was still encouraging with delicate nips and licks. 'Oh yes, yes'm. I sure would.'

Slowly, taking her time, Nelly straddled his face. 'How about my asshole? Would you like to suck at that?' she asked as if in afterthought, flicking the length of bootlace at the tip of his exposed prick. Daisy, her mouth in a huge understanding grin, was finding it hard to hide her glee.

'Oh, yes'm. Oh please ma'am. Yes I would. I surely would.'

'You don't think it would be too much trouble for a young gentleman like yourself?' she asked anxiously, her whip flicking at his belly, which was palpitating with fear.

'Oh no, ma'am. It's an honour, a privilege.'

'You're quite sure?' she asked in concern, reaching for the riding crop Daisy still held. 'I wouldn't want to put a *Southern* gentleman to such trouble.'

'Oh no, ma'am,' he said, his voice muffled by fear and by the inexorable slide of Nelly's thighs down the sides of his head. 'I would be honoured to be of service.'

'See that you do,' said Nelly sweetly. 'And to make sure you do it right, we'll help you along with this,' and she lashed down onto his thighs with all her might.

He squealed and jumped in his bonds. Daisy, entering into the strange game, hurriedly licked the length of the red stripe, and his cry turned to a moan of gratitude.

'First, you must run your tongue around the lips,' Nelly said as she seated herself on his face.

Hurrying to comply, he inadvertently nipped her with his teeth. Without hesitation she lashed at his belly, missing his tumescence by a hairsbreadth. As he set to work she nodded to her cousin, and Daisy bent to suckle at the prominent cock.

At this, Annabelle could contain herself no longer. She knelt on the other side and pushed Daisy out of the way, applying her own mouth to the tumescence.

Peter followed. His cock was pushing at his trousers, and he hurriedly divested himself of them. Clad only in his shirt, he knelt behind his wife and fumbled between her legs, then pushed into the soft, humid spot he found there. She smiled at him with her stretched lips. One eye on Nelly, she continued to suckle at the male stem, obedient to her maid's instructions.

Obedient too was Charlie. Following Nelly's orders, he first ran his tongue over her outer, then her inner lips, pausing to suck at each part. Then she directed his attention to her clitoris, and his lips and tongue began a vigorous sucking action. And from time to time, ensuring his complete obedience, she motioned her assistants out of the way and the lash descended onto his exposed flesh. Nelly's strokes with the lash became less and less directed as she danced over his captive mouth. The spasms of her climax overcame her, and she clamped her thighs roughly over his ears and jammed her pussy deeply against her mouth, then bent over and sucked the entire length of his cock into her mouth and down her soft throat. Charlie licked furiously, unable to control himself, and his own imprisoned member started spasming. Without missing a beat Nelly clamped one hand as hard as she could onto his manhood, while with the other she lashed furiously at his exposed thighs. Streaks of fire blossomed against his flesh and his cock pulsed against the barrier fist, subsiding agonisingly as he struggled.

Panting heavily, Nelly rose from her blindfolded victim. A thin stream of Charlie's spending had escaped her actions and now coated her fingers. She wiped it onto his chest, while motioning to the empty seat she had occupied. Daisy looked at her mistress, whose eyes were glowing at the sight of Nelly's moist pussy, and when Annabelle nodded in assent, she climbed onto the saddle so recently vacated by her satiated cousin.

Annabelle leaped up and grasped Nelly's thigh. 'Do the same to me!' she whispered in her excitement. 'Now, right away!' She threw herself to the floor and dragged the willing Nelly with her. Her mouth engulfed the humid crotch, and began a familiar searching while Nelly whipped her to a frenzy with her mouth and sharp lashes of the riding crop.

Peter, almost beside himself with lust, threw himself down behind Nelly's exquisite backside. With a single thrust he was up her deliciously wetted channel. His balls banged against his wife's nose and forehead as he shafted the maid deeply and with his lust unloosed. Annabelle frantically licked and sucked at the join, while the blows and kisses rained down on her thighs and thirsty twat.

In the meantime Daisy had busied herself with the helpless Southern gentleman so conveniently at her will. Master Charlie's disposition had improved with his training, and he was soon operating to her complete satisfaction. To keep him at his task, she rained blows upon his chest and belly, his thighs, and occasionally, using the tips of her delicate fingers, upon his long bound cock. Nelly raised her head from her mistress's slit long enough to say, 'Don' let him spurt!' before she bent back to her task.

And indeed, when the climax finally overtook them both, the dark mistress and her willing steed, her clenched fist put an end to his abortive uprising, and the white fluid was restrained properly at the base of his tube.

'Oh no,' Charlie moaned as the burning pleasure of the woman's smacks combined with the urgings from his loins. 'Please, please, let me... oh my word. I've gotta spend...'

Daisy, her own shudders still persisting as she wiped her loins by rubbing them on his face, slapped at his cock smartly. 'Shut up,' she said. 'You just do what you're told,' and she bent to inspect her handiwork critically.

The trio on the carpeted floor was approaching resolution. Annabelle, groaning her wordless expression of delight, was jerking her hips into Nelly's willing face and fingers, while Nelly herself was grinding her ass hard against Sir Peter's delving thrusts. Together, the two women stiffened as one, and gave out similar wordless cries of pleasure. Only Peter seemed collected as he withdrew slowly from the almost comatose Nelly, and knelt down to bring his face close to his wife's.

'Darling,' he whispered. 'I would like you to have a new experience. Will you trust me?'

'Of course, my dearest,' she whispered, her interest piqued notwithstanding her near swoon. 'What is it?'

'Why, I don't believe you have ever had two pricks in you, would you like to try it?' He was smiling, and his voice indicated that his question was intended to reassure her. She knew that had he ordered her to do it, she would have obeyed if only for his pleasure.

'Of course, my dearest,' she said, sitting up and rolling Nelly off her. 'Why, what a wonderful idea!'

She rose to stand beside Daisy and her victim. Daisy made to rise, but Annabelle bid her retain her seat. She played with the still erect, twine wrapped cock briefly, her brows furrowed in concentration. Still holding on to the convenient handle, she climbed onto the supine figure and kissed Daisy deeply, then lowered herself. Nelly rose and positioned herself by Charlie's partly-hidden ears.

'You'd better behave yourself now,' she warned, and flicked his chest with her lash.

Gripping the erect prick, Annabelle searched for a brief time between her thighs to position the morsel properly, then with a sigh, impaled herself.

'Ohhhhh,' she sighed as she felt the rough twine rub against her sensitised insides. 'Ahhhhh...' she moaned again as the shaft gradually eased its way into her. Gradually speeding up, she started rocking herself on the captive cock, raising her hips slightly with each forward motion to force the twine to rub against her sensitive little button.

Peter climbed onto the bench and crouched behind her, his erect prick glistening in the candlelight, and held in his fist.

'Are you quite sure about this, my darling,' he inquired

as he nuzzled her neck.

'Ohhhh yes, my love,' her skin quivered, and her hand trembled at the thought.

'Very well,' he said. 'Let us begin,' and he reached for her ass. He parted the perfect pink half moons with the fingers of one hand, and the tip of his cock nuzzled against the tiny puckered mouth. Then he pressed forward, watching entranced as his cock disappeared into her clenching hole.

Charlie could feel his cock sinking into the waiting vagina. His hips twitched as he controlled his response, knowing full well what would happen if he did not. The hateful yet desirable voice beside his ears whispered of dire things, and an occasional biting lash spiced his pleasure with fear. Then he felt a greater constriction on his bound cock as another fleshy cylinder was inserted near his own. The sensation burned the length of his, and he moaned, unable to control his reactions any longer. And when the strange man began pumping into the flesh near his cock, he found himself responding in kind, notwithstanding the stripes that rained down on his chest.

'I can't…' he breathed. 'I just can't. I gotta move. Ohhhhh. Oh yeah. Oh yeah, please lady, please hit me ma'am. I just gotta—!' He screamed, and then knowing that nothing less would do, he set to work to suck at the dark cunt that still enveloped his face. Daisy began her dance again, her hips twitching and her pussy pressed down as hard as she could onto the waiting mouth.

Annabelle was in heaven. She watched as Charlie's former reluctance was shed and he began licking at Daisy's cunny of his own accord. Her own well-manicured nails dug deep gouges into his chest and she wished she could speak; scream out large. Instead, she bent forward and stuck her tongue into Daisy's mouth.

The other girl responded with a deep kiss, until Annabelle broke the kiss and leaned back against her husband's pumping body. Their lips and tongues joined for a frantic and deep communion.

'Oh yes,' she mumbled, breaking away from the kiss. 'Give it to me. In the ass. I love it. Yes – yes – yes…! Use the whip, darling,' she added in a moaning aside to Nelly. Annabelle's eyes were staring out of her head, and she fell into a trance of lust. Nelly grasped her lash and whipped at the conjoined figures before her.

Charlie yelped, but the yelp was now one of pleasure as his climax rose.

Peter and Annabelle had, perforce, to be more circumspect, but they too were whispering encouragement into one another's mouth. Annabelle stiffened, and divining her situation, Peter thrust deeply into her, grinding his pelvis at her as hard as he could. His hands groped her breasts and pinched her prominent nipples viciously. She leaned back into his arms while waves of her pleasure descended and forced her body into a convulsive spend. Echoing her, Peter's bag pulsed once, then again, and he pumped his life-giving milk into her waiting ass.

Nelly, ever alert, dived for Charlie's pulsing cock. She thrust her fingers deeply into the flesh at the base of his stem, and he howled with pain and frustrated lust as her other fist also clamped around the base of the pulsing stem where it emerged from her mistress.

'You had better keep calm,' she hissed at him as his tremors passed. His cock quivered once again as jolts of pleasurable pain lanced from his groin along his spine.

'Ah gotta spend…' he begged. 'Ah jus' have to let go,' he cried, straining at his bonds. Without hesitation, Nelly lashed at his chest and exposed thighs. As Daisy climbed off him he howled for mercy.

'Will you do what you are told?' the whisper again hissed threateningly.

'I'll be good,' he howled, tears running down his stubbled cheeks.

Peter helped Annabelle off their ride. He kissed her deeply. 'Did you enjoy it, my darling?' he asked sincerely.

'Oh yes,' she said, blushing. 'Keep him ready, I'm sure Nelly will want him again,' she said as she repaired to perform her ablutions.

Nelly had been examining Charlie's body minutely as she crouched over him and inserted his fettered cock into her gaping cunny. 'He sure is a hairy beast,' she said, after looking at Charlie's chest and belly. 'Sort of like fucking with a wild animal,' she snorted, moving her hips around in a grinding motion. An idea came to her, and she motioned Daisy to her side. The other's eyes widened in surprise at what her cousin whispered to her, and then she hurried away up the stairs from their basement lair.

A few minutes later Daisy scurried down the stairs bearing a shiny object in her hands. Nelly was dreamily dancing over Charlie's figure, now holding her nether lips open as she descended, now describing intricate arabesques with her hips, now lashing his chest languidly. His hips were in constant motion as his unsatisfied lust rose, a lust she did not allow to expend itself in the massive spending he craved.

Charlie's fear added a sharp flavour to the pleasure he was experiencing. For the first time in his life he was not in control; did not *need* to be in control. His fate was entirely in the hands of this female devil who was riding him to a sweet hell. Even the spikes of pain from her lash were just added spice to the sweet agony in his groin. He felt a jolt of pleasure when she bent forward and thrust her lips and tongue at his, and he eagerly awaited her next use of his body.

The servants of his new love returned. He could hear the tripping bare feet of the two women, and the heavier tread of the man. He could imagine them, the women slim sylphs, their feet flashing enticingly, their brows hidden by dark ringlets. How he wished they would thrash him again, properly, forcing him to spurt at their command.

And the man? A hulking, shaven-scalped brute, no doubt, his glowering low-browed visage a threatening presence. Charlie quivered inside at the thought of that man and what he could do.

There were some indistinct murmurings, and then a cool line was touching the angle of his jaw. With a thrill of fear he suddenly recognised the touch. The touch of a razor. He quailed, and would have lost his stiff-stander in an instant but for the lick of the lash against his sensitive nipple.

'I think we have to shave him,' insisted one of the women, the sharp razor lying across Charlie's throat. His heart pounded as he struggled to speak, as he feared the worse. 'I can't stand an unshaven face.'

'Oh yes, shave me. Pleeeease shave me,' he babbled. 'Anything. Just... please be careful with... with...' He gulped and tried to squint through the blindfold.

The four of them looked down at their victim as Daisy, displaying a rare skill, proceeded to shave the bristly face.

'I have an idea,' murmured Daisy, her eyes on her work. Her memories of the humiliations *she* had suffered was stimulating her thinking. 'Why don' we *really* shave him?' And she looked pointedly at the root of the still-erect member glistening with combined juices.

The two other pairs of female eyes lit up as the

ramifications of what she was saying filtered in. Peter suppressed a grin. 'Just like at the college,' he murmured to his wife's ear. 'Why, I recall doing the same to old Purvis, just before he went up to Sandhurst.'

'No, please,' howled their intended victim. 'No, oh no. I daren't show my face in public.'

Negligently, Nelly raised her lash and brought it down lightly on his twine-wound shaft. 'Be quiet,' she snapped. 'It ain't your moustache we was thinking of.'

Charlie howled as the implications hit him. The touch of the cold steel on his mound would have sent him into hysterics, but for the closeness of the steel to his manhood, and for the sweet bite of the lash. In silence, while his flanks quivered nervously like a horse, Daisy shaved him of every vestige of hair.

When she was done the three women admired the result. Sir Peter also looked on approvingly.

'I say,' he murmured to his wife. 'Quite an improvement, what?'

Charlie staggering towards the welcome lights of the town, tripped and fell. Even the blow from an exposed root could not restrain his impatience, and he hurriedly grasped his shaft and wanked away, his breath coming in gasps. Observed with mixed reactions by a woman hanging her late wash and a curious boy dozing in an abandoned hogshead, he shot a fountain of cream onto the ground, groaning mightily with relief.

'Oh, that was incomparable, wonderful!' he said to the stars, oblivious of his surroundings. 'I sure ain't had nothin' like that before. I do wonder who she is, though,' and tears dropped from his eyes at the thought that he would never feel her firm hand on him again.

'Disgusting,' said the woman, turning from the

spectacle at last, but there was a shine in her eye, and she did not hurry to look away. The boy just whistled between his teeth, wondering why the man should think there was anything so extraordinary about the woman's performance.

The cold of the night tickled Charlie's smooth skin as he staggered homewards, the abandoned sack which had covered his head, and a spot of gummy mud remained the only physical evidence of his passing.

Mr Wildfire watched Charlie stagger by. He had hoped, had hoped so much to use that drunken catspaw to exact his revenge. But the time for using subterfuge was over. He jerked nervously at his gloves in the dark, then turned to make his way back to his hotel. There was a note to be written, a kidnapping to execute, and a revenge to exact. He hoped that his arrangements were in order. There was nothing to do but wait until Captain Williams brought his ship to port, and until he could entice Stone away from his wife.

Silently, Wildfire ground his teeth.

Chapter Seventeen

The heat was oppressive. Annabelle fanned herself vigorously, and when that did not help, she released the buttons of her dress, peering anxiously into the night. Peter was due back, but darkness had fallen and he was still not home. He had been distracted somewhat for the past few days, after she had told him of meeting that charming Mr Wildfire, but he would not confide in her. It was too hot to even light the oil lamps, and she sipped at the glass beside her from time to time, finding it by touch in the dark. The heat had frazzled her nerves, and she had drunk more than she ought of the pitcher of wine that lay beside her, its sides beaded with moisture from the depths of the well where it had lain to cool.

There was movement behind her in the dimness, and her heart beat faster through the misty maze brought on by the heavy, sweet wine. It must be Peter, the tread was too heavy to be one of the maids. She started to rise, when arms came from behind the armchair and hands grasped her wrists, pulling them around to the back of the chair. She squealed in surprise for a moment, then suddenly realised that dear Peter was trying to surprise her with a new amorous trick. Silently she started to battle, trying to suppress, not altogether successfully, her giggles.

As she expected, she found herself soon with her wrists tied uncomfortably around the back of the armchair. Male hands then snaked around and grasped her breasts, not gently, giving each a hefty squeeze and pinch.

'Ooooh, Peter,' she crooned, waiting to see what would

happen next. One hand withdrew, and then returned in a flash, slapping each breast in turn. She gasped happily at the sharp bite of pain, and made as if to struggle against her bonds. The hands moved higher, stroking her collarbone and the softness of her neck, cupping her jawbone, then moved down again to her breasts, pulling and mauling them in a way she found slightly repugnant, but exciting as well.

The hands dropped lower, feeling her belly, then pushed down, forcing her to spread her legs. She struggled vainly as the hands pulled at her soft thighs unmercifully. Then the searching fingers were on her damp moss, scratching at her mons through her diaphanous shift. She bit her lip to avoid crying out again, even though the touch was hardly as she would have wanted it. Behind her she could hear harsh, bestial breathing, and she giggled aloud as she imagined Peter pretending to be what he was not. The fingers took on a new urgency, scratching at her pubic fleece through the fabric, and she squirmed in delight at the scraping pain it brought her.

'I cannot stand it any longer,' Peter muttered in a muffled voice. The hands let go of her mound. The dim light was blotted out by a male figure, and she felt the armchair sag as he climbed on to kneel on the broad armrests. There was a flurry of motion before her face, and it suddenly became clear to Annabelle what he was trying to do. A waft of bitter male lustful essence confirmed her suspicions, and she readied her mouth to receive his cock.

The meaty morsel was thrust at her waiting mouth, and she opened her lips to welcome it in gladly. It was only when the tip had slid past her teeth, when her tongue was eagerly stroking the soft flesh beneath the tumescent shaft, that she realised there was something wrong. The shape was the shape of Peter, but the smell and taste, not to mention the absence of refined movement, did not seem right. Indeed, rather than allowing her the pleasure of licking and sucking at his member, he seemed in a tearing hurry, ramming his cock in and out of her greedily gulping mouth, as if she did not know how to pleasure him properly. She started to struggle, trying to call out and say something, when it suddenly occurred to her that that was precisely what was intended, and without calming her struggles, she settled down to enjoy the sensation of being fucked roughly in her mouth by her resourceful husband. She puffed and sucked at the moving shaft, laving it with her tongue as well as she was able, and soon had the satisfaction of feeling his crisis rise in the balls that were slapping her chin. Fingers tight as an iron vice gripped her face and prodded her cheeks, and he started groaning, bringing the entire power of his hips to bear as he thrust forward.

With a sudden explosion of white liquor he burst into her mouth, and Annabelle hurriedly gulped the salty glutinous drops down. Uncharacteristically, the male member softened almost immediately in her mouth, and he climbed off his perch rather than allowing her to clean him properly. He fumbled about in the dark, and Annabelle wondered what on earth was going on, when a glass of wine was held to her lips. Gratefully, she gulped it down.

A curious lassitude spread through her limbs, and her eyes grew too heavy to stay open. She struggled to understand what was happening, just as the door opened, and rays of golden lamplight shone on the scene. She was barely conscious as Nelly walked in to light the lanterns.

'Who are you—?' she heard, then Nelly's scream.

A rough male voice snarled an answer, and as if from a

distance, her hands still tied behind her, her chin wet with driblets of come, Annabelle could hear the sounds of a fight before she fell into a black pool of unconsciousness...

Nelly woke to a raging headache. The sitting room was a mess, and the side of her head where the intruder had hit her was a sore. She dragged herself to her feet.

'Miss Annabelle?' she cried out tentatively, then louder, 'Miss Annabelle!'

There was no answer, and she had not really expected any.

'Daisy!' she called out sharply, then turned and ran from the room, barely able to support the lantern she had snatched up.

A quick search showed her there was no one in the house. She returned to the sitting room. Her arms and head were sore from the fight but she managed to survey the wreckage. It seemed there was only a short while had passed since the fight. Hurriedly she repaired the damage to her person. Perhaps she might still catch them on the road. Miss Annabelle's little mare was still in the stable.

Annabelle opened her eyes. There was a chill on her skin, and she was suddenly aware that she was completely naked. Moreover, she appeared to be immobilised by bonds that attached her to the framework of the bed she was lying upon. She struggled, slightly puzzled by the turn of events – this was certainly not her bedroom, nor yet even her house – and a man's face hove into view. It took her a second to realise that it was not Peter, even though there were some similarities, but the face of that other Englishman, Mr Wildfire.

'Thank God, Mr Wildfire. May I trouble you for some cover sir, and as a gentleman, would you please avert your eyes? I hardly know how I came to be in this place…'

She blushed prettily, as his eyes never wavered from her uncovered form. 'Mr Wildfire!' she demanded, a snap in her voice.

He raised his eyes to her face. 'And a very delightful form it is too,' he averred. 'Shall I tell you how you got here? Very simple, my dear. I brought you. And though I am a gentleman, I have no intention of removing my gaze from your form.' Deliberately, he raked her with his eyes from feet to crown.

'Release me at once,' she tried to command him. Over his shoulder she saw a familiar face. 'Daisy, quick, run and get help!' she called.

Daisy said nothing, but Wildfire laughed again. 'Yes indeed, Daisy do this, Daisy do that. You do not realise it, but Daisy is sick and tired of doing this and that. Daisy has been my agent all along.' He chuckled evilly. 'She has been informing me of all that has passed in your house, and I have been rewarding her appropriately. Ha ha!' he laughed in triumph. 'You did not realise that your maid, Daisy, has been my agent all along!'

Annabelle looked at her erstwhile maid. 'How could you, Daisy? How *could* you?'

'Oh, do be quiet,' Wildfire ordered, 'stop twittering.' And he waited until he was sure she would say no more before continuing.

'Now my dear, as to why you are here. Your husband has certain papers I deeply require. I have been racking my brains as to how to acquire them, and now I believe I know how.' He beamed at her.

'What has that to do with me?' she asked in alarm.

'Everything, my dear, everything indeed. *Primus*, you probably know where the papers are secreted. *Secundus*, even if you do not, your husband will surely trade them for your delectable person. But since he is a very stubborn man, I believe we shall explore the first possibility. Would you like to tell me?'

'I know nothing of the sort,' Annabelle declared. 'The very idea! As if a gentleman would even bother his bride with his business affairs.' She snorted prettily, though still bound supine.

'I think you are lying, my dear,' Mr Wildfire said coolly. 'But I do know you are an upper-class woman. You are delicate. A few lashes of the whip and you'll be blubbering properly. Come now, I have no desire to be hard on you.' His evil leer betrayed his real intentions.

Annabelle felt a wetness in her crotch, and hoped she could hide it from his eyes. The situation, she decided, though frightening, was quite delicious. 'No, never!' she said stoutly.

'Ah,' cried Wildfire. 'A good and loyal spouse, eh? Well, we shall see... we shall see. Here girl,' he called to Daisy who was standing by the bed. 'Fetch me that box yonder. The young maid obeyed with alacrity and fetched a flat leather box that looked quite familiar to Annabelle's eye. She wondered how he had plundered it from her bedside.

Wildfire snapped open the box and held the contents to her eyes. There was a look of triumphant threat in his maddened lustful stance. 'I inherited it from my father,' he said. 'Shall we try this?' His hands stroked a lovely whalebone quirt. 'Or this?' and he raised a black-lashed tawse. He was practically slavering at the vision of the whips marking her skin.

Annabelle was in shock. At first it was the fear that her captor had stolen one of her most prized possessions, something that had come to her with her marriage, and that she prized very much. The causes of her shock changed, when she realised that there were *two* such boxes, and that one of them was actually owned by this outlaw, for that was how she thought of Wildfire now in her mind.

'You tremble, eh?' He knelt by her side, eyeing her form lasciviously, his fingers trembling. 'You fear this, don't you? The kiss of the lash. I bet no one has so much as laid a hand on you since you were in knee skirts.' His hand deliberately fell on her soft thigh, just above the knee.

Wildfire raised the lash, then brought it down lightly on Annabelle's arched belly.

'Oh, oh, you cad!' she screamed in mock agony. 'How could you, you beast?!'

He laughed. 'Shall I hit you again? Or will you tell me what I want to know?'

'I know nothing,' she sobbed. 'I know nothing at all. And how dare you mistreat me in front of a servant?!' she demanded in outrage.

'You wouldn't mind a man, would you, eh? That would just be an added zest to your lustful nature, would it not? Just like your friend Mrs Jakes. Nice handful that one,' he sneered. Then, he pounced. 'But a maid? Your own *maid*? What do you think of that, eh?' and he rose, and with one stride stood beside Daisy. With one hand he gave her the lash he had selected, and with the other he clasped the dark maid around her waist. 'Strike her!' he hissed. 'Strike your mistress.'

Annabelle saw the look in Daisy's eyes, and knew what part she had to play. She tugged abruptly at her bonds and screamed, 'No, not that! Don't allow that lying bitch to touch me! I beg you sir, if you have any Christian charity in your heart!'

Wildfire laughed heartily, then whispered into Daisy's ear.

With a smile Daisy drew near. 'Ah'll be moa comfortable without this here dress, sah,' she said tentatively, her eyes on Annabelle.

'By all means, by *all* means,' Wildfire sneered, his eyes gleaming. He approached as Daisy unbuttoned her black dress and put it carefully aside. She was dressed as usual in a short shift, her white silk stockings held up by frilly garters, and button-up boots.

'My, my,' said Wildfire. 'You do dress well for a slavey.'

'Ah ain't no slave!' Daisy turned on him, the lash raised in a threatening manner. 'Ah spend mah money to please *me*.'

'Of course, of course, my dear,' Wildfire said placatingly. He turned to Annabelle. 'Now, will you tell me or suffer the consequences of your obduracy?'

'No, please sir. I cannot. Please don't let her hit me, please, I beg of you!'

He laughed again in the artificial style he had. 'No, she shall beat you, and I shall watch. You shall learn that my word is law!' He placed a hand on Daisy's swelling ass. 'Commence, my dear. The thighs first, I think.'

Daisy raised the lash high, and smiled. Wildfire laughed aloud, his eyes bulging. Annabelle quivered in anticipation of the blow, her form exposed to the torture, and trying to control the lustful panting of her chest.

The first blow fell on Annabelle's breasts. Daisy brought the lash down expertly on the soft white skin before her. A faint weal sprung up, a perfect pink line on the milk-white flesh. The pain was excruciating, and Annabelle screamed for real, her eyes on her former maid's face. Daisy licked her lips and Annabelle could feel her juices rising as she saw the hardened nipples on Daisy's brown teat. Remembering her role in time, she sobbed piteously. Wildfire, sunk in his enjoyment of the spectacle of her white flesh being lashed, did not notice the momentary lapse.

'Lash her again, girl,' he chortled in glee.

'Owww,' Annabelle squealed as the fire of the lash spread down to her groin. Her belly quivered. Wildfire's hand squeezed Daisy's ass hard, his fingers penetrating the crack of her bottom. There was a perceptible bulge in his trousers. The lash landed again, on the thigh, and Annabelle screamed with a touch of fire, raising her hips from the bed.

'Beginning to warm up, eh?' sneered Wildfire.

She quivered in her bonds while he looked on and Daisy set to work. She knew that her beautiful breasts were quivering and that her contortions were bringing him to a frenzy, but still she would not say anything. His face, through the lustful glaze, grew thoughtful.

He stroked his chin a moment, then turned to Daisy. 'That's enough. I believe she thinks she is tough. Let us try something else.'

Quickly Annabelle was released. Wildfire looked at Daisy for a moment. 'How would you like a... a prize, eh Daisy?'

'What kind of prize?' asked the maid suspiciously.

'Why...' he licked his lips. 'Here, I'll add another ten dollars. In gold, mind you!' His eyes lit on Annabelle's spread legs. 'Act a man to her.' He nodded his head in his victim's direction.

'Why, I never!' Daisy's eyes widened and she looked at Wildfire in shock.

'Very well,' he said. 'Twenty-five dollars. Mind you, most men would pay *me* for the privilege.'

'Why don't you then?' asked Daisy, in real curiosity.

'That's not for you to ask,' he thundered. 'Twenty-five, that's it.'

Daisy nodded acquiescence, and slowly, as if reluctantly, stripped off her clothes.

Wildfire looked on approvingly as the dark skin was unveiled to his gaze, then turned to Annabelle. 'If you do not tell me what I want to know, I shall have this black woman take her pleasure of you,' he hissed threateningly.

'No, oh no!' Annabelle cried out, closing her eyes. 'How monstrous! How could you violate my person so? How could you allow me to be used so unnaturally? Is it not enough that you have taken my honour yourself, you must also have another force an unnatural act upon me?' The weals on her stomach and breasts were burning with a fire she knew would be hard to quench. Her entire frame was softened, made voluptuous by the lashing she had received, and she yearned for Daisy's body as she had not yearned before.

Wildfire's eyes gleamed. 'Yes! You must obey me or suffer the consequences!'

'Never!' she cried out defiantly, and Wildfire urged Daisy on with a gesture.

Pouncing like a panther, Daisy flung herself on the helpless white body beneath her. She grasped the golden curls and placed her mouth on Annabelle's, exploring her briskly with her tongue, while Annabelle made a well-simulated attempt to escape the embrace. Grasping Annabelle's full bottom with her hands, Daisy forced her curl-covered mound against her mossy hillock and ground down until their lips meshed.

'Stop… oh stop… oh monstrous!' Annabelle mumbled, as her tongue eagerly sought Daisy's.

'Will you speak?' exclaimed Wildfire.

'No, never,' breathed his captive through her teeth. Daisy had taken to sucking on her pert pink nipples, and waves of desire coursed through her frame. The maid rubbed herself furiously against her mistress's hole, squeezing her ass at the same time, and sucking her nipples.

'Oooooh, I can't bear it,' Annabelle howled.

'Beat her, beat her!' Daisy ordered, raising her head for a moment from Annabelle's writhing form. 'Strike her with the lash!'

'Yes indeed, a capital suggestion.' He flung off his jacket and set to work, dancing about the twined figures, dark and pale, and hitting out where he could.

'Not me, you fool!' Daisy cried out at a badly aimed blow.

'Yes, yes,' Wildfire gasped.

'Oh no, oh no, oh *nooo*,' Annabelle swooned as she felt her crisis approaching. The lashing she had received from Wildfire, combined with Daisy's ministrations, had brought about her climax, and to add fuel for the fire, she screamed as waves of pleasure erupted through her, 'I'll never tell you, never, you beast, never, oooohhh…!'

Daisy, her dark skin velvety with sweat, raised herself from Annabelle's feebly moving body. She lifted her eyes to Wildfire, who was staring down at the two entwined females. 'I'm afraid she is one really tough lady, sir. And I believe she has fainted.'

Taking her cue from Daisy, Annabelle hastily closed her eyes and pretended to be in a swoon.

Wildfire shook his head in exasperation. Time would soon be upon him, and some of his previous resolve abandoned him.

'Master,' said Daisy, her own insides quivering in the last twitches of her pleasure. 'Master…'

'Yes, what is it?' asked Wildfire, his shining eyes on the lovely Annabelle's struggling form.

'I have a suggestion,' said the maid, and tugged at his head. He bent forward, and his look turned to one of sly glee.

'Why, such a girl you are!' he exclaimed admiringly. 'Yes, that will do very nicely.' He looked above him and saw the heavy hook that had held a chandelier. He lunged forward, and in a trice, had Annabelle's wrists in his large hands. It was but a moment's work to heave the rope over the hook, and Annabelle soon found herself suspended, hands over her head, her feet barely touching the floor. The two conspirators looked on approvingly at the suspended form before them.

'I must… I must…' cried Wildfire. He surged forward and fell to his knees before the helpless beauty. Parting her thighs forcefully, he buried his nose in her rich pussy hairs. His tongue sought out her little nubbin, and he slobbered at her clit for a long moment, sucking on it like a starved calf, snuffling all the while.

Despite her abhorrence towards the vile man, Annabelle twitched in her bonds, her lust rising again, while he held her open and lashed his tongue into her femininity. Over his head the two females, one white and the other black, exchanged wide smiles. Whatever Daisy had done, Annabelle knew, she had not betrayed her mistress. She allowed her head to fall forward, and allowed herself to be captured by the sensation of the male tongue inexpertly and demandingly exploring her slit. Annabelle looked quickly at the whip, and Daisy, knowing what was needed, raised the lash and brought it down on her mistress's belly, adding another weal to the faint pink marks already placed there earlier. Annabelle squealed loudly, and tried to retreat from the pain. Wildfire interpreted that as an attempt to pull away from him, and his fingers dug more deeply into her ass, restraining her while he continued his frenzied sucking…

The door to the room suddenly burst open and Nelly's banshee figure flung itself through.

The tiny mare had been quick and sure-footed, which had been lucky for Nelly, who was no more than an indifferent rider. Moving through the countryside with the sureness of a local, she soon came up with a closed trap that was rattling over the country roads in the direction of the town. Hardly knowing how she was going to effect a rescue, she urged the mare on, which had been her undoing as the horse stumbled, pitching Nelly off.

By the time she had picked herself up both mare and trap were long gone. Still game, notwithstanding her bruises, Nelly hurried after on foot. Then a memory struck her, and suddenly she knew where she must go. The trap! It was familiar. Indeed, she suddenly recalled, she had seen it several times, as it drove her mistress's friend Heather Jakes!

She turned off the main road and hurried through the smaller alleys in the direction of the Jakes' mansion.

She arrived before the mansion breathing hard. There was no time to lose, she was sure of it. A quick dash around the back of the house and she found that the rundown stables still held a heavily sweating pair of horses. She fumbled at the back door, glad that the age of the house and the poverty of its occupants rendered the burglary simple.

Moving as quietly as she could, she scouted the ground floor. There was no one there, in the mainly empty rooms. It was only as she climbed the quietly creaking staircase that she heard the sounds of the whip, and she ran forward with no thought but to save dear Annabelle.

The man kneeling before her mistress with his back to her was the same she had found in the Stone's mansion, she was sure. Obscured by him she could see Annabelle's pale form suspended from a rope, a familiar dark figure standing by with a whip. Without stopping for thought,

Nelly launched herself into the room, striking out with her hands.

The man turned with surprising swiftness. He grasped her arm and dealt her a buffet on the cheek with his fist. Before she could recover, she found herself twisted to the floor, with the man standing over her. In his hands was a deadly little derringer.

'And where have you come from, eh?' he asked ominously.

'Don't, don't hurt her!' Daisy shrieked.

Wildfire kept the gun trained on the intruder. 'Why ever not?' he asked suspiciously. 'Why, she's merely Miss Annabelle's other maid!'

'She might do us a power of good, to find all that gold!' Daisy improvised.

Wildfire roused Nelly with a cup of cold water dashed in her face. 'You're only a maid,' he said severely. 'Do you want these people to keep on exploiting you, eh? I'll warrant that despicable Stone has forced you to do his will, ain't that so? Don't you want some of your own back, eh girl?'

Nelly looked at her cousin, and Daisy nodded her head slightly, trying to convey that she must agree.

'Why should I?' she asked.

'At least for a share of the… the gold!' he said in exasperation.

'Well… I don' see no gold,' she retorted gamely.

'No, not mine!' he almost yelled. 'Stone! He's the one. All that lovely money, eh girl?' His eyes glinted at her, and he made the suggestive motion of a man jingling a bag of coins in his hand. 'Here, all you have to do is help us get the information from that woman, and you'll have a share,' he coaxed her, pointing at her helpless mistress.

'What have I got to do?' Nelly asked with suspicion.

'Hit her a couple of times,' he hissed. 'You'd like that, wouldn't you? A chance to strike back at your oppressor? And even the threat of being beaten by her servant should induce her to speak!' His eyes widened in triumph. 'Then when I know what is necessary, we can compel Stone to do as we want! All she needs do is tell us where he has hid the papers.'

Nelly had her doubts on both scores, but faced with the firearm which Wildfire still held, she felt she had no other way but to agree. She climbed slowly to her feet, her head still whirling.

The man handed her a whip. It was made of fine braided leather, shiny and new.

She raised it high and examined her victim... Miss Annabelle.

The whip snapped and its lash reddened another streak on the pale flesh hanging before her. Again and again it cut through the air and into the pale skin.

Annabelle writhed in her bonds, conscious of the eyes upon her, and screamed gratifyingly. The heat of her loins was rising once more, and she wished one or the other maid would come and help her achieve another climax.

'Unghh!' she grunted as a particularly heavy blow laced into her skin.

Nelly raised her hand with the whip again, and contemplated her target. She wished Miss Annabelle would play her part well. It would not do to let this madman know that he had been cozened. She flicked the whip once, and the lash curled around the suspended white figure, and clipped into the soft behind.

'Owww!' Annabelle shrieked, louder than was strictly necessary, but she had entered into the spirit of the thing. 'That hurts! Stop it right now, I order you! Stop or it will be worse for you!' and she started blubbering, trying hard to disguise the feeling of pleasure that radiated from the weal to the centre of her belly.

'Again!' shouted Wildfire, insane lust burning in his eyes.

Nelly raised the whip and brought it down in a wicked stroke on the writhing white belly. His eyes glistening, Wildfire pulled Daisy to him, his hands forcing her shoulders down. Without a word being spoken the pretty maid knelt at his feet and extracted his cock. The bulbous tip was glowing as red as the stripes on his victim's exposed belly, and Daisy hastily parted her lips and sucked it in.

Wildfire, in a paroxysm of delight, moved back and forth into her mouth, his eyes held fixed onto the tortured face of his enemy's wife.

'Ha! Lash her! Give it to her!' he cried as his hips twitched uncontrollably and his cock pulsed in Daisy's mouth. Then, unable to contain himself any longer, he withdrew from the maid and leapt upon the deliciously vulnerable lady before him. With one fierce thrust he buried himself in her juicy quim to the roots.

'Oh... oh...!' wailed Annabelle. 'Help! He's ravishing me!'

'Ha ha!' sniggered Wildfire, thrusting more deeply into her helpless body, then he stiffened abruptly, and the two maids could see his bollocks shifting. 'Lash me!' he cried out, his hands clutching at Annabelle's soft bottom. 'Lay on, don't stop!'

Nelly complied and the lash whistled through the air and smacked onto his bottom. Wildfire screeched once, his balls pulsed, then again, and he discharged his entire load into Annabelle's hungry pussy.

'Enough!' he cried out as Nelly's blows continued. She desisted automatically, and by the time she had thought of exploiting the situation, he had his revolver firmly clutched in his fist again.

'I shall now get possession of the last of what is owed me!' announced Wildfire. Some of the madness seemed to have left his expression, and the icy cold persona was back. The girls shrunk away from him instinctively. Even Annabelle, who was sunk in a sexual haze, heard something evil in his voice and her lust seemed to freeze to stillness.

The mansion was strangely empty. Not a person to be found. Peter found that disturbing, and he ran upstairs to a scene of devastation. The struggles of Annabelle and Nelly had left evidence in the shape of disarranged furniture and strewn clothing. And there was the remains of Mr Wildfire's cravat. Peter looked around, trying to master himself. That the object of the raid was kidnapping, not theft, was obvious. But who could it have been? Then his eye lit on the tie pin still lodged in the piece of dark cloth holding a piece of paper, and a cold hand closed over his heart. With trembling fingers he unfolded the scrap of whiteness, and in the light of his single candle, managed to read the bold, familiar hand:

I HAVE HER. BRING THE PAPERS OR ELSE. THIRD PIER AT MIDNIGHT.

Turning abruptly, he rushed down to leap again into his trap and lash the horses into a tired run.

The third pier was a dismal place. Peter cast about for some clue as to the presence of either enemy or friends, and could find neither. There was a small barque, its lights doused, standing off some way from the pier. He was about to hail it when a quick step behind him caused him to spin around. Nelly hurried up to him, a letter clutched in her hand.

'He says sign it, sign it now and he will release Miss Annabelle!'

By the faint light of his lantern he managed to read the brief note:

I, Peter Stone, do hereby renounce the title of Baron Stone of X in favour of my elder brother, Paul. All entailed and unentailed property associated with the title is hereby conveyed without consideration to my brother who is the rightful heir.

'Why, this is nonsense!' he fumed. 'No court would recognise this... legalistic folderol...'

'Then sign it,' she agonised. 'He has promised to release them if you—'

'Sign this?' he cut her off. 'Never! I shall never sign away my birthright!'

Nelly looked at the man as if he had lost his senses. 'But you said it is a worthless piece of paper!'

'You could not possibly understand, my girl. A Stone would *never* stoop to being blackmailed in this fashion, damn me if I will.'

'Ha!' interjected a sudden voice, and a light sprang up on the deck of the ship anchored in mid-stream. 'Have you signed it yet?'

'Never!' answered Peter furiously. 'I shall not!'

'Then you'll never see your pretty wife again!' Wildfire was a monstrous shadow, the struggling figure of Annabelle held close by his side. 'Give it up!'

'I shall never give up my birthright to a cad!' cried Peter. 'You are nothing but a low-born, vile upstart!'

'Ha ha ha!' laughed Wildfire sardonically. *I* am the